I0582366

SHIFTING GROUND

DOUGLAS P. SMITH

KINGFISHER PRESS LLC

Shifting Ground by Douglas P. Smith

The second book in the Fisher of Time series (after the prequel *River Forged*)

Published by Kingfisher Press LLC

Fairview, North Carolina, United States of America

Visit the author's website at www.douglaspaulsmith.com

Copyright © 2022 Douglas P. Smith

All rights reserved. No portion of this book may be reproduced in any form without permission from the publisher, except as permitted by U.S. copyright law. For permissions contact: thekingfisherpress@gmail.com

Cover by MiblArt

Print ISBN: 978-1-7373680-5-2

This book is a work of fiction. Names, characters, places, and incidents are either the product of the author's imagination or are used fictitiously. Any resemblance to actual persons, living or dead, or to actual events or locales is entirely coincidental.

The story was originally published in 2021 as *Resurgent* but has been significantly revised and rewritten with new content added and other content deleted.

Dedicated to those living in unknown times

CHAPTER ONE

Hanging from a cliff face reminded me of how much I hated heights. Really, really hated it. My quarry had led me here, showing that it was smarter than I was. I scrambled up the rock face, which was cold in the cracks and shadows, even in the late summer. If I messed up, it was two hundred feet down to the next ledge that would catch my body. Not lethal for me, but it would be painful for a day or two. Nowhere to go but up.

I finally reached the top, with one last ledge of crumbly rock to crawl over. Not a good time to hurry, so I took my time easing my body against the rock face, then over the lip. Those yoga classes really helped.

It was surprising to see a forest of massive trees before me. The vertical, barren landscape I had just climbed was now horizontal and lush. I sat down and drank some water and rested for five minutes and looked myself over, with cuts and scrapes covering my hands and lower arms, and my pants were shredded as well. The thing I was chasing owed me some new clothes. I thought about how I had gotten here.

I arrived in Anchorage four days ago. Alaska is like few other places, as you immediately notice how vast the place is. Anchorage is on flatland by the ocean and distant mountains hem everything in and fill the horizon. Despite the distance, they seem so tall because they start at sea level, where you are standing, and rise quickly to 14,000 feet. Within that bigness are few people as the population density is just over one person per square mile. Density in the Netherlands is over thirteen hundred people per square mile. People easily go missing in Alaska, and with that vastness, abductions and murders remain hidden for years. But when too many goes missing in a specific area, people notice. The corollary to that was that crimes against nature weren't noticed, much less prosecuted.

I was here because of a spate of missing humans over half a decade in a small town. And lately the sighting of an odd dog-like thing and lots of dead Dall sheep in the surrounding mountains. Another weird convergence of coincidences. The Church had documented the incidents, but several factors had prevented them from investigating until now. They did not have anyone local; the European teams had no experience in Alaska; and seven people missing plus dead sheep were not high on the priority list. But that is why they had me. Experience in Alaska, time to investigate, and I was cheaper than most alternatives. I had volunteered just to revisit Alaska. I spent the past two days in the mountains where the dead sheep were reported, waiting for something odd to show up. When it did the chase was on. A simple trip to catch a killer, yet I did not know how life altering this trip was to become.

Time to renew the chase as I followed a trail into the woods. These were genuine woods, a mature arboreal forest. Not redwood-sized, but still plenty big. I thought this elevation was too high, for both the type and size of trees growing here. Trivia dredged up from one of hundreds of college classes, in particular the class on biogeography. The greenery underneath was a cool jungle. Fern-like plants, and unfortunately some devil's club, grew waist high. The ground was covered in moss so thick it was like walking on a mattress. A mattress interspersed with deep hidden holes that were just large enough to swallow a foot and break a leg.

I stopped worrying about that when I sighted my quarry again. Hard to describe, but basically a dog person. The hind legs and bushy tail of a dog below the waist, while above it was a human torso clad in a flannel shirt, with small human-like arms and hands. The face was hairy, but I never got a close look to see whether it was more dog- or human-shaped. It was agile and fast, almost scampering up the cliff I had labored to climb. No wonder the Dall sheep were getting massacred.

Michael, my occasional employer through the Church via contract, had briefed me before coming over, with files on supernatural beings reportedly in Alaska. I assumed most were myths, but this one was likely an Adlet based on the descriptions provided. This unlikely myth was true.

I started running again, but carefully. Then I sensed something more than saw it and came to a dead stop. A very large humanoid shape in the shadows ahead and off to the side. I stared at the place but could not quite see it. As I stood there, the shape became a tree. I took a few steps closer, then sat down, crossed my legs, and kept my hands on my knees, palms up. I closed my eyes and waited. An Adlet, woods where they should not be, and now this. So much for my simple Alaska venture. But sitting and patiently waiting seemed to be the polite thing to do while going down this rabbit hole.

"Ah, you must be a sensitive one as you have discovered me, even with my cladding. You are not the average hairless being. Well met." Those words vibrated through me as I felt them more than heard them. My skin and bones were slightly ringing with each one.

"That is amazing. I was not even aware that it was possible to shift into a tree, so I still have much to learn." I said the words aloud but wasn't sure it was necessary.

"You are correct on both counts. You have much to learn. And I hear your thoughts, but only when you wish to speak. I would not read your thoughts otherwise, unless you were a threat. Then I would determine your intent. But otherwise, no, that would just be rude. And my people are not rude."

"And who are your people?"

"Ah, that is a tricky question to answer. Regardless, I would defer an answer until I know more about you, and who your people are."

"I am not exactly sure what I am. But not exactly human, which is what I suppose you mean when you call me a hairless one. I believe I am the only one of my people."

"Hmm, now that I study you, you are silvery. Not like the typical hairless ones. Unusual."

"You can see that? Nobody ever told me that but my wife, or our kids. I don't know any other silvery people, but I could always see that my wife and children were golden."

He said nothing for a long moment. "Your wife was a shape shifter that aided the Cherokee tribe? Some time ago, in the low green mountains far to the south and east of here?"

"Yes. How could you know that?"

"I know of you, and that you are the one called the Silver Walker of the Southeastern Mountains. We thought you had gone. But welcome back, it is nice to meet you."

Now I was really confused. How could an Alaskan Bigfoot, or whatever he was, know who I was? Or my wife Hia, a shapeshifter that had died two centuries ago?

"I sense your confusion. We keep up with some of your world closely for different reasons, but usually where your people do the right thing that most helps other species. We are aware of what you and your people did in the Southeastern Mountains, saving substantial portions of it. Your efforts there also helped our kind in that area. We know of your family, especially those of my kind that still travel to that part of the country."

I was not sure what to say, so I kept it simple. "Thanks, and nice to meet you too."

"You are welcome. To thank you properly, we invite you to stay with us for a few days. We can help you with your slant since you already have a talent for it. Could come in real useful someday. I sense you are going to need it."

Once again, I had no clue to the "slant" he had just referred to. But I was continuing to play along. "The entity I was just chasing. I should take care of that while I can."

"That being is of no consequence, as she only hunts sheep. I have persuaded her to leave this area. The one you seek is another hairless one that revels in causing pain. Very ill, that one is. You will capture him after you leave here."

"OK, not sure how you know that, but it is reassuring."

"I should introduce myself. Your wife's people called us the Tsul Kalu, roughly interpreted as 'those that slant'. Many names have the different hairless tribes called us. Our real name is more of a concept than a word. It is not possible to pronounce in your language and defies translation. Our personal names are the same. But in honor of your wife, simply call me Kal."

"Thanks again, Kal. I heard stories that your people existed but was not sure if it was a myth or not. Some tales described something like giants in the forest that could control the animals, and even the trees."

"Part of it is true. As you can see, despite the translation, I am not slanted. It refers to our way of changing things by slanting them with thoughts. Slant is really a discipline or a purposeful way of thought, and how we look at the world and change it, or ourselves, on occasion. A simple trick for us is to slant light to look like something else, which affects your perception. Or persuade someone they need to change their direction if they approach too close. A more complex form of slant is where we bend what you call physics. One thing can become another, distinct thing, if done correctly. For us, slant is a belief, philosophy, process, and way of life that we incorporate to interact with the universe in a way that is foreign to your people."

"Then instead of seeing you, humans would normally see a tree or boulder."

"Precisely. It's a neat solution to alter the perceptions of humans, that we call hairless, and all animals at a superficial level. But I can also be an actual tree and if you approached, you would even feel a tree trunk. Slightly unique process of slant with an application of interdimensional energy. That approach delves into aspects of physics your people have yet to discover. Or you can call it magic. I sense you know something of this way of thinking. You think enough like slant to do the same, with training."

"I have never heard anyone say that I can think slant, but I do realize I think differently. And I think my world just got a lot stranger than I imagined it this morning."

"Your world has been small so far. Stay a few days and learn. It will enlarge your universe."

The prospect of learning from a nine-foot-tall, hairy forest dweller about shifting into animals or objects, using interdimensional energy, just made too much sense to turn down. So, I stayed, and my world changed, as Kal said. The next days were filled with revelations and learning that began transforming my life.

As I passed the days there with Kal, I learned more about his people. They were so much a part of the forest it was easy to overlook them. I think I saw about six different individuals. Kal said there were more around, but I could not tell. They rarely approached us, but Kal said they were listening to us through him, and sometimes he would relay a statement or a question from one of them to me.

I asked how their communication worked. He told me that telepathy connected all of them. They did not read each other's minds unless by mutual consent but sent messages back and forth and answered when appropriate. No sounds were necessary, nor did they need to be close to one another to communicate. They traveled in small groups, more for companionship than need. Kal and his group were traveling in this area for the summer, then returning south through the coastal mountains along the Pacific.

Everyone spent short sleeps on the thick moss without other protection. Rain showers went unnoticed. Kal told me there was a cave nearby they had created for severe weather. Apparently, they could carve caves anywhere, and had a way of heating rock without fire if they needed any extra heat. Food was whatever the forest and land provided. Meals were several handfuls of edible leaves, nuts, roots, and mushrooms, seasoned with seeds and bits of soft bark, rounded out with berries and cold spring water. Kal's people could call up springs wherever they stayed.

A deep crevasse in the rock under the moss was the latrine. At least once a day one of Kal's people walked over, seemed to concentrate, and then odorless smoke rose from the pit. I think they were converting the waste to carbon by incinerating it. I assumed they could do the same thing to heat rocks in their cave. It was about as small a footprint as any group could leave in the wilderness. Between that, telepathy, and their slant camouflage, I realized why they were so rarely seen or encountered.

Kal filled my few days there with thought-provoking conversations, teaching me how the world really worked. Those talks were always profound and disquieting, and I would replay those conversations many times to understand them. Or maybe I was trying to find reasons not to believe them.

Kal was teaching me how to work with slant to achieve things I had not imagined. I needed lots of practice, but time was one thing I had in abundance. The goal of shifting into animal shapes and inanimate objects using the energy from another dimension would likely take time to perfect. I did not wish to end up as a rock for decades until Kal stumbled across me and changed me back, if he even could. Worse yet, was the result if I did not appropriately dissipate that interdimensional energy when changing back.

Kal told me I probably would not survive the resulting explosion, nor would the neighboring area the size of several city blocks. Careful was key in how to approach that business. Kal also referred to the ability to travel with slant. It was even more dangerous, so he mentioned it would be among my last lessons.

One early lesson destroyed any thoughts I had of a simple universe. We were discussing time, and I brought up that humans living in the future were using time travel to interfere with our timeline.

"You are right that they interfere here," Kal said. "They are an immediate threat to all the hairless on this planet, as well as other species. I suggest you make it your priority to oppose them and their assistants here in this timeline."

"I intend to, once I understand more of how to combat them."

"Slant will be your best tool as you develop your talent. I and others can also provide knowledge of this enemy, to help you with strategy."

"I believe they are using some mechanism coupled with quantum entanglement to travel here."

"They do. One reason it was easier for us to block it. But they were thinking much too simply."

"How's that?"

"At its most basic level, quantum entanglement deals with two specific particles that are linked, then separated. Regardless of time and distance, the particles communicate instantaneously because of that link. Correct?"

"Yes."

"Using your own physics, what was the Big Bang?"

"All matter, energy, everything, was once one big blob that exploded and created the universe."

"Precisely."

"Damn. That means that all particles, since they were once all together, still link at some basic level."

"Correct. Everything is linked at all times. The people in your future take a very limited approach and created a limited tool dealing only with "new" entanglements, whereas we approach it differently. Recognizing and then accessing the infinite linkages allows us infinite possibilities. And infinite responsibility, as we travel through the universe and through time. We, as well as other entities, only employ that capability with care. A couple of centuries of training will allow you that ability, if you wish. It takes that long to recognize and avoid the dangers that come with that knowledge. Even some of our own people have decided not to take part in that manner of travel. There is always a potential danger of inadvertently altering a timeline. Plus, there are defenses and traps deployed by some that prefer not to be visited. There may also be travelers you will encounter that do not have good intentions."

"OK, I understand the basic link concept. But since that first beginning of the universe, there have been countless events that could modify 'linkages' on a smaller scale. I'm thinking about stars forming, black holes colliding, or just here on Earth, a volcano creating a new island."

"Yes, all true and you are getting to the heart of what we call the web transits, or linkages. There is the initial, and hardest to detect, link between all particles with each other. Then there are many additional newer levels of linkages between different subgroups of particles. The most complex map imaginable. An entire race of advanced beings could not map or explore the links and transit points even after a million years. But it is just like using the subway in New York. You need only a simple map to get to places that you deem most important. No reason to memorize the Amsterdam train schedules or the Atlanta airport flight schedule, when you just want to travel from Grand Central to Broadway. You just take the green line, then transfer to the yellow line and know which to stop to take and exit the system."

"That... is a most surprising analogy. You travel on the New York subway?"

"I do, as I occasionally enjoy a Broadway play and a slice of vegetarian pizza. I just don't go often, as there are a lot of hairless around." That statement left me dumbfounded.

After four days of constant input of information, I felt the need to leave and continue my hunt. Kal already expected my departure and was waiting for me with his parting words. "If you have a pressing need for us to meet, then take this piece of twig." He snapped a small twig into two pieces and handed one to me. "Then click your heels and say Kal, three times."

I looked at him like he was crazy. He began laughing, which was a very odd sight and sound. He dropped the twig. "I see you have discerned the joke. I believe that was a paraphrase from the Wizard of Oz, a play I once saw. No twigs are necessary, of course. If you concentrate on me, and this place, via slant, then I will receive your thought and will respond."

"Thanks, Kal, for everything these past few days. I assume I will see you again?"

"Likely that is true. I believe we have common business to conduct, and a common enemy. It seems circumstances have conspired to put you in the upcoming conflicts. Safe passage to you on your journeys."

Chapter Two

My head still spinning from all the astonishing revelations of the past few days, I descended from the high forest. I hopped down a steep trail Kal told me about rather than climbing down the cliff to the valley. After all that time spent climbing up, I descended in ten minutes. I was on my way back to civilization and a serial killer. Although in that context, I guess humans really are not all that civilized.

When I reached the valley floor, I headed back to my car. I needed to get back to cell phone range and internet signal. I had been considering my human serial killer and thought I could find him relatively quickly. Since most serial killers were male, I thought the gender designation applied. Plus, there were a lot more males in Alaska than females.

I drove back to town, then started my search when I got to the hotel. On the county GIS website, I looked for records of who bought into the area before the disappearances and then were residents since the first missing person report. I got three possibilities so that was where I would start. I googled all the names and got minimal response, but one name had a hit in the local paper four years back, something about a property dispute with a neighbor. I ran the neighbor's name because it sounded familiar. He had gone missing two years ago and even I realized that was a lead. Police had questioned the other neighbor, but they found nothing. People went missing in Alaska regularly, while law enforcement had a tough job and few resources.

I drove out to the address of the person of interest from the county website. A rundown house, even for Alaska standards, sat on a gravel road outside town proper. Lots of rusty equipment and two trucks littered the property, with a decrepit barn in back. I did not see or hear any dogs, so that was a good sign that I could sneak around undetected. I drove my car half a mile away, parked, and walked back to watch the property.

I had been sitting for an hour in the trees when I heard a truck start up, then saw it pull away from the house. My time to snoop, as I headed behind the house and to the barn. Inside it was a mess of wood, materials, and junk. No bodies, human bone light fixtures, or a sign stating this was the barn of a serial killer. I would need to look inside the house. As I was leaving the barn, I noticed seven license plates nailed to the side. Two from Alaska and five from out of state. They were the only thing not weathering away in place. I took a picture with my phone as I wanted to see where this guy had lived previously.

I walked to the back of the house and found the rear door unlocked. Unfortunately, the house was more of a disaster than the barn. Difficult to believe someone lived in the clutter. I guess it took less to heat it in the winter since the interior was so full of crap. Again, no signs of anything obvious pointing to a serial killer. But I did not even know where to look for trophies this guy might have taken. The place could not have been more than a fifty square meters, but it contained a volume of junk that could have fit in a building three times that size. Old furniture, papers, stacks of cardboard boxes, mattresses, and plastic junk. I hope this hovel had fire insurance.

I left and felt like I needed a shower to rid myself of all the dust and cobwebs. Back at the hotel, it took me ten minutes to find out the guy was the serial killer. It was not exactly my brilliant mind that ferreted out the secret. The license plates matched several people that had disappeared. His trophies were on display for anyone in his backyard to see. Either this was the dumbest serial killer in Alaska, or he was a narcissist with no thought of getting caught.

I thought about what to do with the information. In my recent past, it would have meant a fatal accident for the killer. But I was trying to shed my executioner persona. Michael, my sometime boss, and Jo, my sometime partner, both from the Church, really frowned upon my lethal activities. I was trying to comply and had not killed anyone since I'd taken care of the two that had shot Jo. I would go to the local police and pass myself off as a private investigator from the family of one the missing, since Michael's excellently forged credentials would back me up. I would give them the information I had discovered, then give them three days to arrest the killer. If that did not happen, I would arrange that accident.

I drove to the police department, while calling a trout fishing guide service. Two of the days I would use productively, by meditating on a stream while fly-fishing. The officer was polite, scolded me for trespassing on the property where I had taken the photo, but assuring me they would investigate the matter. Those words inspired little confidence, but I would give them time to investigate. I drove over to the next town to start my fishing.

On the third day, as I was driving back from my fishing trip, I heard on the radio that police had arrested a local man for the murder of at least five people. They had sent teams and equipment to the property to excavate several suspicious sites. They obviously expected to find remains, so no fatal accident would be necessary. I made it back to the hotel to check out, then went on to the airport.

I spent the time on the planes back to Amsterdam, via New York, settled in my seat and listening to my music. Then I began reviewing a series of remembrances from the previous days with Kal, going over all all the new experiences that filled my brain. Before this trip, all my intuition on master vampires, sinister time travelers, and possible aliens were mostly based on observations and deduction. But now it seemed it was all real and dangerous.

My initial forays into slant had also catapulted me into realms of physics and time that I had never expected. Could be exciting, assuming I didn't kill myself with some dumb trick, like shifting and coming out of a transit link in front of a hungry velociraptor, or into the lava pool of an active volcano. A slight miscalculation could be fatal, even to me. It still did not seem real. I realized, though, that I would likely discover just how real it all was soon enough.

The morning of my second day with Kal, we had discussed a general idea of time and the universe. "Time is not what you think it is," he said. "The hairless have a limited understanding of it. Your scientists study some things and have made substantial progress and insights. Yet they shy away from studying the universal force, which is time. They search for atomic forces and subatomic particles, yearn to see dark matter, and sequence DNA. Yet they don't study time. Science can explain what something is, or where something is. Not always, but often enough. But science fails in understanding the 'when' of something, which is more important than what or where. Space, and especially time, are not what your science has reported. In fact, the word you use, time, and your thoughts around it, are not sufficient to even address the concept. In your terms, it would be like using the word 'skin' to describe all the genetics, structure, metabolism and functions of the entirety of one of your beings, plus all the actions it did for a year. Obviously, an inadequate term. Because of the complexity, it will take effort and experience to understand these concepts. With your increased lifespan, I believe you should master those lessons."

"That gives me a great deal to think about."

"Enemies from the future continue to plot the demise of your species, so not much time to think anymore. Now, you already think sideways, which is the first step to develop your slant. To begin, concentrate on your sideways thought, and then using your mind to find that other dimension, pull a tiny amount of interdimensional energy into the thought. That energy fuels the thought into our reality, at least for a short time. The key is to allow that energy to disperse slowly, or it can get explosive. Like Tunguska explosive. We will begin the lesson to access that energy tomorrow. So today is just thinking sideways, then on to slant."

"OK. I'll try it. But I feel like I need to expand my knowledge of these concepts."

"Something you should know about knowledge. It is a good thing, but not as useful as slant."

"How so?"

Slant is how things are done. Knowledge is important but secondary, as much is needed to keep from making the wrong decisions. We keep knowledge within our people similar to your computerized databases. We always have a group based somewhere to act as a library repository, connected telepathically. The rest of us can access them as needed. I can send information or receive information instantly from that database."

"That is amazing. Your people are also your network. Do humans interfere with your network with all our different broadcasts?"

"No, you don't affect us. We don't interact with your kind, but we study you enough to keep adjusting our knowledge and slant to keep ahead of, or away from, you hairless. Your society spouts out so much information hourly that we listen and assemble only a small amount of the important items for our group database. Only a small portion of the information normally applies to us, such as notices of forest clearing."

"Your group is always active, and you choose members to stay in place and act as a library or network?"

"Yes, the group is always active. We span multiple time zones and geographies. But we do not choose members for the group. All of us will go and join the group from time to time, so the members are always changing. Keeps everyone fresh as we rotate back out to the field, then those of us in the field go in and be a part of the system, which also promotes social interaction. That is necessary as we tend to be solitary creatures. We are both centralized and dispersed. Also, keeps our kind in a lower risk status in case of any catastrophes. Say one of your militaries lobbed a nuclear device at the big city you call Seattle but missed and dropped it on us instead. We would likely detect it and slant it to the sun. But just in case we miss it, we disperse our knowledge base so no single disaster can destroy it."

"Then each of you is a personal computer, but each one of you is also linked up to a network server. Just no hardware."

"Close enough. It has worked for us for many millennia."

"I'm not sure I'll ever catch up to all this."

"All of this will take time, perhaps decades. Yet your pursuit of understanding slant will bring great rewards. And soon you will be teaching other humans."

"I will forever be the grasshopper."

He paused for a moment. I realized he was accessing information. "Ah, an apt metaphor. Perhaps we can add pebble-snatching lessons as well."

"We can skip that for now. I really need to keep working on my understanding of all these new concepts."

"Hmm, that reminds me. Along the line of human understanding, we recently lent out one of our words to you hairless. We wanted to determine if you would recognize it and what you would do with it. The word was popular for a short time but now it is in disuse, as only a few of you understood it. I am afraid that the hairless have missed the lesson. If you don't get 'grok' then humans will not understand any of our more complex thought words."

"I'll keep that in mind. Wasn't the protagonist of that book called Michael?" Kal gave his version of a grin but said nothing more.

The day before I left, we were discussing why and how Kal and his people displayed such different behavior from humans. "I don't know how we got to this point, but for all my long life, humans have been killing each other and most everything else that they encounter," I said.

Kal responded with a fresh surprise. "It is not entirely your fault. Your kind was exposed to a terrible virus. Millenia ago, the hairless were more like us. Some even were adept at slant. The virus changed them, closed off that part of them, and exaggerated the violent portions of their consciousness instead. That is when your kind got civilized and started killing on a mass scale. Progress of a sort, I suppose. You had no choice, but your people were robbed of free will. You were no longer cooperative with each other nor cooperative with nature, but driven to aggression and competition, which led to violence. But it also eventually translated to cars, planes, and spaceships. And lots of weapons to wage war."

"What happened to your people? Were they also affected?"

"Since my kind are a much older precursor of what you call the hominids, we recognized the virus could affect us. We protected ourselves and it did not affect any of our people."

"All my people, the humans, were infected?"

"Yes, they were, and still are. I detect the remnants of that virus still in you. But you carry other interesting and unusual things as well."

"Where did the virus come from?"

"The hairless, several millennia ago, called them Sky Lords. They were not from the sky, and not lords in any sense. Just 'civilized' hairless ones. We originally thought they were from one of the other dimensions, but we searched and did not find them. That is when we discovered they were from your future. Your kind progressed technologically in a future timeline. But instead of doing something positive in their own time, they interfered with your timeline. We do not believe in sin how your kind do, and don't even have a word for it in our language, but those Sky Lords committed great evil. I think that qualifies as sin."

"Sky Lords. Could that be the same as Lords of the Sky? A message from a murdered jinn said something about them coming back and ending the earth."

"Interesting. It could be a message of warning related to their plans for your people. We believe the Sky Lords will try to return in force."

"What happened to the Sky Lords?"

"After observation of their actions when they were here, we determined their intentions were malevolent. Even more so when we traced the virus back to them. We expelled the last of them and locked them out so they can't access this world any longer from their place-time. This world is still accessible physically, but that limits those that visit, as it is not near more populous star systems."

There went my head, exploding again. Time travelers were not enough, there had to be aliens too. "None of them can return here anymore?"

"There are always workarounds, and we suspect a very few still come here. But using alternate dimensions rather than jumping from their time to this one is risky for them, so their presence had been significantly reduced. In case you are wondering, we stopped their visits approximately one hundred years ago."

"That was before World War Two?"

"Yes, they designed the first war that consumed so much of Europe, so when we saw them setting up the second one, we intervened. Still did not stop it, as the hairless were already too far along in their endeavors. But locking them out limited the damage we believe they had planned for afterward. Seventy-five percent of the hairless population under one authoritarian regime controlled by the Sky Lords, with nearly unlimited physical resources, was unimaginable. That is why we had to intervene."

"The world really would be a different place if they had won."

"Not just a different place, but a different time and reality. Their ambitions would have not just changed this world but affected this region of space."

"How does the virus affect us currently? Or have you conducted enough research to know all the effects?"

"We are still learning but have discovered they engineered the original virus to make the host extremely susceptible to external manipulation, even several millennia after the initial release. We did not expect that or think it was possible. A particular type of message, repeated and amplified, results in a physiological addiction to the messages. The affected react to your media technology, so when certain emotions, images, and ideas are projected to humans, it affects their brain to block intelligence and heighten certain negative emotions.

"Originally, we believed it to be an unintended artefact from the original virus given to humans, but now we think they embedded that feature to increase susceptibility for the time when mass media was developed and disseminated. It only affects about fifty percent of your kind for unknown reasons. Unfortunately, those affected will eventually resort to violence against the unaffected. That is a significant problem for the hairless, as the affected half tries to kill off the more intelligent half. Soon the affected will be susceptible enough to where they will answer a mass call to arms to cause widespread destruction. We expect that to happen as part of a planned planetary onslaught in the next decade. We don't know yet whether this is reversible. It is rapidly progressing to where we feel this generation of your people may be lost. There will only be trouble to come as your people battle each other."

"Kal, that is worse than I had imagined, but explains a lot. The past few years, people in many countries have split into two camps that can no longer tolerate each other. Is your plan of shutting down the internet and mass communication the only way to combat it?"

"Taking down your internet and computer systems, along with all mass media, could resolve the problem. Following generations would be free of those effects. But that has yet to be decided as the immense disruption may end your society. Many are working on this problem, but without more information, or better yet, samples of the original virus before it was introduced to humans, our progress is slow. There is no other antidote yet."

"That would be a drastic solution. There must be a better way."

"Agreed. We will continue to study the problem and attempt a better solution."

That night I thought about the virus and how to eradicate it. The only solution I came up with was for someone to travel to the Sky Lords and steal the original virus and bring it back. But I did not know of anyone in our current timeline that could accomplish that.

The following morning it was time for me to leave. I walked with Kal to the edge of the forest.

"I realize this is a lot to send you off with, but I would like you to consider all that we discussed," Kal said. "Spend days or weeks with it. At some point, you will need to decide what to do personally, and then whether to bring others into your confidence. But through very unusual circumstances, these are now your enemies and your problems. And, therefore, now part of your purpose."

Kal's revelations certainly explained some thoughts I had already had. Then blew past them with an unimaginably long and complicated history. I would have to consider what to relate to Michael. But it made another decision - to take care of my American family - much easier. And it made my quest to hunt master vampires and any Sky Lords even more important.

I roused myself from the seat and stepped off another airplane. Flying had become so habitual I almost forgot how much I detested it. I took the train back to my Amsterdam house, where I sat on my balcony overlooking the canal, feeling my mind spinning with new information. Which was good, as it kept me fighting the battle of my ongoing depression. Perhaps lots of brain activity and working on my slant would keep me mentally healthy. But with everything happening, I was still disconcerted enough that I called no one, nor rode my bike or listened to music all day. Something was happening in my brain, and it was getting squirmy.

The next day, I had to shake off the lather in my mind and start living again. Time to come back to my present life. I felt half my mind was living in the depression-decorated past, but at least the other half was living in an uncertain but exciting future. But the present had to be taken care of for that future to occur. An easy first piece of business was to call my best friend Thomas and set up a lunch. That would ground me back to the present time and place.

CHAPTER THREE

S omehow Thomas was free, and we had lunch the next day. He was usually too busy with running one of the busiest airports in the world to meet on short notice. I owed Thomas something of an explanation after our last conversation. Telling one of your best friends that you investigate, and sometimes employ force against unsavory characters, needed some follow up.

We planned to meet in the Schipol Airport atrium, then take a long walk to our lunch site. It was down hundreds of meters of hallway that connected the airport to the parking garages and two hotels. Then another trek outside to a set of buildings on the periphery of the airport that was set up as a business campus. There we would grab a sandwich and sit outside, weather permitting. We wouldn't have to worry about anyone overhearing our conversation.

I arrived at the atrium. It was busy, but I saw Thomas right off. He walked over and we hugged.

"Ah, the Alaskan wild man returns."

"Yes, and still beardless and wearing no skins."

"But you could have worn them. You would blend right in with the Schipol crowd."

"Or I could be allergic to wearing dead animals."

"Going into anaphylactic shock could put a damper on your visit. But I would enjoy pulling the AED box off the wall and shocking your body with thousands of volts. Fun for both of us, I'd say."

"Nah, I'll just stick with wearing wool. I would hate to throw up on your shoes at work after all those jolts."

"Always thinking of the well-dressed man. I appreciate that."

We often started our conversations with nonsensical banter. Now that it was done, we started our long walk to less busy places.

"I saw the headlines a while back," Thomas said. "Just what you said would happen. Police captured a serial killer, a crazed religious zealot with a serious homophobic and racist bent."

"Yes, I found him with overwhelming incriminating evidence. I sent the police there for the arrest."

"But you caught him. There was no mention of that in the papers. Not about you or anyone else being involved."

"Nope, just the way it must be. That way, the next one never sees me coming. I had no intention of getting involved officially. Found him, found the evidence, tied him up, and called the police."

"I saw a video of the suspect just after the arrest. He seemed to have trouble walking."

"Might have been. I needed to make sure he did not escape. And I let him stew a little longer than necessary."

"I can't say I'm too disturbed by that. I did not know any of the victims, but some of my colleagues did. We are all glad he is no longer a threat."

"Happy to help. Some folks need to be off the streets."

"Have you done this before, in the time since we've known each other?"

"I think the most recent one was a drug dealer that was killing young teenagers."

"I remember some months ago that they had found bodies of young kids. I thought it was drug related, from overdoses or something."

"No, they died because a vicious drug dealer murdered them."

"I don't remember hearing or seeing anything about a dealer getting caught by police and charged with murder."

"Nope."

"I take it there was no arrest?"

"He made me an offer I couldn't refuse. He sleeps with the fishes."

"So now you are quoting the Godfather?"

"It was a pretty good movie."

"Surely you are not serious. Just how dangerous are you?"

"I am extremely dangerous to criminals, especially those that murder innocents. I'm talking about the vicious thugs that rape and murder girls and boys for fun. Although it is possible that I've killed someone in battle that was not a criminal. I suppose most of that fault lies with the state that hosts the army, though. I am very docile otherwise."

"You are a former soldier as well?"

"Yes, I've been in a few dustups. I plan to stay out of that for the rest of my life, though. Wars seem like they would be black and white, but really, they are mostly gray and confusing. Sometimes hard to tell who the good guys are."

"So, for you, it's necessary to know who the good guys are? Is that why you are working for the Church?"

"It's always important to know who the good guys are. It is just not always easy to tell at first. The Church gives me a few assignments to investigate and then turn over evidence to them on a contract basis."

"You don't terminate the bad guys that the Church is after?"

"I have not yet, and don't plan to unless I get cornered and have no choice."

"I know I'm asking lots of questions, but this is a little disturbing. Your answers are making me feel better. I have felt no hostility in you, but you have an aura of danger and mystery about you. Many of my friends are most intrigued. Now I know why you seem dangerous, but I guess I'm OK with it, especially since you took care if that crazy serial killer. Having him that close in our community is troubling."

"Understandable. Serial killers, by definition, kill multiple people. They do that because they seem relatively normal and can get close to you before you realize the danger."

"That one was too close. I have a slightly different question that you don't have to answer. Is this how you make your money?"

"No, not really. I have accumulated old wealth that I keep in investments that I manage. The Church pays me for jobs, but that is just play money. I would likely do it for free, anyway."

"A philanthropic vigilante that hunts bad men for the Church. I didn't think such a thing existed."

"Yeah, well, a guy has to get by. Gives me something to do other than watch the interest accumulate."

"I guess this explains more about your love life. With that lifestyle, it must be difficult to have a long-term love interest. I assume you would not tell them."

"Right. I can't tell them and so I just don't have serious girlfriends."

"Does Jo know?"

"She does not know every detail, but she knows almost everything."

"She does not seem to be bothered. In fact, I'd say she was comfortable with you."

"Well, the first time she heard about it, she was angry for days. Now I have an agreement with her. I will still do what I must, but not kill anyone unless it becomes necessary. She was recently involved in a dangerous event herself and may understand me better, but I agree with her original objection. Anyone I am interested in would have to be ignorant of my life, which is deceptive, or know about me and be OK with it."

Thomas just looked at me with a half-smile. "So, I am to be trusted with your real life. It may take some getting used to. But I also know I have my personal bouncer if I ever get into trouble. Nice deflection earlier, regarding Jo's comfort with you. I look forward to seeing you two together again at our next dinner."

I had no response to that. I still was not sure where I stood with Jo, much less the new, improved version that I had created. We finally finished our fifteen-minute hallway walk, then went outside and across the street to get our food in the next building.

"How are things with Willem?" I asked.

"Good. Compatible and comfortable. Most unlike me to say that, or to feel that way, as you know. I suppose I don't keep anyone around for too long, but this feels different."

"Damn. Now that sounds serious in a good way. I'm happy for you."

"Thanks. Maybe we can do a double wedding with you and Jo."

We both laughed.

"Yeah, in another lifetime, you ass. Just when we were sounding all mature."

"You never know. Perhaps someday she will like you."

We sat and ate outside, with jokes and small talk. After we finished our sandwiches, we strolled back toward the terminal.

"Thanks for trusting me enough to tell me about your activities," Thomas said. "I think there is a lot more that you have not told me. More to come, I suppose?"

"Yeah, a lot more. Probably best for me to dribble it out a little at a time. It's outlandish, but I'll eventually tell you all about it. You already know me, but I have a long and varied past."

"Don't we all. But yours probably involves angels and demons, wizards and dragons, elves and orcs."

"Well, no wizards or dragons that I know of. The rest of them probably exist. I should have some good stories over the next couple of years."

Thomas looked at me as to judge whether I was serious.

"But you left out aliens. There are definitely aliens." I began laughing, as I could not keep a straight face. Thomas looked relieved, then he chuckled. "Seriously though, a lot of the myths you have heard or seen in the movies are mostly junk. But some creatures from those stories existed, and sometimes, do still exist. That is one reason the Church has contracted my services."

"Anything I need to worry about?"

"You have a much better chance of choking on a chicken bone than ever meeting one of them. For 99.9 percent of humans, other humans are the most dangerous thing they will ever come across."

"That sounds comforting. But then it isn't, really, considering how many humans are on earth. And how close a serial killer was to us recently."

"Exactly right. Keep your eyes on the humans. Let me and my colleagues worry about the tiny fraction of monsters out there."

We were back in the atrium and said our goodbyes. A group dinner was being planned, he told me, and he would send an invitation to Jo and me. I looked forward to it but could not confirm whether Jo might attend.

I took the train back to my place. Later that evening, I sat and began making more plans. I knew I must go back to America, but I had things to do and decisions to make beforehand. Probably not the most important one, but one that had to be started immediately, was to supply myself with weapons better suited to the competition that I was likely to face in the future. I opened the locker that few people had ever seen and looked at the display case across half the room that was protected by an alarm system. Probably redundant, as I don't think anyone could have gotten into this room, anyway. My gladius was in there, as well as a tomahawk, Viking axe, longsword, and several other items from my martial past. The typical set of knives, mace, truncheons with customized spikes or small blades, a longbow with arrows, a crossbow with bolts, and my Cherokee wife's bow and arrows. Plus, a crusader shield and a second Viking axe I had modified with a custom hand guard while plying the Mediterranean and fighting pirates. The gladius was not my original one, as that was long since lost in the river. It was another I had come across during my old Holland days of digging and farming. I found it in terrible shape but had cleaned and sharpened the blade and added new grip material. It was now in excellent shape.

A thought occurred to me, and I added another item to my list. I would call a guy I knew that worked with fine metals over in the city of Haarlem. Plating the gladius and other blades, either fully or partially with silver, seemed like an excellent investment for my future. It would be a pain to keep the tarnish off, but I'd trade that annoyance for a weapon to take on critters that the silver would harm more than a steel blade would. While on that thought, some silver chain mail and silver gauntlets could come in handy. Which begot the idea of silver knuckles, rather than brass knuckles. Easy to wear and conceal, and the silver was a bonus when punching a supernatural baddie in the teeth.

I could also have the metal guy add some small channels along the fuller of the blade. Applying some thick, dehydrated binder potion in the channels could give me even more advantage. The binder was a potent nerve toxin that stopped even supernatural creatures cold. I had no intention of fighting fair with entities that probably did not even know of the concept of fairness. Quick and dirty was always better than giving fair chances in a fight.

I also noticed the blowgun beside my tomahawk. Two weapons I had not thought of using in a long time. But that was another interesting idea to deliver my binder potion. I pulled out the blowgun and realized I needed to get back into practice. I may need to change the darts or make new ones to keep from poisoning myself. Thick binder potion in a hollow needle should do the trick.

I had not tried it yet, but I should be able to evaporate off most of the liquid potion to make a syrup or residue, without losing potency. Might even make it more potent. If it was thick and sticky enough, I could coat many other blades and objects. Lots of ideas to ponder.

Bullets could be another one of those options. I needed to think about how to do that. Coating them would likely not work as it would not stick to the lead, leading to self-poisoning during handling. And the potion would not survive the shooting process. Drilling into the lead and depositing a droplet may work, but the bullet would have to fragment on entry. I would follow up with a weapons expert I knew. He had hand-loaded competition ammunition for serious shooters, including some that competed in the Olympics, so he should know how best to build the bullets. I preferred not to handle ammunition or hand load bullets, but I could if I had to. I could probably get him to do the modifications, but I did not want him handling the potion. Best to do it myself. So, one call to the metals guy, and another to the bullet guy.

Then I had another crazy idea, which I realized was a modification of something I had once read in a fantasy novel. A paintball gun, with the balls loaded with regular binder potion. But I discounted that one quickly. Too many ways for that to go wrong. But it could work if I had enough potion, and then found myself dropped into a vampire or shifter convention. I just did not need to shoot myself with one of those balls in the middle of that convention. Paralyzed, in the middle of a group of pissed vamps, wouldn't end well for me. But I would get to find out how a buffet line felt when a busload of tourists showed up at a restaurant.

All that thinking brought me around to another idea. Perhaps I should prepare an antidote for the potion. If I dosed myself, or another person accidentally, it would be a good idea to know how to treat it. I didn't know how to prepare it, or if it was even possible, but made a mental note to pursue that line of research soon. Another add to the list of things to be done.

I discounted the paintball approach but realized a shotgun could deliver a hell of a physical blow, backed with the nerve toxin binder. The lead or steel pellets in the shell could be coated with binder, then possibly protected with a wax coating. Because the pellets are inside the plastic shot shell, there is no chance of contaminating the shooter. And since there were so many pellets in one shell, the chance of multiple entry wounds would maximize the binder entering the bad guy, or bad girl, or thing. Even better, aim for the abdomen, puncture the intestines, and hit the microbiome directly. That would take down just about anything smaller than a Great Serpent.

My mind wandered to a science fiction weapon, which unfortunately had not been invented yet. A flechette pistol, with the tiny darts coated with binder, would be a great way to take out some riff raff. I just had to wait perhaps another fifty years. My list included a list of several silver weapons, then bullets for sniper rifles and pistols, shotgun shells, and blowgun darts, all engineered to carry the binder potion into the target. Throw in plenty of money to get it done, and probably use all the binder potion I had in the country. Another task was to call Nan and have her start producing more binder. I was uncertain whether all the weapons and ammo would be ready before I traveled back to America, but I would take what I could. Also, I would keep several items in the Netherlands for the European pests I knew were still lurking.

The day after meeting with Thomas, I drove over to the cottage. Even though I had not talked to Michael recently, I already knew he would be there. Possibly some of my slant work was paying off. He welcomed me at the door. He was an imposing figure, made even more dangerous by his career as a professional assassin and head of Church security. I suspected he was that and much more, but his past was a mystery to me.

"Hello, paladin of the great north," he said. "I saw from the news that a serial killer is no longer on the prowl and is in custody rather than in the morgue after an unfortunate accident. The Church thanks you for that service, and for restraining any desire to eliminate the killer. Come in and let us talk."

I nodded a hello. We walked back into the study area and prepared cappuccinos. Michael kept glancing at me and probably wondering about my lack of witty banter. I thought my banter was witty, anyway.

"You look different somehow," he said. "Or you seem to vibrate differently."

"Probably so. I have been communing with the Ents."

He paused. "I'm not sure whether Tolkien based those on mythology, or just made them up for his book. Either way, those are Old World myths."

"Well, when they left Middle Earth, they had to go somewhere. Might as well be the New World."

"You have the maddening ability to drop a note of truth into a melody of obfuscation."

"Thank you."

"Of course, you would take that as a compliment. The rest of us just want to not be tortured by your words. Now let us discuss the case and how you found the killer."

I recounted my story, including details of the hunt, but divulging nothing about Kal's people. I did not feel I needed to keep it a secret forever, but I was not ready to discuss it yet. I told Michael that the supernatural creature, the Adlet, that was killing the sheep complicated the case, as it was a false lead. But then I realized the dead sheep were separate from the missing humans. Dumb luck on my part caught the killer. Michael kept quiet and nodded occasionally.

"I don't agree with the dumb luck assessment. Something prompted you to notice and photograph the license plates. Just as an adept can feel other entities, I believe you can also sense important physical objects."

"Maybe, but I'm OK with luck. Most days I'd rather be lucky than good."

"Regardless, my compliments on an excellent job with the entire case. We have had little exposure to the Adlet, although our Jesuit colleagues have dealt with them in Canada previously. Despite the stories of aggression toward humans, recent evidence suggests they are shy and only attack animals for food. But anything you can add will help our database. Obviously, the removal of the serial killer from society was of significant benefit."

"Sure, I'll fill in whoever you have set up here on the Adlet. Happy to catch a killer, especially when I don't have to kill them myself."

"Well, you can tell Jo all about it when she arrives in two days." That surprised me. I did not expect her to be back in the Netherlands that soon. "I see from your reaction that you were not expecting her."

"No, I have not talked to her lately. I think it will be good to see her. Has she been OK since the change?"

"There have been some rough spots, but overall, she has been quite good. Both physically and mentally. It is time you saw you each other."

"You are right, and it really is time." Although I said it, I was not sure I felt it. I had recently saved Jo's life, by making her like me. Being immortal had its advantages, but I had changed Jo without her consent in order to save her life after a shooting. But I knew from experience how tough it was knowing you would survive all your current friends and family. And she knew it was now something she would face, which had to be a tough adjustment. Things had been strained between us ever since.

"OK. I will alert you when Jo arrives, so you can come and greet her. We can go over her transformation progress with her present."

"Sounds good. I'll see you soon."

As I drove away, I was not sure that it sounded good. Jo and I had a lot of baggage to go through before I would feel comfortable with her again. Or maybe I was overthinking everything. I'd find out soon enough.

CHAPTER FOUR

I drove over to the cottage on a bright morning. The drive was relaxing, at least. Beautiful green fields, weirdly mutilated trees, sky and clouds worthy of any medieval painter. And cowshit, everywhere the smell of cowshit. But even that was comforting after all the centuries I had spent here smelling it, as the background aroma this time of year.

To keep my mind off the impending meeting I also went over the weapons inventory I had readied the past few days. I should have everything I had requested back within a few days to a month. Plenty of time to ship most of my arsenal of new toys to America, plus keeping a few here for my next bout with Caius and his minions.

I was nervous at meeting Jo for the first time since she had left the hospital. She had gone home to her family in the UK for an extended visit, but she cut that shorter than scheduled and returned to the Center. Since that time, we had both been busy with our duties. And probably avoiding each other for various reasons. I wondered if my action of turning her into an immortal, and all the baggage that went with it, might cause her to hate my guts. Perhaps I should just check back in a couple hundred years. With that bright thought, I entered the cottage drive, so it was too late to bolt for greener pastures with less cowshit.

As I walked up the steps to the familiar front door, it opened to reveal Michael waiting for me with a wry grin. I already knew what the bastard was smiling at - my discomfort. I planned to return the favor as soon as possible.

"Goedemorgen" he said in Dutch, just to get me going.

"Back at you," was my response. "What fresh hell have you cooked up for breakfast today?" I asked.

"Just seeing your cheery face is enough to brighten this fine day. But you worry unnecessarily. Jo is excited to see you."

"I am excited to see her, too. I'm just nervous."

"Understandable. But I think you are in for a pleasant surprise."

"OK, let's do this."

He looked confused. "Another Americanism, I suppose. Let us go and 'do this' as you said."

I followed Michael in, with a lingering vision of something like a table lamp flying at me. My last conversation with Jo was professional, but I assumed she was going to be unhappy with me for a few decades, at least. I planned to keep Michael between me and any flying objects, just in case.

Jo immediately stood up and walked toward me with a partial smile. My god, she looked wonderful. I didn't know what to do, so I held out my hand for a handshake. She just shook her head, sighed, and took my hand. Off to another stellar start, I thought to myself.

"Great to see you," I stammered.

"Good to see you as well," she replied as her grip tightened. Damn, she had gotten stronger. I returned the grip more to keep my bones intact than to compete with her. She laughed, dropped my hand, then gave me a full hug that ordinarily would have embarrassed me. It did not in this case, because I had other problems to deal with. The hug came with an intense fog of mixed pheromones that staggered me. I would have dropped to one knee if she hadn't been holding me. I really needed to drop down or sit anyway, as she had instantly triggered a portion of the autonomic nervous system that I had preferred not to rear its ugly head. Too late.

She released me with a grin, then looked uncertain as she saw my face.

"Are you OK?" she asked with concern.

"Uh, not exactly," I answered. "But I will be in a moment."

Michael was watching us intently and looked ready to intervene. I quickly stepped to the table and sat down. She came up behind me and put her hand on my shoulder. Which re-triggered everything. I closed my eyes for a moment and tried to focus on anything but her. I thought she might be invisible to me, like a master vampire would be, but I shuddered as a vision of a blazing comet seared my brain instead.

"Damn," I nearly yelled as I turned around toward her. She flinched back as my face must have been showing the intensity of my triggered emotions.

Michael said, "Jo, I think your presence has affected Sen beyond his ability to control his impulses. It might be best to pause a moment."

She nodded a yes and sat down. Two chairs away from me. Smart girl.

"Michael, please do us the honor of preparing tea, and take your time. I don't think I can manage it at the moment."

"I will. Please tell us what just happened."

Jo was looking at me expectantly, rather than the frightened look I had expected.

"I think I got a dose of pheromones, the like of which I have never experienced before. That led to several complications. Then, when I sat down to focus with my eyes closed, I saw Jo in my other site, like a bright burning vision. Overall, the effect was an overwhelming desire, almost to the point of violence."

Jo blushed at that revelation.

As Michael was finishing his tea task, he said, "Interesting."

He brought us our tea. My hand was shaking, and I almost spilled it.

"What would have happened if you two had been alone?" he asked.

I then had to blush. "Things would have gotten quite heated," I answered as I kept my eyes on Jo. She did not look away nor seem concerned. But neither did she show any obvious reciprocation.

I sat for a moment and did not talk, until I was fully back in control. "Well, that was quite a way to start the morning. Sorry Jo, about my reaction. Sensing you like that was unexpected. Did you pick up anything from me to start that chain of events, or was all that just an automatic, unconscious action on your end?"

"As soon as you walked in, I sensed something like nervousness, and perhaps attraction. When I hugged you, I felt great, like reliving a warm memory. I also felt, well, an attraction. Then, when you sat down, I somehow was aware of you in my head. I felt your emotion, almost to where I thought you might be out of control."

"It seems you two have a bond," Michael said. "Jo, were you aware that you were releasing pheromones?"

"No, I didn't know," she replied.

"Sen, were you releasing any as you came in?"

"No, I have learned to control any type of release automatically. I have met no one before that could release that kind of intense cloud until today."

"Do you think Jo will learn to control it?"

"Yes," I answered. "But I can't decide in my current state whether I want her to."

She smiled. "I'll try not to gas you again. Otherwise, I might have to kick your arse if you get out of control and lose your gentlemanly nature."

"Thanks, I think. Well, I believe that surprise is over for now. Any other issues happening since the turning?" I asked.

"Physically, I feel great. I run and swim much faster and never seem tired. My sight and hearing are much better. I heal from small wounds overnight.

Downsides, if I can even call them that, are that I don't seem to need much sleep, and I no longer have periods."

"But how do you feel?" I asked.

For the first time, she faltered. "I alternate between feeling extremely guilty when around my family and feeling fantastic. It has been a real roller coaster for the past few weeks. Michael has me working with someone on that."

I looked at Michael gratefully. He nodded.

"Any abnormal sweating, aches, or headaches?" I asked.

"No, nothing like that. Speaking with Michael and others, I think I may not have the blackouts and comas like you experienced. I believe the issues you experienced were because of the adaptations to the allergens you ingested. But they have should have attenuated in your body, leaving me without most side effects. But I suppose that time will tell."

"Your grip seems to have improved."

"Yes, along with the strength, came an inch of height and more muscle. I like it because my clothes fit looser in most places, even though my weight increased a half stone."

"What do you think about the change in her reproductive cycle?" Michael asked me.

"Hey, don't ask me, I'm not a subject of the Ovarian Empire. I do not know."

"Again, with the sexist tripe that you call humor," Jo said.

"Yeah, I'm a pig. But understandable, as now you have irresistible pheromones, which is going to make me stupider than usual. I never researched that human function as it never even occurred to me."

"Of course not. And that is why you also won't deduce why I'm already as strong and fast as you in such a short time."

I looked at her blankly. I glanced at Michael, and he seemed as stumped as I did.

"I have an additional microbiome system you don't. Get it now?"

Reasoning finally dawned on me. "You're right, and I'm such an idiot to have missed it. Michael, once again, us old white guys have overlooked something important yet glaringly obvious. The transformation affects women differently, and they have an advantage with another microbiome available to colonize. Which leads back to a possible reason for the change in menstruation."

"I agree," he said. "We don't even consider what should be obvious, so that is a warning to us. However, Jo, I would doubt that it means you are no longer fertile."

"I think my body, along with many other changes, is probably much more efficient and reabsorbs rather than excretes the uterine lining," she said. "And I would rather change the subject. If I have any worries, I will get checked out at the Center clinic."

"Can you sense others around you at some distance?" I asked, both to change the subject and glean how much Jo had progressed with the change.

"Yes, and it seems to get more intrusive. I don't like crowded areas much now, as I feel like my brain is overloaded with sensory input. I don't know what they are thinking or doing, I just know they are there. Today when you came in, it was different. I knew you in a way I cannot explain. Then, when you sat down, it was like you were a comet streaking into my head. You were a bright light moving toward me."

"On the human sensing side, will Jo be able to control that in time?" Michael asked. "And what does it signify that you two are sensing each other so strongly?"

"In time, you should be able to block most of that input without effort," I answered. "It took me a while once I realized what was happening. It comes in useful if there is a threat nearby, but otherwise it is a nuisance. I would say in a few months you can control it. On the other topic, I don't know what it means. I have never had a vision like that before, so I suppose I never met a fellow turnee."

"Will I then always feel you in my head?" she asked.

"I just don't know. But this may be bad. If master vampires can sense us, then we won't have much chance of getting close to them, and they can use it to hunt us."

Michael did not look convinced. "I'm not sure if that is true. I think it is the opposite, that you are invisible to them, as they are to you. But we could test it the next time we catch one alive."

She nodded agreement. "I guess I can either learn to control it or spend more time in the martial arts class with Simon, working out that frustration."

"You should probably do that anyway," I said. "He's an outstanding teacher and highly creative."

"He speaks highly of you as well. The only person he's never taken down. Of course, I don't think he knew about your extra advantage."

"Probably not, and I had no intention of telling him. I nearly had to use that advantage several times to keep him from breaking my bones."

"We should spar later. I need to see how much progress I've made."

"That sounds good. With your new physical improvements and Simon's coaching, you should be formidable."

We continued with conversations on activities happening at or scheduled for the Center. They were still implementing new programs but felt there was progress on studying the microbiomes of turned beings, and on sifting data to find master vampires. It sounded promising, but I was getting bored quickly as the morning wore on.

Michael proposed a break for lunch, and Jo and I agreed. She left to check messages before eating. She gave me a brief smile and went out the door to the back. I went to go get some tea, and Michael stayed in the room, so I poured him a cup as well.

"I should also tell you that Jo has a new position. She is the Vice-President of Public Service and Outreach."

I was having trouble trying not to laugh. I knew the type of people that populated those positions at universities and Jo no longer bore any resemblance to that crowd. "I would hate to be on the end of that Outreach, even if it served the public good."

"I don't think you need to worry about that unless you decide to get really naughty."

"Oh no, I'll behave myself. Why do you guys come up with lame names for your departments and job titles, and then advertise them?"

"The best way to keep a secret organization secret is to hide in plain sight. But always staying very vanilla with titles. I would think you have learned the value of that over the centuries."

"Makes sense, and I have learned that. No reason to change if you've been doing it for that long. On a slightly different subject, now that you have you got the search capability running at the Center, have you been able to trace me?"

"As Jo mentioned, the project is now staffed and software is in training, using you as a test project. Unfortunately, without the file we had already built on you, we would not have detected you until recently. As in the past ten years. You did well with staying off the grid."

"Anybody else show up?"

"A half dozen possibilities. For most of them, they have outed themselves with an opulent lifestyle. And with two of them, a penchant for cruelty accompanied that lifestyle."

"I guess they are due for some serious Outreach?"

"Absolutely. We have surveillance on them, and intervention teams assigned if needed. We want to be extremely careful in case of traps or escape systems. Perhaps their lack of keeping a low profile is made up for in defensive systems. But I doubt it, as the centuries of not getting caught has probably made them lazy."

Lunch arrived, and Jo came back in. The afternoon went by better than the morning as we were brainstorming ideas to improve the search function for master vampires. I added little other than the suggestion to include ancient companies. My little investment company had been around nearly two hundred years, under different names, of course. Then Michael pushed us off onto a tangent.

"You have my thanks for telling us your original theory about the microbiome. Now with Jo's revelation, we'll need to expand that work. But to date, the research at the Center has led to further discoveries we had not expected."

"This ought to be good," I said. "And I'll be glad to hear if the microbiome theory really is true."

"Oh, it is true, but those are just the beginning of our discoveries. Jo, since you have been working closely with that group, please take over. You have a better understanding of the findings."

"Sure, Michael," Jo said. "What the team found was evidence of the organization of the microbiome and nervous tissues. But almost by accident, we saw the nervous tissue extend outward from the gut. Extensive preliminary work shows a neural network throughout the body routed along the lymphatic system. We also found neural tissue concentrations in lymph nodes. Some subjects, but not all, also showed infiltration of the brain through that system."

"That's amazing. I see a lot of possibilities for explaining some of the crazy things walking around out there."

"We do too," Michael said. "Several creatures may have this system."

"It also makes certain entities difficult to incapacitate or kill," Jo said. "The diffuse neural network with 'mini brains' stashed throughout the body, enhanced physical strength and speed, and a supercharged immune system, give them a significant advantage over humans. Although perhaps I should use the term 'us' instead of them." She was looking at me as she said that last sentence. I didn't know whether to give her a 'welcome to the club' speech or apologize. I did neither and kept quiet.

The conversations continued, and as the evening approached, Jo excused herself to take a run and make some calls. Michael and I took a small aperitif and walked outside.

"Would you consider joining me for dinner?" he asked.

"Sure, but only if the food is good. No borrels or dairy cow steaks."

"I'm sure we can do better than that. I foresee roast chicken with fresh greens and potatoes."

"I'm all in for that."

"Good, I'll see the dinner is ready in a reasonable time." He stepped out for a few moments. I sat and thought about the implications of microbiomes organizing into sentient organisms. And how women would be equal or superior to men once changed, with their inherent capacity for a secondary microbiome system. I realized science was entering into exciting new times.

Michael returned a few minutes later. I decided to ask him about the progress of the search for bad guys using the Church's database.

"How is the Center coming along with the digital search for master vampires and other evildoers?" I asked.

"Our computer information branch is doing well. Categorizing relics, cataloguing facial recognition impressions, and researching financial matters concerning master vampires. They are quite busy."

"Sorry that my guy did not work out. He really wanted to keep his independence."

"Understandable. Even more so with computer technology than other disciplines, I can see that we look staid and ancient."

"Yes, that, plus he prefers to operate by crossing over a few lines. Quite a few lines, most of which I've asked him to do and then paid him for. He probably did not want the dad talk. You know, the one about keeping on the straight and narrow path."

"In my defense, I often operate in the grey. Sometimes well over into darker colors when necessary. But I have the seniority to do so and can see that others may be uncomfortable crossing the lines when working with our organization. Concern that the might of the Church might fall on them for the least indiscretion; it has happened before. But I don't operate that way. Basically, I can't operate that way to be effective."

"Good to know. But he can still be quite useful as he is. At least to me, and of course I'll pass on anything he finds that may be of use."

"Understood. As we often work with external contractors or allies that forward interesting information, we cultivate those connections without interfering with their efficacy."

"Makes sense. Like contracting old Roman soldiers that inexplicably still find themselves alive."

"Just so. Remember how we work in 'mysterious ways' in days to come."

CHAPTER FIVE

The door at the back of the room opened and one of Michael's people carried in two plates. We sat casually at the table to eat and make small talk. It was simple, excellent food.

"I think we should talk about upcoming issues that will soon be important," Michael said. "Jo has some other duties for the next two hours, so we will dine without her. It's time to have a candid talk about some things."

"Michael, you damn well better not say any crap like 'Luke, I am your father', or I'll have to skip dinner."

"Ah, I remember that movie. One of our better efforts to educate the masses. But no, I claim no familial relationship."

"Well, that is cryptic. Anyway, I'd say the most important thing about today is that I'll be even more careful around Jo now that I know how she affects me. I have a lot of other thoughts as well, but I need to think about things before delving into a lot of what-ifs."

"I appreciate your thoughtfulness and consideration regarding her. Despite certain misgivings she may still have over her new circumstances, your positive involvement in her life is critical to her well-being."

"It is my intention to do just that. But I'm not always sure my actions toward others are considerate, especially when I'm distracted. But I will make a special effort for her."

"I'm sure you will, and it will be appropriate."

"Speaking of general stuff, while devouring this delicious avian protein, was it a coincidence that I met Brother James in that alley earlier this year?"

"I think that depends on your frame of reference. There are no coincidences, or everything is a coincidence."

"That is a rather intricate way of avoiding my question."

"You spotted that, did you?"

"Yes, even though you tried to sidestep it. But your line of reasoning regarding coincidences could apply to everything in this world."

"Absolutely, as most things exist in dual states, and that is likely planned by God."

"So, God is like Schrodinger's cat, both there and not there?"

He paused. "That is a most acute observation. And exactly right."

"Or in this context, it could also be exactly wrong."

"Now you are getting it." He sighed. "Back to your question. There was some plan in all this. Or maybe some thought about how things could go. But to skip the details, ultimately it came to: We have gotten to a point where we needed you, and I thought you needed us as well."

"In what manner do you think I needed the Church?"

"You have a certain propensity to lapse into mild depression that we have talked about before."

"Yes, in part to have lived this long and see the deaths of everyone I've cared for. I think another part of those depressive thoughts centered on the feeling that I have killed too much in life, as you pointed out. My conscience is full and I'm just tired."

"I would say you have shown remarkable restraint. You spent most of your life in cultures where even minor offenses, like stealing or adultery, were punishable by death. No mystery why you might be more blood thirsty than the average citizen. But I know you don't have that many bodies counted against you, especially in relation to your age and activities. And I doubt many of those bodies were innocent of major crimes."

"True enough, and I understand that consciously. It is just that sometimes my thoughts are bleaker than they should be."

"I understand that as well, and that is how we can help you. Anytime you feel the need to talk, please let me know. I will reiterate that once you work out your awkwardness and feelings of guilt regarding Jo, you two should also talk. You can help her probably better than anyone else as she progresses through her new life. And helping her will also help you. Additionally, working with the Church puts you in contact with those that know what you are. Hopefully, you can develop friendships that will also allow you to converse with them. So that is what I foresaw when we made contact."

"Was Jo any part of your plan?"

He sighed again. "Based on her background, I thought she was the right fit to get you started in our group. If you are asking if I foresaw anything past that, then no, I did not. Never did I imagine that your professional relationship would progress into you turning her after the shooting. So, no plans or even thoughts of those possibilities. The cumulative outcome of all this is a major unintended consequence. Unpredictability has now increased exponentially with no chance of predicting outcomes. Which is most unsettling to me. Yet I admit these times are most exciting. You do not know how many years—well, maybe you do—that I have planned certain actions. Now those plans are invalid and I'm making it up as I go. God has once again surprised us most unexpectedly."

"God is making you work for it, huh? Maybe keeping you humble. But is God a baseball or a cricket fan?"

"I'm not sure what sport is the most watched in certain higher realms. But regarding work, I think you are about to get your share. You have become noticed. And now your very existence is becoming an unintended consequence for a wide swath of our special population that previously was barely aware of your presence. Even your experience with the Great Serpent salamanders has caused waves. Previously, they were only a story in our library, and webbed-foot bipeds don't exist in our catalogs. And yes, before you ask, Jo informed me of that. You told quite a tale apparently, while she was still in the hospital. So, things are getting interesting for you and for us. Through some odd chain of events, it appears you have been led to a place where you now play a significant part in opposing our greater enemies."

"Maybe even God was getting bored."

"You may be right. But when God moves, and I firmly believe that movement has started, then many things go into motion over centuries. I feel like this is the beginning of something major. And that means great things, but also great danger."

"Because when God moves, the opponents countermove. And mortals don't always fare well when the deities throw down."

"Yes. More unintended consequences and collateral damage, possibly on a global scale. And that is when the non-mortals are most needed. I think we are about to have a lot of work."

"How fast can you guys get Jo up to speed with all this, both to use her help and also give her the tools to protect herself?"

"She is already in an intensive program with everything from what we call monster hunting to martial arts and weapons training. We have multiple teams putting in sixteen-hour days just with her. That should tell you how serious we are about both protecting her and preparing her for the coming battles."

"Good. Back to that conversation with Jo on big icky salamanders; there is more to the story that I'll need to add. Also, I'm making plans to be in America."

"Yes? I have a suspicion I'll be having another load of work soon."

"Maybe not. I have a group in North America that could be quite helpful to some endeavors. Small but highly potent, but I absolutely require they remain secret, and safe as possible."

"So, these are allies and neither threat nor competition?"

"No, just a group you don't know about yet, working on the side of the good guys. With training, perhaps they could be quite an asset, at least in America."

"That sounds promising. I hope you can tell me more when you can."

"I will. But I need to spend some time with them for upgraded training. And that brings me to ask for a favor. But not too big a one, I think."

I told Michael what I needed, and he surprised me when he quickly agreed. I think he saw the possibilities in what I hoped to create.

"One piece of advice, following from our earlier conversation. As you develop your project, you know how difficult it is to keep secrets. It's much easier to operate in secret when most of the organization is out in the open."

"I think I get it. I should have my group operate openly in the community in some fashion, while we do the actual work in private."

"Exactly. As you know, the ones that do that correctly have been in operation successfully for thousands of years."

I got up to take a made us both a cappuccino, and we sat in the leather chairs to continue our conversation.

"A question for you, Sen. How are humans made?"

"According to one book I've read, God made the first two, then that couple took care of the rest."

"The book oversimplified a few things, of course. It was more like that God created the first batch, then other batches, then the eventual survivors multiplied. So how do you think God makes angels?"

"Uh, no idea. Wait a minute, are you implying that angels can procreate?"

"Creation, procreation, or other manufacturing processes all have their place. What if the process is similar to the master vampire virus?"

"Now you are scaring me."

"An infinite God can set up whatever system is needed. And if some force intervened by using the master virus to tilt things to its favor, which would have unbalanced the place-time reality, then God can play the game too."

"Angels can be engineered to replace those that fall, or added to balance out the cosmic scale?"

"Why not? Or just call it evolution. Works out the same, given enough time."

"Spy vs. Spy on a cosmic scale?"

"It is on that scale, but more like a ten-billion-year chess game, with billions of pieces to be moved."

"So that implies that all this involves much more than just the Earth."

"Ah, now you get it."

"Crap."

"Your hypothesis about time travel and quantum entanglement?"

"Yes?"

"What is the other component besides time?"

"Space. It works no matter how far apart the two particles are, even in different galaxies, supposedly."

"Exactly. And there is a lot of space out there, with lots of other beings."

"I'm getting a headache."

"Now you are understanding how important this is, as it affects many planets."

"And the Church is the guardian of this knowledge, at least in this world?"

"Not really. But the Church works well enough for many matters on this planet. There really isn't any human organization that addresses what we are discussing, yet we are approaching the time when one is needed."

"OK, back to where we started digging this rabbit hole. Regarding angels, from what I've read, procreation is not what they do."

"Procreation can be a word of wide meaning. Sexual reproduction is only one of those meanings."

"So what other ways are feasible?"

"Anointing, selecting, or even metamorphosing. Sex is also possible, as the rebellious angels proved with human women. But the offspring were not quite angels."

"I guess it makes sense. There must be ways of replacing all those lost angels after Lucifer's fall. And there are a lot more humans in the world, probably requiring more angel work. So, what is the anointing process?"

"Something akin to a bite, or other physical touch. Maybe even something done on a dark ancient riverbank and misinterpreted as a bite."

"Ok, now you are just messing with me."

"Am I? Did you not anoint Jo, in a sense?"

"Damn."

"Back to a prior point. Is there any actual difference between a master vampire and an angel? Other than their ideologies and allegiances?"

"That sounds like they are two different sides of the same coin."

"Perhaps they are. There are enough surface similarities to make one wonder what the larger plan really is."

"The same plan, that, even if you knew it, you would not share?"

"Perhaps. But we are rapidly moving to a time when we will need to share our plans and information."

"Back some time ago at the cottage, when I first laid out my various hypotheses after we met, some took you by surprise, but other things I said did not. It was as if you already knew."

"Your suppositions about your origins, time travel, and the ancient virus were quite intuitive, yet logical. Some things I already, but some I did not.

I am beginning to understand that we are entering a new phase of rapid change."

"Can't the Church's massive database help with that?"

"Not enough. The world is a massive jigsaw puzzle and an incredibly complex place and becoming more so. Everything is constantly changing, and the pace is now increasing. Within that maelstrom, we need to learn and react as best we can. Otherwise, we will go extinct if our enemies control future events."

"That's not ominous at all," I said sarcastically. "The fossil record, as slight as it is, shows that overall life on earth ebbs and flows for long periods, with not much change. Then something happens, perhaps a catastrophic event, and what does not die exhibits rapid adaptations and improvements. Are we progressing to one of those times?"

"Possibly. The other side is pushing many of the negative changes we see today. But we are striving to mitigate what they are attempting. We have been observing and recording this for a long time, so that's how I know a lot of what you said back then."

"Michael, this conversation, as thought-provoking as it has been, is really annoying me. And with that thought, I really should go work out some frustrations. I'll find Jo and get in some sparring practice."

"Be careful. She has progressed enormously."

I left Michael and went through the back of the massive cottage to the far corner nearest the river. They had set a small gym up for martial arts, with a weight room, sauna, dressing room and shower area incorporated as separate rooms to the rear. Jo was already there jumping rope, wearing a sports top and tights. She was looking quite formidable.

"Hey there. Ready to kick my ass?"

"Yes, quite right, I am. Making me wait is going to get you an additional thrashing."

"OK, I'll change into my 'getting thrashed' outfit and be right back."

She continued her routine without comment. I found a locker and changed into loose fitting shorts and a tee shirt. There were clothes as well as towels stocked for everyone to use. I saw sets of women's clothing, added since the last time I had been here with Simon, so Jo's presence was influencing the old church hierarchy. Or at least the local laundry service. No shoes were stocked, so I walked back out barefooted. Usually the best choice anyway, for many martial contests.

Jo was sitting down and taking off her shoes and socks. She popped back up without even using her hands on the floor.

"What is your choice of style or form to start?" I asked.

"Let's go with your style. Simon told me it was something like 'doing whatever it takes to not get thine arse kicked', or some such phrase."

"Pretty close. You ready to rough it up? Got anywhere to be tomorrow, or are faces and hands off limits?"

"Nowhere to be. And as you yanks like to say, bring it on."

"I'm not a real yank" - was my shortened response as she was rounding a kick at my temple. I stepped back, barely avoiding it. While she continued spinning and her back fist grazed my nose. I stepped back again to avoid the onslaught of knees, elbows, feet and fists coming at me with incredible speed. I continued backing and side stepping as I studied her offense. She was quicker than me. Probably not as strong as me, but it was close, and after today's talk I knew she would soon be stronger. All I had for an advantage was experience.

I continued my retreat, stepping to the rear and side in a repetitive pattern. She picked it up and adjusted her offense to catch me by surprise. I caught her arm and leg and threw her behind me onto the mat. I quickly dropped onto her and narrowly avoided another knee and fist. On the ground, my experience and slight strength advantage allowed me to tie her up in double submission holds. She tapped out before I broke anything. I rolled away in case she still had ideas of getting in a cheap shot. We sat on the mat, looking at each other. Neither of us was breathing hard.

"Excellent speed. Excellent offense. Your only mistake was letting me lull you into a false step. Avoiding that will come soon with more practice and experience." I was complimenting her while giving her some advice.

"Excellent defense. Excellent retreating skills. Requisite trickery. Little wonder you don't lose, since you don't really fight." Apparently, she was not completely happy with losing.

"It's a street version of rope-a-dope."

"What?"

"Muhammad Ali. Let your opponent spend themselves offensively while you study them, adjust to their rhythm, trick them a little at the end, then win."

"I've never heard of that."

"Search for Ali and George Foreman. Ali taunted him into punching, while he leaned against the ropes and covered up. The ropes helped absorb the blows. Once Forman ran out of gas, Ali kicked his ass. At least that is the way it worked in the second match."

"So that really is a thing?"

"Yep. A smarter or more experienced opponent can take the best physical fighter out. But watch the old film, anyway. Ali took a beating but had the right strategy to win."

"I will. But you liked my offense and speed?"

"Yes. You've learned amazingly fast. I don't think any human would have lasted more than a few seconds. Now you get to learn more defense, but just as important, more assholery."

"A new style?"

"More like, let nothing hit you square, and never play fair."

She smirked. "I remember that from our Vondel park bike ride. And I'll use it against you."

"I look forward to it."

"You may not think so when you are lying on back after I kick your arse."

"It might surprise you what turns me on. Before I ramble down that awkward tangent, however, I am supposed to ask you something."

"Ask, master rambler."

"The dinner gang would like a repeat performance now that you are back for a time. I am formally asking if you would accompany to dinner. And of course, embarrass me thoroughly in front of the group."

"Oh, I would not miss that. Count me in. Just give me a day's notice."

"Thanks, and I will let you know which night."

I said goodbye and drove back to Amsterdam. Today had been a mix of feelings with Jo. Starting off had been unexpected and rough, but then had gone well, and I was proud of how she had adapted and progressed with her new condition. But I was still unsettled after talking to Michael. I had a feeling he was goading me somewhere, but I did not see where that was yet.

CHAPTER SIX

Similar to our first dinner date, I picked Jo up at her house in Den Haag. But this time she was wearing a sleeveless cornflower blue dress that proved to be quite attractive but demure, with matching medium height heels. I still don't know how some people have such good fashion sense. Most of the time I put on whatever is clean and not too clashing. I knew better than to stare or make any comments, but Jo's new physique was quite noticeable. She looked like a dancer and bouncer, all in one, and it was a good look.

"Good evening. You are looking exquisite tonight."

"Don't I always? Or are you just saying I clean up well for special occasions?"

I took a moment to mull over the proper response. Of course, there wasn't one. Meanwhile, she laughed and climbed in the car as I opened the door. She had me again. I got in and drove toward Amsterdam.

"Don't worry, I shall not hit you with any pheromones tonight."

"Good, as I don't think the car would survive it. How are you doing with the new job? At the cottage you gave a rundown of Center activities, but how are things really going?"

"Same old stuff. Now that we set the departments up, the budget battles have started. And building territory arguments. And parking space jockeying.

It's a wonder we get any proper work done. I'd like to make half of them redundant."

"OK, OK, enough shop talk."

"How are you doing, shambling around in old Amsterdam?"

"Well enough. I did a quick job for Michael in Alaska. Considering some further activity in America. Otherwise, waiting for my master vampire Nazi to stick his nose out from the rock he's burrowed under."

"So, no news on that front? Shouldn't he be trying to kill you by now?"

"Hey, don't sound so positive about my adversary. His cycle shows it may be another two decades before he surfaces. But I'm planning some new tricks to flush him out."

"How was the Alaska trip? I've never been, but heard the scenery is spectacular."

"It absolutely is. The trip itself turned most interesting."

"Uh oh, I hear a great mystery forming. A tale that you won't tell until the most dramatic moment possible. Probably that aliens that live in the sun have adopted you as their next leader, so now you must work on your suntan."

"Hey, that makes me sound like a drama queen. I've always thought of myself as more of a drama princess. No aliens, or suntan needed, yet I need to sort out some stuff and tell you and Michael about recent developments. But no new species, although I guess that depends on your library." She gave me the stare that told me she really didn't believe me. "On a different subject, do you remember those graffiti photos from Utrecht? My computer guy thinks there is a code there. Got anybody at the Center that can look at that?"

"Let me think. A couple of my people may have the right background. We have the computing capacity. I'll write up a request and see what shows up."

"Thanks. It would be nice to have something positive come out of that investigation."

We listened to music for a time, then arrived at the restaurant. We were the first to arrive and the host took us directly to a table for six. We sat and ordered drinks to await the others. Five minutes later, Thomas and his significant other, Willem, in grey and navy jackets, respectively, arrived, with Kate and Anna immediately behind them. Kate was wearing a memorable red dress that highlighted her dark hair, and Anna wore a green dress that perfectly matched her exquisite eyes. Jo and I stood to meet them. Most everyone in the restaurant had glanced up at our group and I could not blame them as we were the best-looking party of six anywhere in Amsterdam this night, perhaps in Europe. The other five were, at least.

Thomas was my best friend in Europe, at least in this iteration of my long life, and Willem was his new partner. Kate and Anna were my other long-term friends from Amsterdam. They were all good people.

We all hugged each other, then air kissed three times apiece. It took a while. The gang was being discreet, but checking Jo out, since she had physically changed since the last time, they had seen her. It reminded me of people admiring an art exhibit. With all the pleasantries exchanged, we sat, and Kate and Anna quickly asked Jo about her new workout routine. I reflexively laughed and almost spewed the sip of drink I had just taken. Jo smoothly answered that her routine was something she had picked up in Italy to offset her long work hours at the office.

Thomas was looking at me inquiringly. He still had questions. And he was intelligent enough to figure out that Jo was also something more than she seemed. I just nodded a yes to his unspoken question. He seemed surprised, then just smiled and accepted it. Willem was watching us and seemed to catch on. Meanwhile, the girls were trading lots of information. Then Kate and Anna wanted to propose a toast, so we quieted down and looked at them.

"I thank all of you for being here with us tonight. Anna and I have an announcement to make. But it is best if you hear it from her," Kate said.

Anna grabbed Kate's hand. "Yes, thank you all for being here. We have told no one yet, but tonight will be my last toast for quite some time. We are planning to enter the parenting world and hope to have a baby next year."

We all erupted with congratulations and best wishes, toasted, and filled our glasses a second time. Thomas had a short but eloquent toast. I wisely said nothing. We ordered dinner, then within minutes, as frequently happens in mixed outings, Willem, Thomas and I were discussing world trade and agricultural business, while Jo, Kate and Anna were excitedly talking about babies. Hah, I thought, that excitement was great, right until the first dirty diaper at 3 am. The evening was going entirely too well, so of course I had to screw it up.

Jo was discussing how best to burp a newborn after feeding. She had ample practice from all her nieces and nephews. She said that gently laying them at an incline along the left arm while lightly patting the baby's back with the right hand was the proper way. I interjected it was easier to put the baby on the left side of your chest while leaning back slightly and carefully moving up and down. Of course, with a napkin on the shoulder to catch the inevitable spit up.

Jo scoffed. "That must be the way Americans do it."

"Hey, don't knock it, it worked well for all ten of mine." Hmm, that should probably not have been said out loud tonight. Or ever.

Jo gave me her best astonished look. I think she was waiting for the punchline. When I didn't provide one, she looked at Kate and Anna, who had also heard me. At least Willem missed it. My unexpected outburst had taken everyone by surprise, including me. Thomas immediately sized up the situation and took charge.

"OK everyone, continue on while Sen and I have a smoke outside."

All of us knew that none of us smoked, but all of us knew it was Thomas' way to put the pin back in the grenade. He and I walked out as the other four watched us leave.

"Thomas, that smoking excuse might have worked once, but I don't see it working again tonight."

"Well, it works well enough to let me get you out of your own mess. So, did you expel that remark to sabotage the evening on purpose?"

"Never on purpose. For me, it's what happens when things are going well. Mouth opens, disaster ensues. Perhaps I should also have told everyone I gave Jo an STD?"

"My god, you may have lost your mind. What are you thinking? Wait, first, do you have ten children?"

"I had ten children. Many, many years ago. They are all long since grown and dead."

"OK, let's come back to that. You are kidding about giving Jo a disease, right?"

"Yes, I am kidding. And another stupid uttering, camouflaged as a joke. I really need to stop trying to be witty. Since we have never come close to having sex, and won't, I don't think it is possible to have given her anything. But maybe someone should give me a gag for talking too much."

"There is that. Now let's go back to the children. You owe me another story, but not tonight. We need to salvage this as quickly as possible and go back to celebrate Anna and Kate's special evening. What is your best story to explain this?"

"Uh, I don't really have one. Maybe I was talking about baby goats?"

"If you are going to be dense enough to step into shit regularly, you really need to develop better lying skills. Most people I have to counsel against lying, while you are the only one that gets into trouble for telling the truth. Let's try this…"

I was amazed at Thomas' quick mind and demand that we fix this up and proceed, while breezing past the fact that I had just told him I had ten adult children that were all dead. The very definition of a good friend.

As we walked back in, everyone was talking but glancing curiously toward us. Willem now knew what everyone else had heard. Jo knew enough about me to guess that I had spoken the truth earlier, although I had never told her about my American family. Now, she might think that I currently had ten kids running around, and that was why I went back to America regularly.

"Sorry everyone, and a special apology to you guys," as I spoke to Kate and Anna. "I said something stupid again but did not have the sense to follow it up with a proper explanation. But this evening is about you guys, so I'm shutting up. Please forgive me. And please, let's talk about who gets to babysit first when you two are ready for a break."

Thomas looked pleased and everyone mostly went back to normal. Jo looked at me with a question in her eyes. I suppose she was acknowledging my apology or my tacit agreement to a later explanation, and probably both. Dinner continued, with no further incidents. I ordered a few rounds of drinks, as Anna would not be drinking for some months. Two rooms over from where we were, a large room was set up for live music and dancing. A four-piece band was assembling, so I suggested that after eating, we should dance. Everyone agreed.

After coffee, we rose and went to the other room. A few couples were dancing, and I had a feeling a lot more people were about to join us. Kate and Anna danced together first. I took Thomas, and Jo and Willem made the last pair. It was an easy mid-speed piece, so I did not have to try very hard. I was quite athletic, but I had never learned all the dance moves necessary to be outstanding. To paraphrase from a book about General George Patton, "more zeal than skill" aptly described my ability.

Thomas took the opportunity during our dance to scold me lightly for my earlier outburst.

"Look Sen, you need to relax. You are wound too tight."

"The problem is that when I relax, something stupid slips out."

"Then relax and not be stupid."

"If only."

"I think most of your issues, with Jo and everyone else, stem from your mysterious life and past. You need to give those of us that care about you, more of who you are."

"I would like to, but that could get me committed or arrested."

"Trust us. Just give us enough to know who you are. We already trust you."

"You are right, of course. And I owe you a long story."

"And I expect one before our next outing. Let's have a long Friday lunch next week."

"Yes, it is time." I sighed. I knew the lunch would turn into a full afternoon of talk and drinks, colliding with dinner. But it would be good to give Thomas what he was asking for. I needed friends that could accept me for what I was.

We traded partners for the next dance, and I got Anna. It was a slow dance. I told her how excited I was for her and Kate. She thanked me and then stared into my eyes. I had a genuine fondness for Anna. In a completely different life, and in another dimension, I could have fallen for her. But I was glad it was impossible, both because I was a terrible match for most people, and she and Kate were such a good match.

"You and Jo seem to be good friends," Anna said. "I know you have excellent reasons to not go any further. But enjoy the friendship. I have a feeling that with time you will meet someone, and things will work out. It will be worth the wait."

I hugged and thanked her as we danced. Kate slapped me on the ass as Thomas twirled her past us in a move highly inappropriate for a slow dance. Showoffs. "Hey, keep a foot apart from my wife," she laughed as Thomas twirled her again.

Another faster dance and I got Kate. We really tore it up. She could dance, I just followed. She made us look good. We came together during the dance long enough for her to speak in a loud whisper.

"Hey, you big oaf, I don't know why you said what you said, but quit being stupid. You ever going to ask Jo out?"

"Sorry, Kate, it's just not that simple."

"Look, I know from experience that being with Anna improves my life. I would have hated to have missed our time together. But sometimes fate can show up and change things. If Jo is not for you, that is fine, but you need to live more than you do now. Go do what you need to do and along the way you'll find your one. Destiny can't happen without a little help." We both laughed at that as the dance ended.

I finally got Jo for the next dance. It was a slow one. We moved closer together but not too close. We could whisper in each other's ear.

"Your friends, now that they seem to be mine too, have lots of advice and stories about you."

"Hah, believe nothing they say. They are good people. They want me to be happy. I think they have some inkling that we should be more than friends. It's just that we don't see it that way."

"Yes, but we can have fun as friends."

"Absolutely. Maybe even pull a prank on these guys at some point."

"You mean act like we are interested in each other?"

"Possibly. Do you think we can pull it off? You are rather repulsive in that dress, after all."

"And you, sir, are a cad. You already told me I looked exquisite tonight."

"Just being nice."

"Oh, I think I could change your mind if needed." She smiled and pulled in a little closer. I got a small dose of pheromones. Oh shit, this could end badly. Then the dance ended, and the band played their last, fastest song. Devil With A Blue Dress On. Damned appropriate.

We put those pheromones into that dance. The dancing was not that great, but our athleticism made up for it. Throwing each other into impossible moves, some that we should not have done in public. Like throwing her vertically five feet into the air, while she spun three times, then catching her in my arms and dropping into a dip an inch from the floor, then throwing her again into another spin. Then she flung me into the air, and I had to show off with a backflip coming down. The music finished, and the stunned room gave us a round of applause. We both looked a bit embarrassed after the circus act. Our friends crowded around us in a big group hug.

We left the restaurant together, and each pair moved off to their car. We had made plans to do another dinner and dance the next month. Jo and I strolled to my car.

"Quite a dancer, Ms. York."

"You too, Mr., uh, well, which last name are you using this month?"

"Oh, never mind, it will just change again. But you really were something tonight."

"Thanks, but flattering me to evade your explanation of ten kids will not work."

"Oh, you remember that, huh. Thought you would have forgotten after that inhuman dance lesson."

"You well know we danced that way to work off the pheromones I should not have given you. Now you get to tell me about how you have ten kids that you have not told me about."

"Yes, I suppose so. I would rather do it somewhere private besides the car. Would you like to come to my house, or we can go back to your house in Den Haag?"

"What about your apartment in Woerden? I have seen your house here in Amsterdam. And if you are telling me all your secrets, I would think you would be more comfortable in your old territory."

"That is a good idea, and sort of on the way to Den Haag. And I don't completely trust talking in your house."

"Good, let's go. We can make awkward small talk on the drive. Or better yet, listen to music."

We drove down to Woerden. I parked in the underground, and we walked up to my apartment building.

"Interesting place at night. It looks different in the shadows than when we walked by it during the day, when we got ice cream."

"This old barracks building, with the arches and doorways, looks more sinister at night. But I like it because I can walk out my door and be in the Saturday market. The town is also small enough to be quiet, but in the middle of the Amsterdam-Utrecht-Den Haag-Rotterdam box. And as you know, this was my assigned station a couple of millennia ago."

"There is that."

I unlocked my exterior door, and we went upstairs, and I unlocked the entrance door. I made us both a drink and turned on a playlist of Americana music sprinkled with some alt rock music, like Collective Soul. Somehow it worked. We sat on my sofa, a few feet apart, since it seemed prudent. She took off her shoes and pulled her feet under her.

"I'm not sure where to begin. I also have to say that once I tell you my story, it could be a burden on you. Because nobody, including Michael, fully knows it, and if word gets out, the lives of my family could be affected, and not for the better. Should I proceed?"

Jo looked thoughtful. She swirled her drink, then sipped it. "Can you tell me enough of the basic story, but leave out any details that could identify anyone or anyplace? That way, I would be less likely to betray anything that could lead to harm."

"Yes, I can, I think. There is one important detail that I cannot tell you regardless, but I'll let you know when I get to that point."

"Agreed. Now tell me your tale."

"Before the American Revolution, I traveled to America. I walked around a bit and finally settled in with a Native American tribe. I met a woman, we married, and had ten children. She told me she was special, not exactly human. That detail is what I can't divulge, at least not yet. But she was not evil, rather the opposite. After a little over twenty years, she died, but had already lived for nearly two hundred years. The British governor killed our eldest son just before the war broke out. Some years later, I left America and took my revenge in London. Since then, I only returned for brief stays, except for roughly the 1960 to 1990 period. All my children are dead, as are my grandchildren. I have later descendants that I sometimes see. I have protected that knowledge from everyone, especially the Church. That is my short version."

"But why the secrecy? I understand you probably did not want the Church poking around your descendants once they found out about you. But it seems strange that you would protect them after all this time."

"There is more to it, Jo. My descendants, at least some of them, carry my wife's special nature. That is why I protect them. They have been under the radar for centuries and it is best it stay that way for now. I need to keep them away from notice of the old guard of the Church, those that still believe in exterminating those that are different. I'm also, for now, keeping them from being pulled into what we do, or from being hunted by our enemies. They are not ready yet."

"I think I understand. But when you say they are not ready yet, what do you mean? Are you planning something?"

"Yes, I am. Sometime soon I will go back to America and begin training them. I have already told Michael I need to return there for a training project but did not tell him they are my family. Knowing him, he probably already knows or guesses the truth. I'm doing this because they need to be ready for the world that is coming. And they may be our allies in this fight, but only if they choose to be."

"Ah, I see. I just did not want to find out you had ten toddlers waiting on you back in America."

"No, nothing like that. A wife in Laren for a few years, several centuries ago, with no kids. A wife in America, two centuries ago, with ten kids. There has been no one else. There will probably be no one else."

"Why no one else again? Surely you must have thoughts and desires. Could you really go without someone for centuries to come?"

"There will be no one else because of the life I have. Watching all those you love die, time after time, wears upon your soul. Now I have passed that curse on to you. There, now I have said it."

She looked at me with an inscrutable face. "You took me to dinner, then dancing. Now I'm on your sofa with my shoes off and sipping a drink. And you have told me something that shows your vulnerability. That should make me think differently about you and relax my guard enough to consider other actions." We just sat there and looked at each other. It was not a pregnant pause; more like a nursery-full-of-newborns kind of pause. "But I won't. And I think you know that perhaps better than me. I'm not looking for a relationship, and even if I was, I would need much time working on the complications you provided me with. Now you need to drive me to Den Haag. I have to go to work in the morning."

"I agree."

"To what?"

"That we don't need any complications, and that I need to drive you home. We are work colleagues, hopefully becoming good friends, and there is no need to mess that up. Plus, we both need time to sort out all the recent events. Maybe a lot of time. Oh, and you can buy gas for the ride, my friend."

"Whatever. Let's get to the car."

I was uncertain what to do or what else to say. Complications with Jo were not what I needed right now. And I thought it would be a terrible idea for her as well. So, I drove her to Den Haag, and we spent the time in a comfortable silence other than the music. I drove up to Jo's house and parked. She got out but told me to stay in the car. I watched her walk to the door and go inside as I pulled away and went home.

CHAPTER SEVEN

S chiphol Airport was busy, as always. I still had a habit of arriving early to relax before the flight. I boarded the plane, settled into the seat and started my music, then pulled out my notebook and pen. This would be a working flight as I designed the American project. I glanced out the window as the plane rolled across the fog-laden tulip fields, an eerie sight from a jet. The plane was in the air minutes later and across the global curve to Atlanta.

The plane dropped into a slightly smoggy Atlanta, then off on the little jet that landed along the French Broad River in Asheville. I walked into the garage and found my rental, the newest model of bland SUV. I left the airport and headed northeast while staying off I-26. The eternal construction project, coupled with flocks of out-of-state tourists that were inexperienced with hills and curves, could literally be deadly. Seriously, Florida should require its driving courses to have elevation changes and curves instead of a flat grocery store parking lot. Apparently, anyone can get a license there before traveling to the mountains to cause mayhem.

I drove on and past the outskirts of the Biltmore Estate. It brought back old memories of things done there in a time long past. After downtown, I started gaining elevation after passing through the old neighborhoods. Old being a relative term compared to Europe. I came to my gate and punched in the code, then rolled down the short gravel drive to my mini estate. Mini because

I had little use for a large house, but an estate because I did like and need privacy that only acreage and vegetation provided. And I had an excellent view over the valley and downtown from my mid-century modern perch.

This time of year, Asheville had warm days and cool evenings with bright blue skies. Normally dry and pleasant, although the occasional storm up from the Gulf Coast could make it feel like the Netherlands with heavy rain. But it would pass in two or three days, while storms in the Netherlands could settle in for what seemed like weeks. I learned there to soak up the sun when available, since you never knew when you might not see it for weeks.

My cell phone vibrated on the table for the dozenth time. More business to do, from paying real estate taxes, shunting more money into long-term accounts, to keeping estates and trusts up to date. It was maddeningly tedious. But in my case, it was a necessary evil to get me through my charade and eventually turn everything over into a trust and start all over again with a different name and identity. It was always fun, especially since I did it on two different continents.

After a day of chores and then slumming in town, it was time to get busy with the new project. I had been scanning the online real estate listings in western North Carolina for some time. I needed a large enough acreage to where nobody outside of our training group could watch us or stumble into our activities. The property would also need some buildings for students to live in and space for at least one classroom and a cafeteria. Other outbuildings for storage and trainings, and preferably a large barn. What I had in mind was an estate or compound on a thousand acres, contained in a small, dead-end valley, with property lines to the top of the ridge on three sides, and enough buffer on the fourth side to keep out the curious. I had seen similar properties that were old church or Boy Scout camps, and even some prepper listings that had bunkers. I also wanted it to be far enough from civilization to minimize possible traffic around the property, but not too far out, so there could be access to a grocery store and airport.

Now it was time to call agents. The market had been crazy lately, so it seemed everyone was now taking classes and advertising themselves as the newest and smartest realtor. I looked up a few that I knew had been working the area for over twenty years instead. There were only a few properties available that could work. I found two promising options in the Burnsville area and made appointments to see them. Meanwhile, I drove up that evening to get an unofficial look at both. The nighttime perspective was just as important to me as the daytime viewing. Much of our training would be in the dark.

The first place was a likely candidate. The land lay as I had envisioned, although the valley was narrow. It also had only one building, a nice house, but I really needed more buildings. An old barn left over from the previous owner was too far gone to salvage. But the entire place was private. The night sky was bright, and the valley was quiet. Because of the narrowness, the ridges blocked more of the night sky than I liked.

The second property was also a suitable candidate. A larger tract of 800 acres, tucked into a dead-end hollow but was wider between the ridges than the first place. It had a couple of houses, barns, an old milking parlor, and various small sheds. It was a former dairy farm that had also seen some use as a camp or compound. All the buildings needed repair and were ratty. But remodels would be faster than building from scratch.

I used my new Monk-encrypted phone to call a few local family members. I told them I was in town and would like to gather for a training project, and everyone seemed inclined to take part. Jennifer, my great-granddaughter, was in North Carolina, and showed the most interest. I said I had a facility that should be available in a few days, and I would be ready for the first batch of volunteers. I sent texts to Oklahoma to Nan, another great-granddaughter, and Henry, and old family friend, with the same information.

The next day, I met the real estate agent and toured each property. I think she expected me to choose the first place, but I told her to make an offer on the second property. I made the offer based on a twenty-four-hour acceptance and an immediate closing. It was an unusual request, but money can speed things up. I had no intention of waiting longer as it was time to begin.

I heard from the real estate agent that the owner accepted the offer. Since no one was living there, I also had permission to take possession immediately, although the lawyers would take a few days to get the closing finished. I was paying in cash and paid close to the list price, so I don't think the owner was worried about me being there. As I drove up again to inventory the buildings closely and start putting a list together of materials and supplies, I called Henry. I had known him for many years from prior stints in America, and he was also a man of mystery, in a Native American way, and the most solid person I knew.

"Henry, I got the place we need. Want to take a vacation? Well, a working vacation, anyway."

"Why not? Should be cooler there anyway. I've got a couple of my guys ready to head that way. You call the boss yet?"

"Nope, but she is next. Do you know if Nan has had any luck recruiting anyone there?" Nan was a shapeshifting great-granddaughter of mine, a product of my marriage to a Native American shapeshifter before the American Revolution.

"I believe she has, but I'll leave the surprise for you. But despite some early misgivings, I can vouch for all of them."

"Good enough for me. I'll look forward to whoever shows up."

"See you soon."

I ended that call and dialed Nan.

"You heading back east to the homeland?"

"You know we have multiple homelands. But yes, we will travel to North Carolina the day after tomorrow. Are we booked at the Biltmore Estate Inn?"

"You wish. No four-hundred-dollar rooms for my family. We are going a bit more rustic. Bring sleeping bags."

"Great. But you owe me at least one spa day."

"Done. In fact, the Biltmore will be one of our group trips. I think everyone will appreciate that after having to build their own shelters."

"Yeah, that really is rustic. But you better have indoor plumbing and private showers for the girls. Otherwise, it will be a brief session."

"I will have that ready. See you in a couple of days. I'll text you the address."

"Bye."

My last call was to Jennifer. Although she was local and my great granddaughter, I didn't know her well. I hoped to rectify that with her and her brother Seth. It embarrassed me to admit I had never met Seth. They were both shifters and should be a great addition to the program.

"Hi Jen. Wanted to let you know I have a large place near Burnsville to set up as a training center. You still in?"

"Yes, both Seth and I can show up and spend some time. We have recruited a couple of girls, first cousins to each other. They are a little rough and wild, but they have signs of being shifters. Some training away from civilization should be good for them. Also have John Henry coming. Nice kid that is trying to get a college scholarship. Not sure if he is going to be a shifter yet. But he's from our line, so always a chance."

"Good. Be nice to see you again and meet Seth. I imagine the kids will work out as well. Glad you mentioned college. For any of these kids that want to go to college, trade school, or get jobs, I plan to support them as part of the training bennies."

"That sounds good. John Henry, at least, will be happy to hear it."

"See you in a few days."

I arrived at the property and unloaded my Land Cruiser. There was plenty of work to start. Making it more private and ensuring there were working showers was a priority. I put in two twenty-hour days at nearly full speed. Things got done faster when no one was watching.

Henry's big blue truck was the first to arrive at the place. I had already put in a gate with an electric opener and had given everyone the code. I saw him with a half grin as he approached and could have sworn, he was saying "dumbass" behind the window. He got out and introduced me to Samuel, from the Moffett, Oklahoma adventure, and to a new guy named Watt. All three were long time acquaintances of each other and distant family in some way.

"Hell of a place you got here," Henry said. "Looks like it needs a bit of sprucing up."

"Yep, good thing we got plenty of kids coming in that work for free. All I have to do is make sure Nan has a nice place to stay."

"That should be first on your list if you are smart. Got some easterners coming in as well?"

"Yes, Jen and Seth. They have a few kids they are bringing. Time to get the east and west back together."

"Good luck with that. We been apart so long we don't know each other, so at least old grievances won't be an issue. Bunch of new kids together will be hard enough."

"I know. That's why I have so many adults here with them, at least at first. Plus, the stuff I'm going to tell them just about guarantees they will freak out a little."

"You telling them the truth? The whole truth?"

"Yep. Everything. Then I'm telling them they are in charge of it, and that the fate of the people, maybe to some extent the world, depends on them to get it right."

"Damn. That should keep them distracted. I need a beer. Watt and Sam, come get a beer."

We sat in old camp chairs and finished a couple of beers. In my case, cider. Henry, Sam, and Watt all came and went as they slowly unloaded their gear from the truck while pausing occasionally to sit and drink.

I asked about the unfinished Moffett business. "Anything else come up on those strange prints on the river in Moffett?"

"Not really," Henry answered. "Watt and Sam were with me when we saw them. We been asking around the old ones but getting nowhere. We ran across a half-crazy old man in the hills that said something about it, something old from far away, but he would answer nothing else. He just said to forget about it before we got them stirred up. Not sure how lucid he was, telling tales about the Moon People. That's all we got."

"Well, the world's largest database of monsters and curious critters has exactly nothing, so you are ahead of them."

"You still working with them Church folks over in Europe?"

"Yep, still am. Had an assignment recently in Alaska that went well, but also a little sideways. Have to tell you about it soon. You also got a surprise coming in a few days."

"Hope so. Halloween will come up in a few weeks. Need some treats."

"No problem. We'll take the kids trick or treating in town. Then we will celebrate Sinterklaas as well."

"What is that?"

"Think Halloween, Christmas, Mardi Gras, disco, and blackface all in the same gigantic street party, with a Dutch accent."

"Damn, don't think I know that one. Sounds interesting but may be politically or socially incorrect. Besides, we don't go around appropriating a foreign culture."

"Henry, I just realized you can give the lecture on diversity, equity, and inclusion. Maybe even be the DEI representative."

"Yeah, screw that. Say, you look different somehow. This hard work must agree with you."

"Maybe. We'll talk later."

Henry looked at me speculatively. But he asked no more questions.

A Suburban pulled up with Oklahoma plates. Nan opened the door, along with four familiar faces. Stacey, Melissa, Jimmy, and Ned. So that was the surprise Henry had alluded to. But since he had vouched for everyone, Jimmy and Ned must have had a change in attitude. Jimmy and Ned had been along for the ride on the Moffett adventure, when I killed the world's largest neurotoxin-spitting salamander. It happened when we went to rescue Stacey and Melissa after they had been taken as a snack for baby salamanders the size of alligators.

We all met and hugged and shook hands. Everybody knew everybody else. The older guys went to set up their lodgings while I toured Nan and the kids around. Nan was happy to see that she and the girls got the house with hot water and two showers. The boys got barn loft privileges, complete with a water hose. To my surprise, they seemed excited to be camping. Maybe they really had come around. But lots of presence of Nan and Henry in their lives probably had that effect. We unloaded all their stuff and got them settled.

Then Jen and Seth pulled in. Jen was in her Subaru with two girls, and Seth was in his pickup with a boy. Right then I realized I needed to change my pronouns. I would give myself permission to refer to the entire group as kids, but no more boys and girls. All of them were technically adults. I walked over and met Jen. The two with her looked me and everyone else over but said nothing nor introduced themselves.

"Hey Jen, glad you found it." We gave each other a brief hug. "And obviously you two are Emeline and Elendor. Welcome. We can get your stuff and get you settled in the house, then meet everyone else." I continued to get the silent treatment as Jen eyed them but said nothing. "Jen, you three will share the house for now with Nan, Stacey, and Melissa. Should be room for everyone and plenty of hot water and shower space."

I walked over to Seth. He looked a lot like Jen. "Hi, you must be Seth. And you are John Henry. I'm Sen, the warden of your new prison farm." Seth smiled, and we shook hands. John Henry looked at me for a second like he was about to bolt. "I'm kidding. This is just a farm that has a bunch of extraordinary people, which includes you. Let's get your stuff and get you settled before meeting everyone. Seth, you are in the other house with Henry, Watt, and Samuel. John Henry, you get the barn with Jimmy and Ned."

Now that everyone was here, I was expecting some awkwardness, but I hoped after tonight most of that would be past. As evening approached, we had a simple dinner in the second barn, where I had set up tables and chairs. Either this barn or the old milking parlor would end up as the mess hall, but we would figure that out tomorrow. Everyone met each other, and the older adults seemed at ease with each other. The younger adults, not so much. That would end, starting tomorrow. After eating, I asked everyone to go out to the clearing behind the house. I had set up a large fire pit and benches. Henry lit the fire, and once it was going well, I started the dialogue by giving a monologue.

"All of you here, as I understand it, are related to each other. Some closely, others distantly. But if you can trace your lineage back to Hia, then you are part of this family. Also, all of you are part of the people. You have many other family ties as well. We have recruited you here for training, after which you will go back into the world and help your people. But you are also responsible for recruiting and training the next group that comes here. Therefore, all of you are required to rotate back through here, over time, to train future groups. Then they will do the same. I plan to have the first few groups through here that are all chosen from the people. But then we will need to branch out to bring others in. We are creating a unique organization, designed to deal with significant threats, some of which aren't yet known. But I would like you to be trained on other matters as well, including social responsibility. This is not a cult, or a bunch of preppers plotting against the government. Some things will be hard to believe, but we will prove to you that all of this is for real. Just to get your attention and start the process, my name is Senecus, but call me Sen. I was the husband of Hia, and I believe I am a distant ancestor to most everyone here. And with that, I'd be happy to answer questions."

Chapter Eight

I had asked Nan and Jen to give their recruits a basic lesson on their ancestors prior to arriving. A couple of the younger crowd got it, as they realized how long ago Hia lived. Stacy and Melissa already knew much about my past, but the others did not and looked at me incredulously.

"Uh, Miss Nan told us that Hia was from near here but lived about two hundred years ago. So, uh, how are you, her husband?" Jimmy asked.

"You are correct about Hia. And I was her husband, although even back then I was much older than her. But that, plus many other things that sound crazy right now, you are going to find out are true. We intend to show you the world that we really live in. The people here will show you things you may not believe, but after seeing it and living with it, you will find it to be true. And not just us, I have others coming from Europe to assist. Your world is about to get a lot bigger."

The older adults perked up when I said that. I had told no one about outside trainers, other than insinuating it to Henry.

"We heard a lot about old tales up in the mountains, crazy things. Witches, shifters, monsters in the woods. Been reading about magic. Is that what this is about?" Emeline asked. It was the first evidence I had that she could talk.

"Monsters and shifters are real. Don't know about the rest," Stacey said.

"How do you know?" Elendor asked. Her tone made it obvious she did not believe it.

I waited but nobody spoke up. "Stacey knows this better than most people walking the planet," I said. "But you don't have to believe my words. You will see for yourself, Elendor. In fact, you might be a lot closer to some of that truth than you know."

A part of me wanted Stacey to shift and prove my point, but I knew it might be traumatic for her so soon after the ordeal in Oklahoma. Tomorrow, though, once Nan, Jen, and Seth proved shifters were real, then Elendor would understand.

"What do you mean by that?" Elendor asked.

"This family is special, and tomorrow will prove it out. As part of this family, you are also special. Again, you don't need to believe my words, as you will see for yourself. We are not monsters, but they are out there. I'm not very familiar with witches, but I have heard they exist. Magic is an unknown to me, as I don't know where advanced science ends and magic begins. But plenty of stuff that is real probably looks like magic."

"Oh hell, Sen, let's just do this tonight," Nan said. "I'm not bashful. But you better not steal my clothes while I'm changed."

"Wait, Nan," I said. I grabbed a towel we had been using as a cushion on the bench. "OK, you go."

Nan stood up, walked up closer to the fire, then became a golden hawk standing upon a pile of her clothes. It made quite an impression on the younger crowd, although Stacey and Melissa knew what was coming.

"Holy shit," Elendor said.

"Kind of is," I said. I walked over to Nan and held up the towel. She turned back into human form behind the towel and put her clothes back on. Those younger in the group that were not shifters, or at least not yet, were quite impressed.

"Everyone in this family carries these genes," I said. "For reasons we don't understand, some exhibit this ability when they reach the age of about twenty, while others do not. For the younger crowd here tonight, some of you have already discovered this ability, and some may yet find out soon."

"You mean we might be that way?" Emeline asked. Her faced betrayed a mixture of wonder and disbelief.

"Yes," Nan said. "We will start tomorrow with some further inquiries and perhaps be able to tell you soon if you are a shifter. But even if you are not a shifter, you have other attributes that, with training, can be used for other specialties that the world needs."

The young folks looked impressed and thoughtful. That reaction encouraged me.

"OK, people, now that the excitement is over, I'd like to spend the rest of this fire with more introductions and social time. Starting tomorrow, life gets real with a lot of work and education. Speaking of that, when you leave here, I'm funding all of you for whatever you want to pursue. College, trade school, jobs, or business startups. Over the next few months, we will figure out together what you want and get it set up. Meanwhile, I'd like Henry to start and give his story, and then go around the fire. Say whatever you want to. I'm excusing myself because you will get my story tomorrow."

The remainder of the evening passed quickly enough. The kids were buzzing but the adults were relaxed. After the round of introductions, we had snacks and drinks, then everyone began drifting back to the buildings. As I got up to do the same, I noticed Nan and Jennifer staring at me.

"You look different," Nan said. "Still silvery, but you have a slight greenish-blue shine. It's a pleasant color, but I have never seen that before. What is it and what have you been doing?"

"Like I told someone else recently, I've been hanging out with the Ents. They must be rubbing off on me."

"Which is your way of telling us you will not tell us," Jen said.

"Yep, other than is what happens when you go bowling with Bigfoot," I replied.

"You are so weird," Nan said. Jen nodded agreement.

"I will tell both of you all about it at some point. I first have to work out some kinks and figure out some things. Then all our lives may get more interesting."

"If you are into something that can change your color, then you really are going to have to tell us," Nan said.

"I promise I will, and soon."

That seemed to mollify them, and we all walked back to the camp.

We all met in the largest barn the next morning. I started the session with some mundane lists of things we needed to do as a group. It took a while but needed to be done. Each day, there would be blocks of time devoted to classroom instruction. Topics would vary widely and wildly. Everything from science and math, politics and social institutions, to basic espionage, monster lore, and weapons instruction. Another daily block of time would be for outdoor training or martial arts. And a third block set aside for working on the farm to get the buildings into better shape, both for us and future students. We also had to divide up the daily chores of cooking and all the fun cleaning activities. Each person handled their own laundry and kept their personal area clean.

After that, I reintroduced myself. "Continuing from last night, I am Senecus. My full name is Seneca Marcus Aquila. I changed it to Senecus, and I usually call myself Sen. There have also been a lot of aliases as well since I have been alive for a long time. Although I have some fine stories, most of my existence has been very low profile. I don't think I ever got into any history books. If I did, it was by accident. I'm not immortal, but whatever changed me gave me a very long lifespan. Perhaps before I get into the specifics of what all this training is for, you can ask me questions."

The group began asking a series of almost random questions.

"We started talking last night and I heard that you were a Roman soldier even before Christ. Is that true?" asked John Henry.

"I was a Roman soldier in the Ninth Legion, but some three hundred years after Christ. I spent many years, during the end of the Roman Empire and the early Middle Ages, asleep because of my condition, as my body changed and adapted. But I have lived a long life and have seen and done many things."

"Are you our direct ancestor?" Jimmy asked.

"Good question, and I believe a genealogy lesson is necessary to give everyone an idea of where they came from. Our line is mixed up because some are shifters and live long lives, but others are not. Even in the same direct family, so it gets confusing after a few centuries. I married Hia some two hundred and seventy years ago. We had ten children, several of which were shifters. Most of you here, if not all, are descendants of that marriage. But there were many other shifters than Hia, so it is also possible you are not Hia's descendant or may be related through intermarriage of other ancestors. But it doesn't matter, ultimately, exactly who your ancestors are. The key is that you are special, and you are here."

"From most of the stories I have heard about people living that long is because they are a vampire or something bad," John Henry said. "Are you a vampire, or are you something else?"

"Neither I nor others think I am a vampire. I certainly do not have any of the symptoms you know about, other than a long life. I believe that something attacked me, and through a unique series of events, I became what I am now. Not immortal, but very long-lived. Someone in the Church has put forth other theories about my origin, but I'm not convinced yet. And I'm not sure I'll ever know."

"If you have been alive that long, have you been in wars and done bad things?" Emeline asked.

"I have stayed out of most conflicts over the years. When I took part, I did so surreptitiously. For example, I did not openly fight during World War II, but I killed off quite a few bad Nazis. I try to do good overall, but I sometimes do things I should not. I believe that qualifies me as a human."

"Have you ever had to torture anyone, like a Nazi, to get information?" Emeline asked. She seemed to focus on violence.

"No. But I did it once because I wanted to. It was not long after the Revolutionary War. A British governor had my oldest son killed, so I thought I needed to do something atrocious. Afterward, I realized that the aftermath of doing that terrible thing resulted in the loss of a piece of my soul. Every action has consequences, and karma is a bitch. I don't intend to repeat that."

"Are you the only one like you, or are there others?" Elendor asked.

"Until last year, I was the only one. Then I had to decide; let someone die or save that life by turning them into a version of me." The kids didn't seem fazed, but the older folks in the room looked shocked.

"So, if there is another of you, where is he? And how did you do that? Can you make anyone into you?" Jen asked.

"Not he, but she, instead." The older ones in the group continued to look shocked but interested. "Perhaps you will meet her if I can persuade her to join this training. She is with the Church in Europe. I am also allied with the Church on a contract basis to investigate evil humans and monsters." Jaws of the older crowd, that had not heard yet finally dropped.

"I don't know if I can turn everyone, but it may be possible. But that is a decision I made once, and I don't know when or if that circumstance will arise again. I saved her life, and gave her near-immortality, but now she gets to watch all her family and friends die while she does not age. I took on the burden of her hate mixed with gratitude towards me since actions have consequences."

"What are we being trained for, exactly?" Stacey asked.

"To learn as much as possible to make the best decisions and then decide your futures. All to prepare for what is likely to be a large-scale conflict, as we have enemies ranging from master vampires to evil humans traveling from the future. Before I get into that, let's take a brief break. This is a good time to get caffeine and change the subject to the purpose of the camp."

From the looks on some of the adults' faces, I also need to do some explaining to them. Nan was less than happy, Jen looked confused, and Henry had an odd look on his face. The kids filed out, and some looked excited, and some were thoughtful. Their lives had just gotten very interesting.

Nan and Henry immediately came over to me. Jen hung back a step so she could hear, without getting in between anybody. Nan started first.

"What the hell, Sen? You can turn others? And the one you turned is in the Church?"

"Yes, I did. The choice I had was to turn her or let her die. And she is a researcher for the Church. But the real question is, do I start changing the kids in this class that aren't shifters?" Henry started laughing hard, which I had not seen before. Nan went from looking angry to perplexed and sat down. I thought that was a good thing because she would have further to go to get to me when she tried to kill me.

"I know the idea sounds bad, but everything, and I mean everything, is on the table now. When I tell you the details you will have a much better understanding of the situation. But believe me when I say you have heard nothing yet. We are facing enemies we can't easily defeat; we are going to need a way to survive the coming battles. And it would be great if you came up with a suitable alternative, because I really, really don't want to turn these kids. Sorry to be so direct, but we may only have a few years to set up and train a small army."

Henry chuckled again. "I think you have quite a story to spin. We need to talk tonight."

"Better to have some spirits and sit around the fire. I need to tell you both some things. And Jen, you and Seth need to hear it as well. Henry, you can relay it to the rest of your guys as you need to. Then, soon after, I intend to tell the kids. Full disclosure might be harsh, but they need to know what is ahead."

"It's bad, isn't it? I can't imagine any other reason for you to act like this," Nan said.

"It could be extinction for humans, or worse. But that is not a foregone conclusion. There are just as many humans and entities trying to prevent that, as there are those trying to make it happen. Unfortunately, we have other players involved that outmatch us to an extent. Monsters are already here on earth. Time travelers are coming from the future to tip the balance to the bad guys."

Henry looked fierce. "They be human, or near enough to it, then we can still take care of them."

"Exactly right. We have to be smart enough and careful and unpredictable to fight them. That is why we are here. These kids are the soldiers that we train to die along with us in that effort."

"No, no. That can't happen. Oh my god, what have you got us into?" Nan sounded desperate.

"The time travelers called the Sky Lords got us into this some few thousand years ago. We now think they created the Uya. Nan, as a Nunehi shifter, you have been created by the side of good to fight the Uya. You have been in this battle all along and just didn't know it. The Great Serpents are likely another creation, or an offshoot of a virus sent by the Sky Lords. I do not know how many other things are out there. I am finding out that many things I thought were myths are real.

"But the most dangerous to us are the master vampires and other humans. The virus sent be the Sky Lords infected all humans, but has negatively influenced half the human population, which can be triggered with mass media and messaging. Those humans become high functioning zombies, incapable of logical reasoning but with a high propensity for violence. Now billions are in the fold, ready to listen to and follow marching orders to kill. Now the affected are clamoring for a despot to lead them at any cost. It has been happening worldwide wherever mass communication and social media outlets are widespread. The other half of the population continues to be unaffected by the virus but are likely to be attacked by the affected humans. The master vampires are helping as well, as they get to eat half of humanity."

"That's terrible," Nan said. "Three billion plus bad humans and other powerful beings. Why do these kids have to fight and die, when the odds are so much against us?"

"I don't want any of these kids to die. I plan to prepare them, and have you prepare them, so that it won't happen. They need to survive to lead the future. But it could happen anyway, and some or all of us die. My other Church friend, sometime boss, who is probably not human, has already sensed that God is making a strong countermove, so we have allies. Yet, the other side is reacting, and we could be in for a few hundred years of a battle here on a galactic scale. Yes, extra-global, outside of Earth. Now you know the basics of what we face."

I was running out of adjectives to describe Nan's face. I was just going to stick with "troubled" the rest of the day.

"Damn son, you don't do things halfway." Henry had a way with words.

"It seems not," I said.

"So, tell me about who you turned," Henry said.

"She is a little firecracker of a blonde Brit librarian. She's smarter than me and can probably kick my ass."

"This I got to see." He smiled and sat down. I was talking about the world ending and he was thinking about my new turnee.

"Let's finish this up for now. We need to get our heads together for the rest of today's training."

Nan still was not talking. I guess throwing together time travelers, gods, aliens, and turning her relatives was all too much to hear at one time. I commiserated with her, but I felt they needed to hear the news, then digest it and get ready to help with strategies.

CHAPTER NINE

We had another session with everyone later. I started off with a general summary for the group.

"I know you asked what you are doing here. We plan to give you the skills to make you think, then decide, and then act. You are about to be on the front lines of a war almost no one knows about yet. Basically, a coalition of humans and other entities plan to dominate the world for their own benefit. The ones I know about are master vampires, Wendigos we know as Uya, and humans from the future called the Sky Lords. I have been told there are a lot more and bigger things on the other side that I have not seen yet. They are playing softball right now, throwing viruses and climate change at us to weaken us. Those much older and wiser than me think there will be an open conflict in a few years.

"To prepare you, we will train you in physical and mental skills. Along with all the knowledge we will throw at you, each day there will be a session which will deal with ethics, moral obligations, and political ambiguity. The other elders and I can assist by answering questions and providing examples based on our experiences. Each of you in time, according to your strengths, will become a leader and a decider. Hia told me that her people were special, so as her descendants, it is incumbent on you to help the people for a greater good. Despite the odds against us, I intend for every one of us to survive. After the future is secure then you can use the skills that you learn here to build your world in a better way."

Later that evening, all the adults stayed at the fire while the younger crowd drifted off. I needed to give the adults the full story.

"OK guys, some of what I will tell you is common knowledge among certain groups that are concerned about events on this planet. They are already waging war against a series of entities they apparently have fought with for some time. I have some other information given by individuals that are part of that group, but may not be widely known, even among them. I will tell you what I know right now, which is not nearly everything. The people I'm talking to should dribble out more information as they feel more comfortable and trusting in me. So, here it goes."

I told them everything I knew from Michael, from Kal, and everything I knew beyond that, or suspected, at least. Battles being fought between good and evil, on a bigger venue than just the earth; climate change and natural disasters being used as weapons; master vampires; allies that were from mythology; and a dozen other things I could think of. Details I remembered about the virus and its application to our world. There were some surprised looks, but nobody objected to what I was saying. These people were very solid.

I finished up with a brief description of what I wanted to do. "As you know, I have partially allied myself with the Church in Europe for reasons of my own. Either the Church or I can end the agreement. Whether it is an excellent decision, I can't yet determine. But it was a decision I needed to make, and I believe I have gotten ideas about their more successful training methods. We can learn from them. I think another component of this program should be to identify a few people to form a research group. We can access the Church's resources for a database of things we are likely to face, then add in our own unique entities. I also want to add a section on all the potential allies circulating out there. We are way behind on that knowledge compared to the Church, but there could be advantages if we have allies they don't, or that they don't even know about."

I got an interestingly shrewd look from Henry after that last sentence. There were no questions from the group, so we broke up for the evening. I felt there would be a lot more discussion once everybody had time to digest this first round of information.

The next day, I drove down to the airport to pick up my special guest. His plane was just landing when I arrived. I met him inside and we picked up his small bag as he traveled light. We traded a few teasing insults and drove back to the Farm, then had dinner together to plan the training sessions. The rest of the camp was buzzing about the mysterious new guy, as I had said little about his arrival. Michael had been gracious enough to lend me Simon. He was the most skilled personal combat person I had ever known when we trained together at the Church cottage.

I had the entire group meet in the barn around the sparring area the next morning. Henry had been working with the kids on general tactics, hunting, and basic firearms skills. We had briefly discussed the importance of personal defense but had not started it yet. That was about to change.

I introduced Simon to the group. "OK, people, this is the guy that is going to work your butts off, while making you both incredibly dangerous and difficult to hit. He is obviously not from around here. But we sparred for a few weeks recently. Simon, what do you call this particular style?"

"I named this style Sim-Sen after its two inventors."

I had to laugh. "Hah, that is a little different. How does it work?"

"The idea is to turn every move and countermove into an advantage to deliver additional damage. Every one of your actions inflicts significant pain and damage on your opponent, all while moving away and minimizing counterstrikes. For example, this move is to gouge the eye while turning your arm and angling your body away from the opponent; changing angles again to step aside while kicking and breaking the knee. Stepping and angling again to slide your arm down and dislocate their opposite shoulder, or, if they are falling the opposite direction, to chop and break the collarbone."

Henry grunted approvingly. "I like it. Bar fighting with style."

"Yes. You want to inflict three incapacitating injuries in six or fewer seconds. Extremely efficient and very dangerous. The idea is to create a cascade effect. As soon as you score the first injury, the second should come fast and the third even faster. At that point, your opponent has no offensive capability and limited or no defensive capacity. I believe the cofounder of this style called it 'whatever it takes to win and keep your ass from getting beat' on the first day that we trained together."

"Yeah, that has been working for me for a while," I said.

"We should probably warm up with other styles, then carefully train with this method, Simon said. "That will help keep the injuries to a minimum. As this style is still developing, we will also add new twists during training. If you have ideas or suggest ways to improvise moves after we start, let us know so we can check for countermoves. If it looks good, we will add it to the regimen. Questions?"

The balance of the session went well. Simon was incredibly talented and professional, working with everyone and improving their moves. I started noticing the younger women asking for more help than seemed necessary, or volunteering during the group activity. I did not know what Simon's preferences were, or even his marital status, but opportunities were about to blossom here. Everyone was an adult, and I knew Simon was not the type to do anything casual. After lunch, Nan came by to tell me she would have a chat with the younger women to give Simon some relief.

Simon came up after the second day of training. "What the hell is going on here? Some of these teenagers are stronger and faster than they have any right to be. I see you have that set grouped together, while the normal teenagers are in the other group."

"You are right. The normal group is athletic, but the other group is special. As you have noticed, they are going to be two to three times faster and stronger than normal humans. They are human, but have enhanced physical attributes, mostly from my wife's side of the family."

He looked at me and grinned. "I believe there is quite a story there. Also makes me wonder if you were holding back on me on our first sessions."

"Yeah, maybe a little. But I'm a whole different animal than those kids."

"I didn't realize you're married. Is your wife here?"

"No, she passed away over two hundred years ago. Most of these kids are great great grandchildren, or even further down the descendant list."

Simon looked intrigued. "Yes. Very much a story there. I think you are even more dangerous than Michael insinuated."

"Perhaps. Can't let all my secrets out, though. But now that you have seen the two groups here, I can tell you more about my plans for their training. Even though the one group has physical enhancements the other group does not, I need to get multiple strike teams put together with various combinations of all of them. I think very similar to teams that Michael has put together."

"Ah yes, I see. We put one Advanced with an Adept and two backups, with the backups trained in intelligence procedures and sniper school. After training that strike team will track and take down the worst of what the Church uncovers. Would you would be assigned as an Advanced on such a team?"

"Probably the Advanced, the Adept, and the sniper. I don't think I have the training or skills for the intelligence aspect."

"Hmm, you were holding back on me."

"Maybe, but I was having a lot of fun and learning something new every day we sparred. In fact, for this training, I have an idea. I heal within a day, so let's run through a full speed, full contact session and show the students what this style really looks like. We can go through a few rotations and then, on the fourth rotation, you take me out with a few broken bones. It will hurt, but I will be back up and good as new in a day."

"We can do that, but are you sure?"

"Yes, I would rather them see it at full speed to see the advantage of the style, but also show them the danger involved if they get carried away with it."

"OK, it is your bones and joints. Will be an interesting change for me. We try to never fully injure our training partners, other than the occasional bruises and sprains."

"Just don't make cry in front of the kids."

"Sure. Back on the training question, what roles do you see for these students?"

"That enhanced group will all be Advanced, and I think most, or all are also Adepts. The other group will be the backups. But I want all of them cross trained at all positions, so they will understand all roles. I think that is the best strategy to make the teams successful."

"Agreed. That will give you the best use of personnel. I can tell that you are both a small organization and a new one. Otherwise, you would not be agile enough to be so forward thinking."

"Agile is always good."

"Jo would be good to have here."

I choked on the water I was drinking. Simon noticed and grinned at the effect his words had on me.

"She is the only one, since you, that I have seen with such physical potential. She did not have the technical skills at first. But now she is already beyond my level and could be co-teaching this along with you."

"Could be, but she is where she needs to be for now."

"Of course," was his response. He was still grinning, tossing a little mental jujitsu my way. "Did you know Michael was considering sending her here with me?"

"Damn it, Simon, you really are trying to choke me. Don't want to wait until tomorrow to take me out?"

"Just having a simple conversation about a colleague. I can't help it if you are having a choking episode."

"OK, you got my goat today. But I was considering asking Michael to have her come over for a few days, anyway. She can give the kids quite a background on some critters that they are likely to run across."

"Even better, they can watch you two spar at full speed. Will be quite the show."

As Simon was drinking, it was my turn. "Some ladies around here seem to be hot for teacher."

He spewed water and then laughed. "Yes, turnabout is fair play. This happens often with small groups. I doubt there will be any problems with these young women. They seem mature enough. In fact, I would bet they would drag a man around by the hair."

"I'm not worried. You are a professional, and as you say, the women are stronger than you anyway, and everyone here is an adult. Oh, and don't tell her I told you, but Nan is ninety years old."

Simon choked on his second long drink of water. It was juvenile but I had just won the choking score.

CHAPTER TEN

Most of the group had spent the day at Biltmore Estate, enjoying time away from the farm, as I had promised Nan. All the kids and most of the adults had gone to sample the spa, skeet shooting, horseback riding, shopping and restaurants. Afterward they were staying overnight at my house in Asheville. Henry did not go as he saw no purpose in the trip, and Seth did not since it was not his kind of social outing. It was just the three of us at the fire and we all retired early. Henry seemed edgy but did not say anything about what was bothering him.

Henry came in to wake me up, but I was not asleep. I was getting ready to sneak away to the other side of the property and practice my slant exercises.

"Sen, we got something moving on the edge of the property," Henry said. "Not sure what it is, but it isn't supposed to be here."

"Something dangerous?"

"Doesn't feel like it, but better to run it down and find out."

"Get Seth, he might be able to track it in mountain lion form."

"He's already outside waiting."

"Hey Henry, how did you even know something is out there nearly a mile away?"

"Just had an itch all evening. Kinda feels like something familiar, but not."

"OK, let's go get this thing."

Seth and I ran behind Henry as he seemed to know the general direction to the intruder. We cleared the pasture quickly, then moved a little slower through the woods. Near the edge of the property, Henry stopped and motioned that we were close. Seth dropped out of his clothes, put them in a small bag and tossed it to me. By the time I caught it, he was in mountain lion form. His head swiveled around a few seconds as he inhaled heavily to catch any scent. A second later he leaped away, and Henry and I followed.

We were not going to keep up with a mountain lion, but we did hurry along. We ran through fields, woods, farms, and past an occasional house, moving roughly east and slightly north. A couple of times we stirred up dogs that barked, but always at a distance. Whatever we were chasing was staying away from humans. Seth's form was always out of sight, but he occasionally chuffed, which gave us an idea of his direction. I did not know where what we were chasing was going, but eventually we would be at the Toe River, and I did not think there was a bridge across it nearby.

After nearly an hour the chase ended. Henry and I ran up to Seth near the river. He had already changed back to human form, so I tossed his bag of clothes back him to get dressed. We were all breathing a little heavy, so conversation was slow to start.

"What was it, Seth?" I asked.

"Don't know what it was, but it's gone," Seth said. "Never got a good sight or smell of it for long. Maybe a man but did not move like one. In fact, it was kind of odd. Like it was flashing out of existence every time I got near it. Then it showed up a hundred yards away and I could hear it running. I'd give chase, but when I got close, it would blink away again."

"You mean, like it was flying?"

"No. It was just gone."

"Henry, you ever run across anything like that?"

"No, there is not anything like that around here."

We stepped down to the edge of the riverbank and Henry and I turned on flashlights. Henry pointed out a medium-sized bare footprint in the mud at the edge of the water. Roughly human-shaped and very lightly embedded in the mud. The body belonging to the foot could not have weighed much, so the foot was likely disproportional to the body. What really stood out was that the toes were webbed. That put a whole new wrinkle into the mystery, and the chance of it being a fluke that this thing was both on the Arkansas River in Oklahoma, and now here at the Toe River in North Carolina, was vanishingly small.

"This is what we saw on the Arkansas River near Moffett, after we rescued the girls from the Great Serpent," Henry said.

"I've never seen a print like that," Seth said. "I'm going to look and see where it came out of the river."

We walked and checked both sides of the river for a mile up and down where the footprint was found. There was no other sign of any kind that the thing had ever come out of the water. It must have gone in the river and never came out.

There was nothing else for us to do so we started back. We had a few miles to go and dawn was coming soon. But we had time to mull over and chat about our unusual visitor.

"Think it might be here to stalk Stacey and Melissa?" I asked Henry.

"Not sure that fits. All the girls were gone tonight over to the Biltmore. Seems like it picked an odd time to be looking for them." As he finished, he gave me a look.

"Nah, don't look at me. I have enough weirdness happening in my life without this. Makes more sense that it was checking on you. Maybe it took notice of you tracking it back in Oklahoma and wanted to get a closer look."

"Maybe, but don't feel right. Suppose for now it's gonna remain a mystery. Maybe we should not tell the rest of the gang when they get back."

Seth and I agreed. We would not tell everyone, but Henry would tell Nan, and Seth would talk to Jen. They could keep an eye on the Oklahoma girls and not send them out alone at night for the near future. Henry, Seth, and I would also keep a close eye on the kids and do some perimeter patrols. I made myself a mental note to get with Kal about setting up a detection system around the property.

We continued jogging, which would have been a full run for most humans. We did not talk much but I'm sure we were all thinking about the evening. Henry had no problem keeping up, and that, plus his other uncanny abilities, made me think he was more than just a regular guy.

Everyone was back at the Farm the next day and in a great mood. They all had an excellent time on their day and night off. We heard how Elendor and Stacey had bested the guys while skeet shooting, and how Jimmy enjoyed the hot stone massage at the spa. Jen had gotten Simon to try banana pudding for the first time. All the good restaurant food in town and hot showers at my house had helped buoyed everyone's spirits. I decided it was a good decision not to tell everyone about the trespasser that might be linked to the Moffett, Oklahoma events a few months back. It would have put a strong damper on most of the kids. Nan, of course, picked up on something amiss, so Henry talked to her while the kids were still telling stories. I saw Seth pull Jen aside as well. Otherwise, the day went smoothly. Late afternoon was not so smooth for me, as that was when Simon got to impress everyone with busting me up.

The next morning when I woke, I momentarily wished that I had not. I needed a big breakfast to push through the healing process. Simon had been thorough in breaking my bones the previous afternoon. The kids were most impressed with the loud cracks and possibly a few groans I emanated. But they now had new respect for Simon and what he was teaching. And I was hungry and grouchy.

I was not sure which pains were worse than others. But I hobbled down to the makeshift cafeteria. A lot of food today, no physical training, and I'd be well by tomorrow. I thought about turning Simon just so I could beat him senseless. Nice thought, but probably not the best idea, as he would likely be invincible. I thought about leaving a dead possum under his pillow instead. Sophomoric but effective. Knowing him, he'd probably have it for breakfast in front of me.

Simon was fitting in well, and the guys, especially Henry, were spending extra time with him. Reminded me of a much earlier period of my life when a warrior from another Legion would travel and spend a few days with us. If they were good at what they did and had new techniques, like adding a few yards to a javelin throw, the men would hang around and pick up every tip they could. I then cut off that line of memory when Caius entered my thoughts. Catching and killing him was a priority, which reminded me I needed to go back to Europe and hunt him down. That led to further contemplation about a British colleague.

I thought about my call last night. Michael had been gracious to have Jo come over. He only gave her three days as travel would eat up most of another two, and he needed her in Europe for other purposes. I still was not sure it was the right thing, but it was too late now. She was already traveling, and I'd be picking her up at the airport late today. So now it was time for me to eat up and put my happy pants on.

After I watched some of the group training sessions and taught a class, it was time to go to Asheville to pick up Jo. I could have sent someone, but right now I was the least important person at the Farm. That is what we were calling it now. Sort of fitting, as I had told the kids to look up The Farm near Williamsburg, Virginia. We were a long way from being a CIA training center, but we did have some assets they did not.

I pulled up to the terminal building, then remembered I could not park at the curb. Until recently, it had been one of the last airports to allow parking by the building for short waits. Then some moron had to show up with an inoperative pipe bomb and that was over. I walked in and soon I saw Jo walking down the hall from the gates. We smiled at each other, and after hesitating, I gave her a brief hug. I was still thinking about our encounter at the cottage, and she probably was too.

We went to my house in Asheville first. No real reason other than to show it to her, plus there was no schedule for either of us back at the Farm that afternoon. She seemed to like it, but we spent little time there. I thought she felt as slightly awkward as I did. It was odd having Jo in America and driving around familiar places. We left the house and headed north toward the Farm. Other than a stop at the grocery for some s'mores and hot dog supplies requested for the campfire that evening, we went straight there. More music and silence than conversation, except for the last few miles.

"Michael did not tell me much about the purpose of my visit or what you are doing with your people. I assume it is about what we talked about after dinner recently?"

"Yes, this group includes my distant relatives. Many of them are shapeshifters. That was the part I had been keeping secret for a couple of centuries, but no reason for that anymore. You and Simon are finding out firsthand. Of course, these are not the evil, chaotic cannibals, but the gentle helpers. Except, of course, when they meet the bad shape shifters. Then it is all out war."

"Just how distant are these relatives to you?"

"The closest one is my great-granddaughter, Nan. Jen is a great-grand-daughter as well, but became the generations are so offset, she is a lot younger than Nan. The rest are more distant, with some of the non-shifters ten generations out."

"And what are you are training them for?"

"My goal is to get them self-sufficient at defense, to help themselves and their people. Ultimately, it will be more than that, including enough offense to fend off the expected new threats. A mini version of how Michael sets up teams."

"Will you join up with Michael's forces?"

"Not soon, since we are just too few. The group you are about to meet only numbers thirteen, with only five known shifters so far. We hope to get more over the next two years. Even with the extra abilities of the shifters, we obviously can't do much for quite some time."

"So few. You really have a tough task."

"We hope to recruit more and will contact other groups. But we think there may only be a couple hundred shifters left in the country. Because of some old complications of tribes, politics, and philosophy, we will probably never convince more than half of them to join us. The non-shifters are also important for support. But as you do the math, unfortunately, I don't think we will ever have over two or three hundred people in total."

"What is my role, then? Education of the entities they may face, or did you have something else in mind?"

"Yeah, I'd love to have you teach a compressed course on the known entities, especially those they may face in America over the near future. Anything you may know about the other side of the pond that is OK to share. And I believe Simon is really hoping to watch you kick my ass during sparring."

"Speaking of that, I noticed you were moving slower than usual. Training accident?"

"Nope. Simon and I did a full speed full contact spar session yesterday. It was an opportunity to let the kids know how dangerous the martial training is. At the end, I had Simon bust me up. Limped off with three broken bones."

"Well, at least that shows dedication. Will you heal enough by tomorrow to get broken up again?"

I laughed. "Petty sure of yourself, huh? Simon told me you were still getting better. I suppose after our last session, you are also getting sneakier."

"Very much so. Should be fun, especially with an audience."

"Great. Hurt and embarrass the old man. I get no respect."

"You will need to earn it. First, we will see how good a s'more you make."

I laughed. "S'mores, I can do."

CHAPTER ELEVEN

W hen I drove in, I noticed there were more people lounging around the house than normal. I bet that Simon and Henry had notified everyone of the new arrival and they were hanging around to get a look at her. We got out, and I introduced Jo to everyone, since everyone was already there waiting. Jen showed Jo to her temporary quarters while Nan just looked at me.

"You're a bit late getting back. Did you get everything?" Nan asked.

"Everything I needed," I responded. "Chocolate bars, graham crackers, marshmallows; and hot dogs, buns, chips, ketchup and mustard. The dogs are the non-meat, vegetarian kind just to piss you off."

She laughed. "I bet you got packs of chicken, beef, and pork to make everyone happy."

"Actually, yes, I did. Happy bellies make happy campers. And killers."

I carried the groceries in. Then I found Henry and Simon to ask about how the afternoon activities went.

"Jimmy, Ned, and John Henry are really coming along," Henry said. "Stacy and Melissa are kicking it up a few notches. Elendor and Emeline not so much, but Jen is bringing them along. They have had a rough upbringing. But both Nan and Jen think they are going to be shifters. You know how much that will change things for the better."

"How bout Nan, Jen, and Seth? Everybody getting along? And Watt and Samuel?"

"Everybody is getting along fine. Jen is a real killer, action all the time. Seth is interesting. He sits back and watches, then makes unusual strategic moves that work real well. Watt and Sam doing their usual thing. Altogether, the makings of a real team are here."

"Simon, how about on the fighting and tactics side?"

"Everybody is new to most of this, but they are learning fast. Nan, of course, is already above most anything we can teach. I really like Jen and Seth. I'd steal them for my team if I could. As Henry said, Jen is all non-stop action and Seth is a real unpredictable tactician. All the younger ones have the talent to be on teams once they have more skills. You already know that both Watt and Sam are excellent snipers and hunters, now they are doing well at anchoring the young ones."

"Good, so we are on target so far."

"Yes," they both said.

"That Jo is some looker, huh? Heard she is smart, too." Henry just stood there grinning, knowing I would not respond. Simon had on his best Cheshire Cat smile as well.

"Let's get the fire started. Everyone should be hungry." I left before I started laughing at Henry's comment.

An hour later, as it was getting dark, everyone was on benches or chairs around the fire. We laid out a table with all the supplies for a messy dinner. After tonight, most clothes would bear mustard and chocolate stains.

As we gathered, Jo had Nan, Jen, and Henry on one side, plus the younger women on the other side of her. I was across the fire with Simon and Seth. The three young men were milling around, eating large quantities of food.

Jo and I were occasionally trading glances across the fire. I never expected her to be sitting around a campfire in America. But I was glad to have her here.

She could really add to the training, both in content and to show the group that, between her and Simon, the Church could be an asset. Nan seemed to pick up on our glances and I caught her shaking her head. There were no secrets in this small a group of accomplished people. It was kind of funny, though, that Nan was picking up on something that really wasn't there. We finished up the food, and I asked Jo to tell us more about her specialty. She did for about five minutes. Then it was time to finish the fire and get ready for tomorrow. Everybody said goodnight and headed back to their respective lodgings.

Nan nudged me as we walked back. "Want to trade rooms with me tonight?"

"No thanks. That is a kind of trouble I don't need."

"Damn Sen, you just might mature here in your second millennium."

"Yeah, well, don't celebrate too soon. I'm sure I can still behave well below your expectations. Maybe I'll drive down to Asheville and kill a random mugger."

"Now don't get edgy. Besides, you know you need to control that side of things."

"Yes ma'am. Now, goodnight, I'm off to prowl the fields before bed." My late-night prowls were an excuse to go to the far end of the property where I could practice my slant with no one observing me. Once I felt comfortable with the basics Kal had taught me, I started thinking out of the box. Things got interesting and I understood why most current humans should not have certain abilities.

Slant, to me, was a kind of sideways movement and thought that deflected then channeled vibrations in unusual patterns. I could also see it work as a defense if someone or something came at me. But it was more of a philosophical lifestyle that changed my perception of the world. I understood that everything, literally everything, was resonance, and all vibrations were linked at some level. Time was the force that kept the resonance going. And it was likely to take centuries, if not longer, to figure out what it all meant.

The next day continued the pleasant weather. Climate in the North Carolina mountains, this early in the fall, was typically good, and this day was no exception.

Jo was a hit with the kids. Attractive, with a British accent, and obvious intelligence when teaching the course on nonhuman entities. If they were impressed now, they would be even more so after the afternoon spar session. Nan and Jen cornered me at lunch. Nan went first.

"What is the deal with Jo? Why is she really here?"

"I thought we needed an expert in monsters and creatures."

"Possibly, but there is more. Try again," Jen said.

"OK. Because I lost a bet with Simon? Or because I like her and want to carry her books at school?"

"Don't be foolish."

"At least that isn't a complete lie," Nan said. "Maybe we can help you out." She was failing at suppressing a smile.

"Really? OK, what advice can you give? Or maybe we should spend some time on actual issues, like how do we set up training sessions for next week."

"Hey, let us have our fun," Nan said. "Let me think what is on the list. First, you could forget her, move on, and turn the other cheek. Second, you could hire a sex worker. Either of those could work."

I could not help but laugh. "Great. But let's find a solution that makes me look less like a loser, and maybe prevents me from getting a sexually transmitted disease."

Jen took a different approach to teasing me. "You should probably try another Cherokee girl and leave the white girls alone. They are too fickle."

By this time, we were all laughing.

"Oh, did I tell you two that Jo has the same hearing ability that we do, if not better?"

Nan and Jen stopped laughing, looked at each other in surprise, then reflexively looked over at Jo across the room. She was smiling serenely at them. Jo had obviously enjoyed the conversation as she started laughing. Then the three of us did too.

"Well, that was most instructive," I said. "I believe I will take a rain check on the advice, however. I'll muddle through my love life in confusion, just like everyone else. Again, I'm pretty sure my it is not important right now compared to everything else happening. Besides, while you wannabe match-makers are having your fun, Jo and I are not a thing. This must be a professional relationship, and Jo is not interested in anything else either."

Nan and Jen just laughed again. At least I had my sense of comedy still working. Maybe it was tragedy, rather than comedy? Wasn't one form of tragedy also a spectacle? Yeah, I could do spectacle, especially in America.

The afternoon was wearing down as Henry was finishing another session on outdoor survival and hunting. It was time for Jo and me to spar. We would go a few rounds of three minutes each, full speed. Nobody knew quite what to expect except for Simon. The rumors were likely circulating that Jo was the one I had turned. But they probably didn't know she was at my level or beyond. Should be fun for the spectators.

We went into the barn, chatted with Simon as he was going to call the session, and then we started. It was so sudden and intense the small crowd there didn't even realize we had begun. A few minutes later and it was over. I won two of three bouts. Tomorrow, that could easily swing the other way. We were both bruised, but no broken bones or major sprains. It was a success as the display wowed the spectators.

We toweled off the sweat and walked with the crew toward dinner. Everyone was loud and in a good mood. I sat with Jo during dinner, then I went to get a shower before the meetup at the nightly bonfire. As I came out of the house, Nan greeted me. She put her arm in mine and dragged me out into the field, in the opposite direction of the bonfire. She seemed to be contemplative but said nothing. We kept walking until I finally spoke up.

"Nan, I have suspicions that you either wanted to talk to me away from the others, or you needed a companion to walk over to Raleigh."

"Sen, she's the one, isn't she? The one you turned recently?"

"Yes, she is."

"I could tell from the sparring. Also, I'm not sure, but I think she has a slight silver glow."

"I had not even noticed. It must be just beginning."

"And you are sure there is nothing between you two?"

"Mostly sure. I mean, she is highly intelligent, great in her field, and physically attractive. But there is not likely to be anything developing."

"Hmm. I understand your explanation easily enough, but there seems to be something more brewing."

"Uh, why do you think that?"

"Nobody, even your kind, fights like that unless there is attraction or hatred. Not that there is much difference sometimes."

"Well, hate to bust your theory, but Simon and I have some good bouts as well."

"You can try the denial route, but it won't work. You and she could end up together someday or could kill each other."

"Both?"

She laughed. "Possibly. It certainly happens with some people. But Sen, you mentioned you should be able to turn anyone. Is this what you meant when you mentioned turning the kids?"

"Yes. I certainly do not want to do that, however. I hope the training, and the teams that come from it, will be good enough to protect the people without resorting to turning anyone."

"I don't know. After seeing Jo in action, the benefits of turning someone are so obvious. Yet I am not sure about the ethics of changing someone's life so much. How did you decide to turn Jo?"

"I didn't want to. But as I said before, it was that or watch her die. I only had a couple of minutes to decide that."

"That must have been tough."

"It was incredibly difficult. But maybe I acted on selfish instincts as I didn't want to lose her, even though I knew I was damning her to another type of life."

"That wasn't complete selfishness. You did it to help her. And maybe there is something more slowly taking shape. I would think the turning episode has really changed the game though. So you probably don't have any idea what to do with her from here, now do you?"

"Not really. I guess I don't really plan to do anything with her at this point. She has a lot of things to deal with. I had the benefit of learning about this kind of life over centuries. She has barely had months. Other than working with her, I won't plan anything further."

"I understand. But you may be the only that she could really talk to about it. She may need you, so don't be a dumbass and withdraw from her while trying to be a gentleman."

"I really had not considered it from that angle. Although an old Church assassin said something similar."

"Of course not. Some things go missing on that Y chromosome. Sometimes you underthink, sometimes you overthink. But she really needs a friend to go through this with."

"You are going to get into her and my business, aren't you?" I said as we turned and walked back to the bonfire.

"Someone has to navigate that blind pig toward the acorns. But I'll be gentle."

"Yeah, heard that before. I can just hear some old sea captain screaming 'ramming speed' at the helmsman."

She laughed. "Give me more credit than that. Besides, she is only here another day or so. I'll just try to get to know her better. See if I can help."

"Hey, I appreciate that. I know that you, by nature, help and heal others. Jo probably needs friends like that, especially those that know her secret and are comfortable with her."

"That is exactly what I hope to accomplish. And you need to do the same for her. Changing the subject back to earlier, you know if things are going to get as bad as you think, there may be no choice but to turn these kids, plus others. I just worry that some of them won't adjust well. And what happens when you have someone with that ability that turns out bad?"

"I've thought of that a lot. There are only a few choices. Don't turn them. Or, once turned, and things don't go well, they either have to be given the binder and cleanser potions or killed. So dead, or crazy and locked up, are the two options. And these kids are my family, even though distant. I just don't know that I can make that choice."

"I hope you don't have to. But I also know that if it's necessary, you will do it."

"That is what I'm afraid of. I suspect this is how those nuclear scientists felt while starting the Manhattan Project."

We continued back in silence. At the fire that night, I sat beside Jo while Nan sat on the other side of her. After the fire, they walked off together and were mostly together for the rest of Jo's stay. I realized I should not have been surprised. Nan was a wise person and had always been a healer. She would be empathetic to Jo's pain. And she could learn from Jo what it was like to be turned unexpectedly, especially if she was going to have to deal with a group of kids I had turned into, well, whatever the hell I was.

The next day was similar, with lots of class time and outdoor training for the kids, meals taken together, a late sparring session, and then the bonfire. The following day, I shook things up, both for us and our two Church guests. It was time to incorporate the shapeshifter aspects into the training, to show what could really be done with shifters on the team. I planned it with Nan, Jen and Seth, with Henry acting as the coordinator. I basically got the right people together, then shut the hell up. It was called effective administration.

We gathered as a group near one end of the Farm, and everyone had binoculars. I set a timer to mark the start of the exercise. Details were vague, and all we knew was that Nan, Jen, and Seth would start in the woods a mile away, cross the several hundred yards of pasture, and use pistols to shoot three targets we had tacked to a shed set up near the fire pit. We were observing how well they stayed hidden and how much time it took them to hit the targets.

At the appointed time, I fired off a shot to begin the exercise. Ninety seconds later, we could see three figures in camouflage leave the woods and sprint across the pasture. Another ninety seconds and shots rang out, and the targets were down.

"Damn, that was fast. My strike team would need six minutes to make that trek," said Simon. "Your untrained team did it in half the time."

"Yeah, they are pretty fast," I said. "But they want a second go to improve it."

"I don't know how much faster they could do it."

I gave the three of them a few minutes to get back to the start location, then fired a second time. Less than ninety seconds later a hawk plummeted from the sky to a brown lump that appeared near the shed. We had not seen the shape as it sprinted across the pasture, below the tall grass. As the hawk landed, it turned into Nan, and she pulled a pistol from a pack strapped to the mountain lion. Three shots and three seconds later and the targets were down. Ninety-three seconds to cross the mile and take down three targets with two people, or rather two shapeshifters. Simon just stood, shaking his head in disbelief.

"That is remarkable," Jo said. "My god, I didn't really believe shifting was real. But it's an insanely successful tactic, and so fast that no one could defend it."

"Now you see the potential for these kinds of teams. We will need more training to get better. Then they'll really be dangerous."

Nan pulled out a robe from the mountain lion's pack and put it on. Then the lion shifted back into Seth, and he pulled out another robe to wear. A few minutes later a nonchalant Jen walked up. Her only job had been to strap the pack on Seth after he changed. But she could have easily changed into her hawk form for backup or extra surveillance.

To say it was a successful exercise was an understatement. Everyone was buzzing, and Jo and Simon were asking lots of questions. The kids were even more into the training after seeing the possibilities. I knew it was a simple example, but damn, it was effective.

CHAPTER TWELVE

Jo was highly popular with everyone, possibly because she occasionally kicked my ass during our sparring sessions. Our bouts were basically even so far. There really was something to the double microbiome theory, or I was getting old. At the end of the third day, wins were four to four, with one draw, so I told Simon we needed one last bout. We should do it outside and have no rules. He readily agreed, and Jo seemed interested as well. The three of us walked out of the barn as the others followed. Just as we stepped outside, Jo took me down in half a second. She and Simon stood there, smiling down at me. Jo reached her hand down, and I grabbed it and hauled myself up. I slapped Simon on the back and hugged Jo.

I stepped back and announced to everyone, "I hope you just saw what happened. I have been telling Jo for some time that deception and surprise will win most fights. She just proved it, and now I can retire as her teacher. She is sneakier than me, and I am proud."

Everyone congratulated her as we headed toward the fire and more treats. The sunny day was turning into a cool, clear night. After the fire, I walked with Jo back towards the house. We kept going past it and into the field. The stars were out, and I was happy to be outside. We sat down in the field and leaned back to see the night show.

"Have you passed on the sneaky crown to me?" Jo asked.

"Yes, and glad to do so. Always remain sneaky and you will go far. Meanwhile, I'm working on a new level of sneakiness."

"I am glad I came here. I was not sure that I should come, but now I see you and the others are building something special here."

"Thanks, and I'm very appreciative that you came. I had mixed reasons for asking you here. But it seemed to work out."

"Everyone seems happy here. It is strange seeing you here though."

"What?"

"You have always seemed like such a solitary figure. It's strange seeing you in a group setting, working with and joking around with everyone."

"It is different. It has been a long time since I've been around more than just a couple of friends."

"It looks good on you, so you should keep doing it."

"I think so too. I didn't even realize how much I missed it and how much fun it could be."

"Are you coming back to Europe soon?"

"I would like to spend a few more weeks here, but honestly, they don't need me very much. If Michael needs me, I will be back sooner. But I think I will always come back here when I can. Although here won't always be here."

"What does that mean?"

"I have a feeling that we will move elsewhere, maybe more than once. I don't think we can escape the notice of our enemies forever. As this training becomes successful and we start field operations, they will eventually come for us, like they did for you and others at the Center. I just hope we have a couple of decades first."

"Do you think you have that long? From conversations with the Church analysts and Michael, the consensus is that major trouble is imminent."

"I don't like to think about it, but your timeline seems right. But I believe we are safe here tonight."

"I think so too. But I need to go back and pack up my things. As you know, my flight out is midday, so I'll need to leave after morning class."

"Yep, and I'll be your chauffeur again. Let's head back before we start any rumors."

"A bit late, don't you think? Nan and Jen already have us paired off. But Nan is great, so I don't mind the light teasing."

"That is kind of what they do. They grow on you if you have the patience not to strangle them."

We walked back and traded goodnights. I moved back to the field for a while. Later, the sickle moon rose and kept me company. These were the nights I liked best. Clear, cool, and quiet. One owl at a long distance was the only sound. Stars were disco dancing, so there must have been some high-altitude winds, and I watched occasional satellites cross over. They were getting annoyingly common.

I sensed a presence nearby. I could not get a good read on who or what it was, but my threat detectors were not on alert. Or I could just admit to noticing a large tree in the field that had not been there a few minutes ago. A true detective I was.

"Kal?"

I felt a deep, rumbling laugh. "Ahh, the Silver Walker is back in his mountains. How do you like this glorious night?" The tree changed into an intimidatingly large being.

"I like it much. I still miss my Old World, but nights like this remind me why I will always come back to these parts."

"Good. Part of you belongs here. You and the mountains here are mutually beneficial. Remember to return after your many journeys."

"Is that your way of telling me I'm going somewhere?"

"We are all going somewhere. Just remember..." And we both said in unison the old joke, 'No matter where you go, there you are'. We both laughed. I was getting more used to Kal's unusual laugh. "No, I did not come to talk to you about physical journeys. I was nearby on other business and stopped by to share some night sky with you. And to ask how your self-training is going. Any questions?"

"Thank you for stopping by. I don't have questions right now. My efforts so far have been very revealing. So very much of our universe is in front of us every day, but we don't really see it. And we do not know how to use it. Maybe that is for the best. Humans are dangerous enough with the primitive weapons we have."

"Yes, with wisdom will come acceptance of self, and eventually the repeal of aggression, or so we hope. Those changes would come sooner if we can reverse the manipulations of the Sky Lords."

"Were the Sky Lords also master vampires created by the initial virus or later versions?"

"Some were, and still are, master vampires. But a few remain here. Without access to the future and the resources there, it limits them in their mischief, but they are still dangerous. We will continue to look for those Sky Lords still here and eliminate them from this timeline."

"I am still hunting for one master vampire, a colleague from my oldest days. He has been difficult to find."

"I believe that you hairless have another of our words to describe your situation. Karma. It applies to both you and your enemy. Prepare well, as you will surely battle again. As a warning, we have observed the master vampires working with the Sky Lords to carry out their plans in this timeline. That makes them even more dangerous."

"I plan to be careful. On a similar subject, how do I protect the people in this place from those that would seek to harm them?"

"Ah, you cannot protect them, not fully. Is there a specific threat that concerns you?"

"Not really. I just have a strong feeling that what we do here will threaten many. And Sky Lords and their local thugs would be near the top of the list. You said that you had cut their travel off, but I still don't have a warm and fuzzy feeling that they are gone."

"Yes, true. You can defend this place, but it needs more layers. You may also consider moving it to a more time-secure location."

"Yeah, things like 'time secure locations' don't compute for me yet."

"I will consider your issue. Meanwhile, you need more understanding and self-training. Keep up your slant efforts. These concepts will soon come to you much easier."

"I will. I just need time to work on it."

He stared at me. "You already have all the time imaginable. You just have to learn to employ it."

Those words seemed simple but meant little to me. As I began to respond, I realized I was by myself. Kal was simply and completely gone. There was no hint of air moving, nor any noise or light. He simply did not exist anymore where he had just been standing. That exit, plus his last words, hinted at what was possible. Now I just had to find it for myself.

I took Jo back to the airport the following day. On the way, I took a few minutes and drove through the Biltmore Estate. I briefly described how that factored into my previous life, and now affected my current life. I left Kal out of that explanation. Although I would tell her about Kal eventually, for now, I felt it best to keep that quiet. At the airport I went with her to security. We hugged for a moment, then she left. I drove back to the farm and blended back in with the daily rhythm. The four horsemen of the teasing apocalypse, Nan, Jen, Henry, and Simon, kept at me in a good-natured way. A few days passed in relative peace and hard work. But all things must end.

Michael called Simon one afternoon while we were finishing a class. Simon was needed back in Europe as soon as possible for a mission regarding a possible master vampire. After he talked to Simon, he called me.

"I suppose you heard about my conversation with Simon?"

"Yes, and any chance this master vampire might be Caius?"

"Definitely not. In fact, we are not sure he is a vampire yet, but need to get our teams on him as he fits most of the search categories. How are your efforts going there?"

"Everything here is good, and the training has been successful. Thanks for allowing Simon and Jo to take part. We just need more trainees and a lot more time."

"Is your presence required there for the foreseeable future? I'm asking because as this mission develops, it would be good to have you come over and take part. I feel this is an excellent training opportunity for our people, regardless of the outcome."

"I can break free here most anytime."

"Good. Can you make it to Scotland a week from now?"

"Certainly. It is always good to see Edinburgh again. One of my favorite old, haunted cities."

"It definitely is that. The operation is a little further north in Inverness. But from America, Edinburgh is your best bet for an airport. Send me your travel information, and I'll have Simon and his team expecting you."

"Sure, talk to you later, Obi-wan."

I heard him mumble something as he hung up. I must have distracted him to let me get away with one like that.

Simon left that evening to get on a flight to Scotland. I spent the next week on training sessions and going over political and social studies classes with the kids. It was slightly less fun without Simon and Jo around.

The kids were doing well. There was some consternation when I started the political ethics class. My topics were difficult for them to digest. I did not blame them at all as the topics were complex or controversial enough to vex most seasoned adults.

I found Henry one night, and we walked out into the fields for some discussion. He started it off.

"You really think you could change enough folks to start an army?"

"I am not sure, but I don't think so. I think it will work on the non-shifters, but I do not know if it will work on the shifters, or what effects it might have. Unfortunately, if our enemies move soon I don't know what other choice we will have."

"You sure about not working on the shifters?"

"I guess it is possible. I just have a moral and ethical dilemma turning kids into near immortal super kids. I just don't feel it is the right thing to do. But getting swatted by a god or nasty time traveler does not make me happy either."

"Damn, that is some rock to carry."

"Yep, and I know it will come rolling back down the hill and squash me."

"You could step out of the way. Get less squished if you see it coming."

"How are you and your guys, plus Jen and Seth, taking all this? And how do you think it is affecting the kids?"

"All of us in the older group are taking everything in stride. The kids are doing well. They have a slight sense of astonishment, and maybe still wondering if all this is real. They will find out the truth quick enough when they face their first enemy. And at least they'll be prepared for it."

"Henry, you ever hear of the Tsul Kalu?"

"Oh yes, but never really spent time with one. They give off a distinct vibration. I run across that a few times in the woods over the years. You got a new little tingle about you, so must have been spending some time around them."

"What are you, Henry? You know a lot that others don't even suspect."

"Just a guy that keeps an eye open."

"The third eye too?"

"Gotta use all you got. By the way, if you have TK friends, learn all you can."

"I plan to."

Then it was time for me to fly out. I was going back to an old haunt and maybe getting a shot at a master vampire. It would be good practice for taking down Caius when I found him.

Chapter Thirteen

I was on the plane, in my seat by the window, on the flight from Asheville to Atlanta. Since it was a small plane, even in first class, there were two seats together; the seat beside me on the aisle was unoccupied. It stayed empty until just before the door closed. A nondescript man with brown hair and a brown suit sat down beside me. He was the guy that you would never notice, nor remember five seconds later, even if you noticed him. That was the first clue. That and the familiar glow from my other sight.

"Hi Kal, good to see you. Although a bit strange that we meet on an airplane. I am sure you don't need one to get somewhere."

"Hello there. Good to see you again as well. I have traveled by plane before, mostly to get a feel for the technology. But you are right, I normally don't travel by this archaic method. Today I am here to talk with you."

"I see. Do you have a particular subject for this visit?"

"Yes. As I told you before, you and others have been pulled into a larger conflict, much of which you are not aware of yet. Your quest against an old master vampire, who is likely working with or for the Sky Lords, is just a small part of that conflict.

"For you to succeed, you will need to arm yourself with certain skills. These include learning to travel the links in a responsible way. Other skills involve protecting yourself and your people from the array of dangers the other side will throw against you. The fastest way to immerse you in these new ways is to meet up with Odin. He may not be easy to find, but it is in your best interest to make that contact. You have met before, if only briefly, in a previous time and place. The circumstances of that previous meeting also illustrate the inherent danger that comes with actions that affect the future. Those harmful actions are easy to commit once you begin traveling the links."

"That seems unlikely, as I don't remember meeting Odin. And I definitely don't recall changing the future. But I will take all the help I can get."

"Odin was probably in disguise. He was present in old Germany because of an altered timeline, which required his direct involvement to correct and remove a paradox. Although we did not realize it then, you caused that alteration. Some centuries ago, your adventures included meeting a group of Vikings and traveling to Germany."

"Yes, I remember that time."

"Entwined in that story are larger lessons in the understanding of place-time streams, paradoxes, and the danger of affecting future events. If you could tell me of those events, I can explain the place-time cause-and-effect ripples."

"Sure, I can do that. I'm not sure we have time on this short flight unless you are going to Edinburgh as well. It is a long story unless I leave out the details."

"No, I will not be flying to Scotland. I try to limit my time on an airplane. But, in this case, details are necessary. Besides, we have all the time in the world."

I noticed he was looking at the window. I glanced out too and noticed the plane, suspended in the sky and not moving.

"OK, Kal, my understanding of physics tells me that if the plane is not moving, then it is falling out of the sky."

"Not to worry, the plane is operating correctly. You and I are currently in a small bubble of pre-time. There are physics, and then there are physics of a larger universe. Your physics do an adequate job in most cases of explaining things inherent on your plant. But there is a greater body of physics that govern the universe. The links, interdimensional energies, and different versions of time are of that system. If it is easier, just consider that level of physics as magic."

"OK, glad we are not plowing into the ground soon. But what kind of watch would I need to keep up with pre-time?"

"A very cheap one would suffice, since pre-time does not exist in your world."

"Oh, that makes perfect sense. I guess someday I'll need a class about the non-existent pre-time zone we are currently in."

"Agreed. And that brings me to a tangential story about our planet, from a very long time ago, and another entity you'll need to meet."

"This should be interesting. Your tangents tend to be astounding bits of information."

"Thank you. First of all, the earth is an organism. The outer body is the land and water and atmosphere above the surface. Solar winds and bits of other planets and solar systems stream by and sometimes seed the plant; volcanoes rumbling up through the surface as tectonic plates buckle allows the lava to seed the surface with what is below. Underneath is another environment, of heat and pressure, caverns and crystals, some of which are sentient. But overall, it is one thing. All the life forms that inhabit the layers are all connected as well. Some forms have developed enough to understand this, whether primates on land, or the cephalopods and mammals in the water, or the crystals underneath. Previous species on this planet also developed to the same level or beyond, but the universe had other plans and killed them off, or they developed far enough to leave for other planets or planes of existence.

"We know one species escaped before a major extinction event. That event was not an accident. An entity, with malevolent intentions, engineered circumstances over time to aim an asteroid at the planet. It killed off a great deal of life, including most of the dinosaurs. It did it to destroy the advanced race on the planet, but evidence suggests most of them escaped beforehand. The asteroid impact highly annoyed the planet. Ten million years later, which is remarkably fast for a planet, which spends millennia just thinking one thought and breathing, it responded. It slung a comet back at the offending entity. It impacted the small moon around Mars at enough speed to destroy the entity."

"Damn. Remind me not to piss this place off."

"Wise words. Others should heed that advice, but we doubt most will."

"I will, at least."

"The earth species that was targeted for extinction had advanced enough to achieve interstellar travel. They probably could have defended against the asteroid, but they saw an opportunity to evacuate in secret, and to appear extinct. That kept any other entities from pursuing them. Of course, they were eventually found again, but by then they had developed enough that they could protect themselves.

"The asteroid hit was an act that unbalanced the two sides competing in this region of space. Therefore, the offending side was placed into the penalty box by a higher authority until the comet hit the Mars moon. It took a few million years for that ruling to be made.

"Our side got to rebuild the planet without initial interference. They experimented with several types of species, including primates and my people, then seeded the planet with various improved primates, then you humans, when everything was ready. The prohibition against the other side being involved in affairs on this planet ended about ten thousand years ago. But we have proven that they had secretly interfered with the planet during the ban with the virus that subverted human DNA. Catastrophic climate change and natural disasters were also used to prevent advanced development. Now they are interfering again, introducing triggers to the original virus, which acts through your virtual systems to hijack the logic and emotion centers of human psychology, as I told you earlier. The previous World Wars were small proxy fights to test their products and advancements.

"Wow, that was quite a tangent. Why tell me this now?"

"You need allies, so you will need to meet both Odin and one of the original inhabitants that escaped the asteroid. We call the former inhabitants the Ascended."

"I have appointments with both a god and an ancient alien?"

"Yes. You will recall I never said any of this was simple or easy. But now, for reasons we don't fully understand, you have been called forward to participate in this conflict. It is incumbent upon us to prepare you."

"Thanks, I guess."

"Now, back to the original intent of my visit. Would you recount your tale of Viking adventures?"

I began to tell my long story to Kal. Although lengthy, I guess we had all the pre-time in the world. After leaving Laren when my first wife died, I ended up at the sea and became a fisherman. My two mates, Pater and Paul, and I were accosted by a battered Viking ship. I fought them off, then agreed to become a crewman and join their venture. Over the next weeks I made peace with a scheming captain and crew, and their even more dangerous earl at their home village. Meanwhile I got to ply the waters of Germany, Denmark, Sweden and Finland with an interesting group of warriors. Along the way I minimized the damage intended by raids by warning the local people of an imminent raid at one of our stops. We also captured a damaged trading boat along the way, laden with riches and the son of a wealthy merchant. The earl sent us back off to ransom the son to his father in Germany. I kept the son, Klaus, alive and tried to deliver him back to his family. But at the very end, when we escaped from the Vikings, Klaus was intentionally killed by his own people at the city gates. Apparently, his own father wanted him dead for some reason.

"So, Kal, that is my tale of becoming a Viking for a time, and my even shorter time in Germany. I don't know what portion of that interests you, nor when I met Odin or how he fits into that narrative."

"Your inadvertent actions during that place-time caused quite a stir. Several entities discovered a significant anomaly had developed. That was probably the first time that others realized the existence of something that was not supposed to exist. That something was you, of course, but no one was aware of that yet. Your existence was simply not possible or predictable.

"To get to the point of this conversation, your interaction with Peter and Paul was positive. They continued to live and provide for families that ended up giving a basis of stability to Frisia over the years. Their descendants still live in the Netherlands. Had you not been on the boat, they would have died that day. The family that you warned about the impending Viking raid also survived and provided a positive outcome. The original place-time streams projected a likelihood they died in the raid. Instead, they lived and produced descendants that stabilized the Oldenburg dynasty.

"Klaus, however, was a significant problem. Our side called emergency meetings after he did not die at sea, either in the storm or from the Viking attack. His death from either cause was a necessary event for the time stream that you and everyone else now inhabit. But you saved him. It could not stand, so Odin himself oversaw the operation. The older gentleman you saw on top of the battlements when they killed Klaus at the gates was a manifestation of Odin."

"But I don't understand. I really felt that Klaus was a good kid."

"He was. But he would have chosen a darker path some years later, and his descendants would have been much worse. Without going into too much detail, World War I would have continued past 1918, as Germany achieved several successes on the Western front. England would have lost another 400,000 soldiers over that extended time. America would have sent over and lost more than 300,000 soldiers. The net effect is that some years later, Britain would not have survived the Nazi blitzkrieg, and America would have never entered the war. Your time stream, along with billions of others, would have drastically changed. The Sky Lords and master vampires would control most of this world and its resources."

"OK, I get it. I think there is a lot more to this timeline thing, but I'll let it ride for now. But one question - what other time-place problems have I caused? Listening to all this, I'm worried our side will kill my colleague because she was supposed to die."

"You speak of Dr. York. Yes, we know about that, and it has caused quite a conundrum. Not because she is a target, but because she cannot possibly exist. To allay your fears, she is perfectly safe. We just do not know what her role will become. One explanation is that you both are part of a larger plan at a level above our understanding. 'Time will tell,' as your hairless say."

"OK, that makes me feel better, but it seems just about any action I take could lead to complications in the timeline."

"Yes, in fact, there are unlimited possibilities. And at this stage, too much information could easily sway your behavior and contribute to other problems. So, back to my visit here. Things have transpired more quickly than reckoned. It would be good for you to contact Odin, and soon. He could, if so inclined, make a difference in your personal timeline by just meeting with you. We believe that contact could be quite helpful to you later. Odin can also assist with protecting your people at your training site. My people will help with that as well. Your visit with the Ascended one is not as urgent but will need to happen soon."

"So how do I find Odin?"

"You are a smart hairless, I trust you will find a way. One piece of advice, though, is that he is more easily contacted in Europe than America. Closer to his home address."

"Thanks Kal. Say, do you know my part-time employer, Michael?"

He made the odd sound that passed for laughter. "I must leave you now. That is a conversation for another time."

Kal disappeared, and I was back in "normal space" still sitting in my seat. The plane was moving through the clouds, and the flight attendant did not seem to have noticed anything. Physics or magic, I didn't care if the plane kept flying.

I began thinking about how to find Odin. I had plenty more hours of flying time to come up with something, but I wouldn't attempt anything while in Scotland. My knowledge of the old Wodin myths from Gaul, and the slightly newer Odin tales from Scandinavia, led me to believe that Scotland was not his country of habitation. I had some ideas about where to start when I got back to the continent.

CHAPTER FOURTEEN

The plane dropped into Edinburgh, late, just as I expected. It was part of my love-hate relationship with traveling in the UK. On-time flights were more of a guideline than a rule. I also seemed to have worse luck with train rides and hotel bookings in the UK than in many other places in Europe. Although Brexit had not improved anything, my pet theory was more supernatural in nature. Enough complaining, it was only travel, and I had more time to waste than most.

I was happy to be back in Scotland, although I liked it a lot more than it seemed to like me. In particular, I had a history with Edinburgh. I always ended up entering or exiting from there whenever I traveled to or from Scotland. The city itself appeared haunted. Tendrils of dark stains spilling down the stone buildings seemed to infect them with a dour outlook, which was the same for the elaborate tombstones as they aged. It must rain black grime here.

But the people were lively, the food and music were good, and other than the ghosts, the city and surrounding areas were scenic and inviting. Whenever there I always climbed castle hill and walked part or all the royal mile. I tried to do it when the crowds were minimal, so midnight was usually a good time, except for the ghosts, as they followed me around. I can always spot them in the corner of my eye, haunting my peripheral vision.

The ghosts felt familiar, and I probably knew some of them at one time. Some people in Scotland had liked me, and some had hated me. I seemed to have that polarizing effect on people, and on their ghosts. I attributed my travel woes to all the unfriendly ghosts. The Scottish ghosts always made my plane late, kept the trains off schedule, and caused hotel reservations to disappear. They just wanted to mess with me. It probably didn't help that Scotland was one of the most haunted places in the world. The old castle in Edinburgh was rife with them, many of them much older than Scotland itself. I had to admit that I had been directly involved with creating some of them in times past.

But I was not staying long in Edinburgh as my business was to the north. I tempted the ethereal realms once again and took the train. Mainly, it was because of my reluctance to travel any distance driving on the wrong side of the road. Country roads were harrowing enough, the narrow lanes closely bordered with hedgerows and rock walls, but busy city streets with tiny signs and roundabouts flooded my brain with visions of horrible automobile crashes. I'd survive, but others might not. I also just liked to sit on the train and read or watch the scenery go by. I spent one night in Edinburgh, had an enjoyable meal, a late walk with a few hundred of my dead friends from the castle, and then hopped the train the next morning.

Lots of farmland, some coastline, the Firth of Forth, and quaint towns and villages went by. Then the highlands, with distilleries scattered all along the route. The places that made that awful, undrinkable brown swill called scotch. I had never developed a taste for it and often verbalized the sentiment. One argument about the stuff a couple of centuries ago had turned violent and nearly led to another ghost being created. Since then, I have kept my anti-scotch sentiment to myself while in Scotland.

I finally arrived at my destination, Inverness. A favorite city of mine, small enough and friendly, it sat on a river near to a coastal inlet. The river was the

Ness, exiting from the famous Loch Ness. Despite my history with rivers, my business was not finding the legendary monster. I was interested in having salmon for dinner, however. I expected that to be the extent of my dealings with aquatic creatures.

I exited the train into a mostly cloudless day, a rarity. I was hoping to cross the street to my favorite coffee and doughnut place. It disappointed me to see it was now a burger shop. Now I had to walk further toward the river and find other coffee or cappuccino opportunities. I wondered if the shop had changed because of normal restaurant attrition, the pandemic shutdowns, or Brexit. My default on all things negative in the UK was Brexit, so that it was. I wondered how much longer Scotland would stay in the fold or go their own way. I did not ponder that thought very long, as I had no dog in that fight.

I stepped on the bridge but stopped halfway across. I enjoyed standing on the bridge sidewalk and peering into the water as it flowed by. Very clear, so that the rocks on the bottom were visible. The sun glinted off the wavelets, giving the river a scaled appearance. I resumed my walk before my thoughts went down the river monster rabbit hole. There was an oddly shaped small fellow on the far side of the bridge that had appeared without my notice. I sensed no threat and a moment later, he had disappeared.

As I continued, I remembered there were a few stores off the beaten tourist path that had decent wool and cashmere for sale. I was early for my appointment, so I took the time to shop. I walked slowly along and looked into shop windows until I noticed a familiar reflection in the window into which I was peering. "Can I buy you a kilt?" I asked.

"No thanks, my spindly legs might embarrass the Scots," Simon answered.

"They let you out into the wild to dabble in some field work?"

"Yes, I was told I needed to babysit some yanker until he could ride without training wheels."

"Did you mean Yankee or wanker?"

"Yes," he answered.

"Ass."

"I learned from you the art of insult to both distract and divert an opponent prior to action."

"I'm not sure it worked."

"Oh? Have a look to either side."

A dark-haired man was thirty feet away to our right with his hand mimicking a gun. To the left of us, the same distance away, a striking red-haired woman was doing the same.

"OK, point taken. How about you introduce us, and we get some food and have our briefing?"

"Sure, if you have finished shopping for doilies. Guess you have lots of old furniture to cover."

"Again, you are an ass. Just for that, I may crochet you a kilt."

Simon just grinned as the other two walked up to us.

"This is Erin and Davis," Simon said as he nodded to the woman and man. "And this mythical creature is Senecus," as he nodded toward me.

"Good to meet you," I said, as I shook hands with both. They each gave a half smile but said nothing.

"Well, Simon, this would be a good time to grab a bite and catch up on our briefing. Know of a good place?" I asked.

"Yes, I know just the restaurant. Not too quiet, but private. Just two blocks down and one block over."

We walked in a loose group to the smaller place overlooking the river. We sat, perused the menu, and ordered. I began the discussion after the server left. "Forgive my bluntness, Erin and Davis, but what are you? I know you are not exactly human."

Simon looked shocked that I could discern that they were different. Both Davis and Erin gave another half-smile but appeared only slightly surprised.

"Erin, please do the honors. It seems Senecus really is an adept, as we were told," Davis said.

"Yes, you are right, of course," Erin answered. "We are selkies, a people of the fae realm. I'm Irish and Davis is Scottish, so in the waters we can't be together, as our people forbid it because of the old clan ways. But as humans, there are no restrictions on us, so we stay together in this form most of the time."

"Please forgive my ignorance, but what is a selkie?" I asked.

"Ah, so, when in the sea, we are in the form of a seal. We are not merpeople, before you ask. Once ashore, we can shapeshift into human form, but no other forms. We are species-fluid as we can live with humans and mate with them. In human form, we have an uncommon ability in that we are gender fluid. Unless I were pregnant, which would prevent me from turning into a human male form." I was about to ask about that when Davis turned into Erin, and Erin turned into Davis. The server had just arrived to bring drinks and was a little confused. He was not the only one.

"Thanks for the explanation," I said. "I have no experience at all with selkies, but I bet that really helps when you have someone under surveillance."

"It does," Davis said. He had changed back to himself. "If we wear the right type of clothing, we can morph into just about any human form, and the clothing won't give us away. It allows us to tail anyone, and with frequent form changes and turning a jacket inside out, or taking off a scarf, we can be nearly undetectable. But you spotted us."

"Yes, it is some sort of ability I have. Normally it allows me to determine if humans are in my vicinity, and whether anyone is a threat. But now I'm finding it has other uses, and I'm using it to recognize non-humans. I knew you were not a threat, but obviously did not know what you were. Do you live mostly on land or in the water?"

"As selkies, we usually prefer the sea, unless one of us meets a human and decide to mate," Davis said. "Then we stay on land. Many of us are also living as humans in recent years, as the inlets and estuaries have more boat traffic, more houses on the coastline, and more pollution in the water. We like to stay near the water, though, because in the evenings we can return to it whenever we have the opportunity for a swim."

"Sounds like an elegant solution," I said. "Except that you end up hanging around inelegant humans like Simon."

"I think I have been insulted," Simon said. "I'm not sure exactly what the opposite of elegant is, but it sounds unappealing. But before the food arrives, we should start briefing Senecus on our project."

"Sure, but before we start, I'd like to ask Senecus a question," Erin said. "What are you? Your form seems slightly familiar, but I can't quite tell, which is unusual."

"Good question, and one that I will answer messily. I really don't know. I was attacked one night by something I never saw, fell into an icy river in old Holland, and got into a fight with a large fish. I've since ended up with more than human abilities. And am immortal, or mostly so, since that all happened 1700 years ago when I was a Roman soldier."

Davis and Erin looked at each other. They began speaking in a very odd language. Within a few seconds, Erin asked, "Do you know what type of fish it was?"

"No idea. It was dark, and the river was icy, and I was losing a lot of blood. I have studied general fish proteins since then, but I never thought about the type of fish. Do you think it matters?"

"Perhaps," Erin said. "It could matter a great deal."

The food arrived, and the conversation ended as we concentrated on the meal first, then moved on to the purpose of the gathering. Michael's team was investigating multiple master vampire possibilities. They had recently identified one in the UK. The suspect had several business interests in the country, in London, Glasgow, and Belfast. Outside the UK, his business interests were in Kiev, Gdansk, and Budapest. He had a house near Macclesfield as I suppose he wanted to be close to the footballers. Also, a massive apartment in London, a summer estate near Inverness, and a waterfront estate in Belfast.

I was here to look at the surveillance team and tactics, and coordinate with Simon and his team on potential strike strategies. They had not planned an imminent action, so this was more of a meet and greet with the principals during the surveillance period. They planned similar activities in other locations where alleged master vampires had been located. When positively identified, the plan was to hit all of them at once, and not attack just one and have them give notice to their colleagues. But because all of them had multiple homes, like our target in Inverness, we had to plan for all locations. It was going to be complicated.

The Inverness estate of our target was the preferred location for a strike since the London location was too visible and had too much chance for collateral damage. The Belfast house was well-protected, and he only spent a few weeks a year there. He was only at the Macclesfield house a few weekends during the soccer season.

The estate house in Inverness sat on the north shore of the inlet across from downtown. It was on the water's edge, with steps down from the yard to the shore, which had a landing. There was not a boat docked there full time, but occasionally a yacht would pull up. The setting allowed Simon's unique selkie surveillance team to get up close to what was happening at the house. When the suspect left the house and went to town, they could easily follow without detection by constantly changing human forms. Most of the information so far had been collected by Erin and Davis, but they had only watched the target for just over four weeks, so there were unanswered questions.

"What are his business interests that you have found so far?" I asked.

"Most of this is from Michael's analytical team," Erin responded. "He has a clothing line, mostly marketed to young women. Swimwear, beachwear, and yachting outfits. He recruits girls for modeling the clothes. He does some amber exports, and his sham companies operate several boats for shipping. Overall, not enough business in total to support his lifestyle, but he has inherited a huge amount of money."

"He meets most of the definitions of a master vampire lifestyle," I said. "I need to be in the same room with him. Not for very long, and no closer than a few meters. With that, I can get a good read on him and minimize the chances of him detecting me. Does he come into town for shopping, dining, or anything else?"

"He has lunch at least once a week at a place nearby and usually has people with him. The dining area and bar are large enough that you could be in the same room but some meters away. Would that work?"

"Yes, that should be a good setup. But just in case he detects me, we should set up a potential hit immediately afterward. Otherwise, it could get bad if he starts a fight in town."

"We can get set up for that with Simon's strike team," she said, as Simon nodded in agreement. "Based on his schedule, he should be in town for lunch tomorrow."

"Good, let's go over the details of what we might need. Also, if you have an extra copy of that dossier, I would like to study it tonight."

"Sure, here is your copy," Davis said as he pulled an envelope out of a messenger bag.

We continued the discussion a while longer. Then I spent the rest of the day walking along the river, or in my room looking over the dossier. Four weeks just was not long enough to document an entire life, especially one that could be centuries long. But the target gave off alarming signals. The location of the business operations, plus the line of girls' clothing and models, gave a strong indication of human trafficking. Amber exports could be a cover for drugs, especially opium and heroin. There just wasn't enough information yet to confirm if he was a master vampire. But tomorrow should give me confirmation about just how dangerous this guy was.

Chapter Fifteen

Then stars were just appearing as I began my walk out to the inlet. I stared across the water to where the target's house was located. I was not sure where Beauty Firth ended and Moray Firth began, but it did not matter. It was all water to me. The night was exceptionally clear, so I stayed out late to enjoy the crisp breeze and the stars. I had a lot to think about and ready my plan of action for the next day.

I felt a presence nearby, but saw nothing, and even with my other sight I could not get a positive fix. It was concerning, but there was no aura of threat, so I relaxed. I walked further and whatever was there did not follow. Paranoia cane to mind, but then a lot of odd things had happened recently around water, from the giant squid attack on the beach to the web-toed intruder at the Farm. I put the thoughts away and walked back.

We met the next morning to set up the operation. Simon had his team ready to deploy outside the restaurant, although they would not take positions until the target and his party were inside. We planned a contingency for a takedown on the road back to the house. I insisted Erin and Davis not take part in the strike. But I wanted them ready to monitor the house if everything went sideways and the target escaped back to the residence. I was being overprotective, but I knew Erin and Davis' people were very few, and I did not want my actions getting them killed. They protested when I brought that up and told me that I was the most endangered species on earth. I countered with the fact that I was only one specimen, and therefore didn't qualify as a species. They were not happy, but they obeyed and would be on watch at the house.

Late morning, I walked over to the lunch restaurant. I took a small table in back and out of the way, partially behind the bar, with a newspaper and data pad with me to appear like everyone else dining alone. I perused the paper over a coffee while waiting. Just before noon, the target and two others arrived and took a side table. Two of them sat with backs against the wall while keeping a clear view of the room, indicating they were not amateurs. One of the extra men looked like a bodyguard, while the other looked more like a business associate. I was too far away to get any read on them, and there was enough chatter that I could not eavesdrop. My order arrived, and I finished quickly. I left payment and tip on the table, then made my way out. I passed about five meters from the table as I typed on my pad. Other than a glance from the bodyguard, there was no notice taken of me.

Once outside, I spoke into my hidden lapel microphone, "Stand down, stand down, no action." I kept walking to the corner and hopped into the waiting van.

Simon was inside and coordinating with his team to fall back. Everyone would rendezvous back at the team's house in town.

"No action, so he did not react to you?"

"No, they barely noticed me. Not that they would have. All three are human. Bad people by my read, but no master vampire here."

Simon seemed relieved, yet disappointed. I felt the same way. Relieved that action wasn't needed, which might get our people hurt, but disappointed that we were on the wrong target.

"OK, I will get my people back to the house, packed up, and on to the next suspect."

"Wait, I think that this might be an excellent training opportunity. We can follow this to completion and take this guy down if he is truly bad. Give some resolution to the surveillance and strike teams, without alerting other master vampires."

Simon considered for a moment. "I agree that this would be an excellent exercise. But I need to run it by Michael for approval, although I should have an answer today. But that means we would do the strike at the house."

"OK. You get approval and we meet up later today for planning."

I now knew the target reeked of malice and evil. My best guess was he was from a crime family, or he was an example of just how much evil a person can devolve into in a lifetime. I decided that even if Michael opposed the takedown, I would visit the target myself before I left Scotland.

Michael gave the OK an hour later. His provisions were that Erin and Davis were surveillance-only, and that I was to be an observer and backup-only. I was not happy, but I understood I should leave the action to the team to give them the needed experience. I told Simon that I would stay on the water in a small raft near where Erin and Davis were stationed. Simon planned for his strike team to approach the house from two sides and take out the target. The takedown was on for tonight.

I was pushing my small raft off the bank about to get in and paddle to my position. I was out of the sight of the back of the house, as there was a promontory between me and it. Erin and Davis were already in the water in their marine forms. If they saw anything unusual, they would radio it in. But we did not expect any surprises, which is always a mistake.

Davis radioed in a report that a boat had docked at the landing as the sun was setting. Two men had wheeled down a cart from the house, then unloaded four bodies from the boat, and returned to the house with the two men from the boat. The bodies looked like young girls, probably drugged. The night had just gotten crowded and more complicated.

I called in to Simon. His team was expecting three to five men in the house, and potential for innocents. Now he had eight men in the house as another car had come in the front with one occupant, plus the four innocents from the boat. I wanted to know if he was going to abort for better odds later.

"Penguin, operation status?"

"Operation still active," he responded. "Change order. Overseer to back for coverage, selkies in water for support. Fifteen minutes." I was now to head for the rear of the house and take out any baddies that appeared. Erin and Davis were still in the water in case anybody else showed up.

I chimed Davis. "Selkie One, any kiddies out in the pool?"

"No, Overseer."

That was odd. This guy had been careful guarding his other locations. It was not like him to leave half his property unprotected, since anyone could approach from the water. "Selkie One, do not leave the pool for any reason. Selkie Two, need you further out to scout for other incoming."

"Understood."

I was not sure what it meant, but I saw a subconscious red flag waving around. Meanwhile, I paddled the raft quickly around the point. I pulled it ashore and put it behind a sizable rock not far from the landing. Then I crept up the rock steps to the lawn. I could see in the massive glass windows at the back of the house, where it looked like a small party starting. Four men with drinks sitting or standing in a large room, four scantily clad girls in chairs or on the sofa. The girls did not seem to be conscious yet. Four men unseen, and possibly guarding the house. I radioed in a brief version of what I saw. I got two clicks back for acknowledgement.

Simon's men planned to come in force through the front as quickly as possible, eliminate the guards, and toss flash bangs into the social area. Nobody wanted live rounds in that area with the girls present. I would not go in the back but wait for anyone that was coming out to escape.

At the fifteen-minute mark, I heard the front door blasted. Almost immediately, gunfire erupted. One of the men in the house pulled out his phone, then metal shutters sprang down and blocked off the rear doors and windows except for one door. Crap, I could no longer see in, but at least they only had one way out. But for a supposedly undefended house, it was rapidly looking defensible.

I heard a report from Davis. "Four bads incoming from the pool."

I turned around and sure enough, a sleek boat was speeding toward the landing. The lack of a rear defense was not a lack at all; they clad the back of the house in armor while the backup goons showed up in a boat for support. They must have been at a nearby house to arrive so quickly. Simon's team was still engaged in the house, so I and the selkies would deal with the reinforcements and let the strike teamwork through their assignment.

"Penguin, Overseer is back to the pool for four incoming." Two clicks were the only response.

I sprinted back toward the landing. As the first goon topped the last step, I sprang forward and bench pressed him as hard as possible, back and down. He knocked down the other three lined up behind him - bowling for dullards. I jumped down while they were trying to get clear of each other to start blasting me with their machine guns. I popped all of them as fast as possible, leaving four sleeping uglies laid out on the landing. Davis popped his head up over the landing. For a second, I did not recognize the non-human face. He grinned and went back down. I zip tied all four and headed back to the house. I heard no more shooting, so perhaps the party was over.

When I got halfway to the back door, it banged open. The target had one of the barely conscious girls by the hair and was using her as a shield as he backed into the yard with a pistol to her head. He did not see me in the dark as he was watching Simon ease out the door with his gun raised. The target was spouting the usual nonsense about he would kill the girl unless they left him alone, he was taking her and the boat, and nobody had better follow. It might work in the movies, but out here in the real world, it was a zero-sum game. I knelt down and picked up a baseball-sized rock, thinking that sometimes simple is better. But it wasn't needed, as Simon calmly shot him in the face. It was a beautiful grazing shot, knocking him down and unconscious without killing him. The downside for him was he would be ugly the rest of his life. Simon cleared the idiot's pistol and zip tied him. I picked up the girl and handed her to one of Simon's team at the door, but the girl was so drugged she barely reacted. I dropped my rock and walked over to Simon.

"About to go Cro-Magnon and brain him with a rock?" Simon asked. "You really are old school. You remember you are carrying a pistol and hatchet, right?"

"Didn't want to waste any bullets or pollute nature with a lead bullet. And do you know how long it takes to resharpen a hatchet blade after embedding it in a cranium?"

"Actually, no."

"Me either, anymore. But I'm not as good a shot as you with a pistol, so I would rather risk the rock being off target than a bullet, with the girl so close."

"I suppose that makes a certain sense."

"How did you guys do inside?"

"One of ours wounded, possibly seriously. Their four goons down. The other three partiers gave up without a problem. This guy wanted to play. Now he's going to have trouble shaving one side of his face for a while."

"Scar tissue will gum up a good razor."

"You handle the other four back here?"

"Yep, they are on the landing, taking a rest and zip tied. Davis is keeping an eye on them. Other than the usual unanticipated screwups you can't plan for, looks like a green operation."

"Yes, so far. Good practice. Let's clean up and get out of here. We have a truck coming to pick up bodies, live and dead. We will meet and debrief in the morning."

"Sounds good."

We loaded up the garbage and left. A Church van picked up the girls to take them to a safe haven. Erin and Davis towed my boat away, then they stayed out to swim, chase fish, or each other, for the rest of the evening. Sounded like fun, I guess, if I was a fish, or part-time seal.

Simon and one of his team met me, Erin and Davis the next morning for coffee. We walked back to Simon's house he had rented for the operation. They had lifted his wounded man to a Church hospital in Glasgow. He had taken a shot above the vest, but his collar bone had deflected the bullet and saved the lung. He would make a full recovery, but a broken collarbone was no fun either.

Simon provided the latest information from a brief search of the house and the latest from Michael's analyst team. Our target was from an old crime family in Russia that had moved to the Ukraine. His specialty was smuggling underage Eastern European girls into the UK. He and his staff picked them at the teenage beauty pageants in Kiev and Budapest, then lured them for dinner and spiked their drinks. He also filmed porn on the side, usually rape and snuff films using the girls that did not cooperate after the drugs wore off. I wished Simon had gone more center mass than for the grazing head shot. The amber trade was legitimate and used as a cover for the international shipments that included trafficking. It was not the major bust of a master vampire network, but it got a dangerous maggot off the grid and saved a lot of girls.

I then had a nasty idea. "Simon, instead of shutting this down, why not keep it open and have the Church run it?"

The room erupted in incredulous shouts.

"Wait, wait, the part about snatching girls obviously goes away. In fact, the Church can put extra people in those areas to clean up the turds still operating. But keep everything else running a while. Find out who is buying the girls, then when they order, send them a batch of Church commandos instead. Won't work very long but might be a chance to take down some more scum."

"That might work," Simon said. "We could fill a couple of orders with our commandos before someone realizes the customers are disappearing. Erin and Davis, are you in? We will need some extra bodies to run this right."

"Hell yes," Erin answered. "Let's take some more of this trash down. Since he's had operations in Belfast, it's good bet we can clean up some of the Irish garbage, and I can be home for a while." Davis nodded his agreement.

And just like that, I got the Church into the business of sex trafficking underage girls, at least the imaginary kind. I'm sure Michael would understand, but I was glad I wouldn't have to sign off on any of his people's expense reports. He would forgive me eventually. Of course, that was not actually going to happen, except on paper for a few days. I would have loved being there when some wealthy group of male perverts opened the cargo truck, expecting underage girls, and instead got machine guns and pissed off Church commandos.

Now I just had to leave Scotland. I expected a few cancellations and delays, even though the flight to Amsterdam was less than an hour. True to form, the Scottish gremlins showed up, and it took me a day to get back. I really needed to sacrifice a chicken or something the next time I was in Scotland to appease whichever minor deity there that I had pissed off. Or the dozens of mischievous ghosts that worked for him.

Chapter Sixteen

When I finally got back to Amsterdam, I had lunch with Thomas at the airport. I gave him a few more details about my life. He was understandably incredulous, but overall took it well. I also gave him a copy of a book, illustrated and published two hundred years ago. It had an illustration depicting Hia and I, as we had met the author when his study of botanicals had led him to Cowee Town. That should give Thomas something to think about until our next chat.

The next day, I got a ping from Monk. He was my computer and information specialist, probably the best in Europe. I hoped he had found more information that could lead me to my Nazi vampire friend. Monk and I did our song and dance while he cleansed my phone and, as far as I knew, danced on the grave of some tech wizard to magic up the airwaves. It was as good an explanation as I could decipher from the technical jargon he spouted.

I answered his call after the required delay of five minutes. "I have bad news," he started off.

Damn, this could not be good. "Go ahead. Make my day."

He continued after a few seconds of confused silence. "Oh, yes, Dirty Harry. Appropriate. Now to business - you remember the recent job offer I received based on your recommendation. Which I turned down?"

"Yes, of course."

"That organization was the source of the operations you inquired about some weeks ago. The elimination of a scientist in Italy and nearly so of another in the Netherlands."

"Dead sure?"

"Dead sure. And it's back on. They approved termination of the original Netherlands target."

"Can you meet me at location B?"

"Yes, at ten o'clock."

"See you then."

Whenever I had to meet someone for a private conversation that could not be overheard or recorded, I had two go to spots in the country. The first was the National Park, De Hoge Veluwe. Extensive open heaths of waist-high grasses stretched for long distances, interspersed with managed forests across the park. The heaths provided wide open space away from people. It was easy to meet someone at the Kröller-Müller Museum on the grounds, then bike ride out to a suitable spot for conversation. It was north of Arnhem, site of World War II's Market Garden operation, and included an extensive abandoned Nazi airbase. After a meeting it was also nice to walk through one of the best outdoor sculpture gardens in Europe.

The second site was the massive dam and roadway the Dutch had built in one of the world's largest land reclamation projects, the Afsluitdijk. One enormous dike, and it would be one of the world's largest tragedies if it ever breached. The dike separated what used to be the Zuider Zee bay from the North Sea. Now the Zuider was freshwater and called the Ijsselmeer. A highway covered the dike along the thirty-two-kilometer length, and there were a few places to pull off along the four-lane road. It was wide open, noisy from the wind, and quite private at certain times of day or season. Few people wanted to be out on those days of sixty-kilometer winds pushing the sleet into horizontal waves in January. Some days in other months of the year could be just as crappy. The surf and wind made it virtually impossible to detect any sound if you needed privacy. North of Amsterdam, but accessible by car, it was a good meeting spot.

I parked along the Afsluitdijk and waited in the car at one of the overlook parking lots. The grey clouds were scudding along at a fast past while the darker waves hit the front of the dike, producing a dirty white froth quickly dispersed by the wind. The weather wasn't terrible, but not great either. There was some blue sky showing around the edges of the clouds. A dark sedan pulled up and parked a few slots over. The tall young Dutchman that got out was wearing a long overcoat and scarf perfect for these days. He jogged over and got into the passenger seat.

"Hi Monk, how's it hanging?"

"Most things hang well on me. My Dutch heritage provides the perfect blend of height and leanness, allowing a superb presentation of our fashion sense. Thank you for asking."

"You are welcome. Might want to work on your American slang, though." He looked confused. "Anyway," I continued, "what do you have for me?"

"Before that, why have you code-named me Monk?"

"Oh, before we met, I pictured a guy in a basement by himself working on a computer sixteen hours a day. A modern monk." I didn't tell him the rest, that I imagined he'd be in his underwear, surrounded by days of empty pizza boxes and cat litter, and considered untouchable by most human females.

"I see, but obviously not the case. With my looks, I must socialize a lot."

"Of course. Now, what do you have for me?"

"Someone at your part-time employer authorized the disposal of an asset. The same one that was targeted before but miraculously lived. Apparently, that outcome was unacceptable."

"OK. Anything else, or even better, an identity?"

"No, to both. The message was brief but direct. Sent out to several questionable business organizations in northern Italy."

"So that is where the target currently is. Can you get me a specific location? And was it a rush order?"

"Expedited contract, within five days, but not a rush. As soon as the contract is accepted the location will be forwarded, and I will intercept it. I should have it later today and will send it to you. Because of the nature of this information and the chance of detection, I shall disappear for a few days of vacation."

"Do you have a good escape plan?"

"Yes, of course. I will implement it. I don't think I am discovered, but I will be out of town just in case. The only way to reach me is the special line."

"Smart plan. Goodbye and good luck."

Damn. I guess this new hit was a consequence of saving Jo for the first time, and I should have anticipated it. I needed to warn her without setting off any alarms that could speed up the contract.

I started driving in the general direction of Woerden. I needed to pick up some things and decide how to approach this problem. Could it be Michael? It made little sense, but that could be because I did not have all the information. Did he set up the first shooting so they would wound Jo in order to force me to turn her? Maybe, but that did not explain the other murder. And made no sense at all to kill her now.

The Church was a massive organization, so orders could have come from elsewhere within it. But with Michael as head of security, somebody would have to have major juice to do that. Somebody powerful that still wanted Jo dead. Yep, time to go deal with this. But how, and with whom? Best to keep my plans simple and stupid, since that seemed to work best for me.

As I neared Utrecht, I pulled out the special non-traceable phone Monk had given me. I put in the special code then waited for confirmation. Our phones danced back and forth in the ether and finally connected.

"Monk, I need the target location faster than waiting on the contract details. If it speeds up your search, the target is Dr. Joanna York. She works at the Center, a new group with the Church. You already know she is somewhere in northern Italy."

"You mean she works for the same people that want her dead?"

"Yes, and that is something I'm trying to remedy. Can you do it?"

"I need as much detail as you can give me if you want this fast. I assume it is also dangerous to be searching for her and her location?"

"Of course. I only give the dangerous shit to you. It's a token of how much I respect your work."

"Satirical flattery will get you nowhere. But bullion will."

I then gave Monk all the details I could think of about Jo and the Center. It only took about a minute.

"I can work with this, as I'll trace her travel first, at least narrow that down to the city. I should have the specific location quickly by tracking cell signals. The contract information with location has not shown up yet, so your information will make this faster."

"OK. I am driving but contact me when you have something. Better yet, just text me the coordinates when you get it. Thanks."

"Thank me after you see the invoice."

I expected to hear from Monk in a few minutes. The best computer guys are always sandbagging how long something takes, so they can always complete the project early and look like geniuses. I drove back toward Woerden to pick up my supplies. I got a text from Monk on the special device he had given me previously. Some sort of untraceable, unbreakable coded text device, better even than the special phone. I parked in the open, along the edge of a massive green field in the middle of nowhere, or as nowhere as it could be in the middle of the Green Heart of the Netherlands. The fields were so large and flat you could see harrier hawks hovering over a mile away. It took me a minute to interpret the text coordinates and then search for maps on the internet. It had taken him ten minutes to find Jo's location.

I called Thomas next. Probably my last call for a while since I needed to disappear from the network until the crisis passed. He answered on the second ring, a record.

"Thomas, I need an enormous favor."

"Coming from you, this could be big."

"Nothing you can't handle."

"Is it legal?"

"Not really."

"Necessary?"

"Absolutely."

"OK. What do you need?" That's why Thomas was a great friend.

"A way to fly anonymously to Trent, Italy."

"Let me think. OK, I can do that. Do you want to be comfortable on a private plane, or uncomfortable in the cargo hold of a commercial plane?"

I thought about the possibilities.

"Private plane, but Verona instead. And then the same scenario outbound from Verona but for two passengers, and the destination is Finland."

"Finland is tricky. I would suggest the cargo hold for that leg. No, wait. I won't be able to get you out of the Helsinki airport if you go in that way. If you are ready to leave Verona within 24 hours of arrival, the same private plane that takes you there can get you to a smaller Finnish airport like Tampere, and you will arrive anonymously with no questions on arrival."

"Let's plan for that. If you can swing it, I also need a private car at Verona waiting at the hangar, as I can't use the rental agencies."

"Anything in particular?"

"No, just anything with four wheels. Or could be a motorcycle if a larger model for two, plus gear. Whichever is easier to get. I'm giving you a credit card number that is untraceable, so none of your fingerprints will be on any of this. I suggest any calls you make are not from your office or cell phone. Same for email."

"Sounds like you have some practice with this."

"More than I could tell you. But I can give you quite an interesting story next time we are out."

"Is Jo a part of this?"

"She is passenger number two for Finland. She's in a jam, and I need to evacuate her as quickly as possible."

"Then even more so, whatever you need, I'll make it happen. I like her better than you."

"Thanks, brother. I like her more than me as well."

We both laughed.

"My price is a beer and a tall tale."

"Done."

"When do you need the plane?"

"Is today a possibility?"

"Hmm, the price is now two beers. I will text you in five minutes about the hangar to be at, and the time to be there."

"Thanks. I'll bring you a six-pack just to be safe."

"Be careful."

"Always."

I hung up and started moving, arriving at my place in Woerden a half hour later. I grabbed a few things, ran across the alley to the Hema store to grab an assortment of women's clothing, then back to the car. Driving as fast as possible to Amsterdam Schipol, I parked in the long-term lot and then grabbed a taxi to go to the other side of the airport. Just before reaching the private aircraft area, I got out to walk the rest of the way, preventing anyone from tracking the taxi destination. I eventually found the correct hangar, then entered through the side door. Two men dressed as pilots were checking the exterior of the plane. Two others in coveralls were standing by the office. One of the pilots saw me and came over to me, while the other two in coveralls went to open the hangar doors. The pilot asked me for my name, fake as usual, and when I answered correctly, he turned and walked up the steps into the jet. The other pilot came behind me and pulled up the steps without saying anything. I was not perturbed at all by their abrupt behavior since the less we knew about each other, the better. I sat in the back, and a minute later we left the hangar. Fifteen minutes after that, we were taking off.

A company leased the small corporate jet as a charter for various businesses in Northern Europe. This trip was getting billed as a post-maintenance check flight. The plane seated ten in a long tube, with relatively comfortable seats. A tiny head even smaller than those in commercial jets and a small galley. The pilot and co-pilot up front in the cockpit, with me siting solo in the back with my backpack and a duffel.

I had one pistol, a thick stack of euros, six burner phones courtesy of Monk, and five credit cards. Those were in various names and encrypted by Monk and tied to a special account. I had three passports from my old stash, none provided by the Church. Three changes of clothes completed my backpack load.

The duffel had extra ammunition, various items like binoculars, and an encrypted GPS unit. A rain jacket and an extra pair of boots. An empty backpack and those couple of changes of women's clothing from Hema, quickly estimated to be Jo's size as I was standing the store. That might be tricky, but better to have them and not need them than the other way around.

CHAPTER SEVENTEEN

The flight was a basic up and down over the Alps. Once the plane was on the ground, it taxied directly to a hangar well away from the commercial terminal. A black Jetta sat outside the hangar. The plane pulled up and stopped, then the copilot jogged back and opened the door and dropped the steps to the pavement. I walked past him with a wave, down the steps, then tossed my two bags into the car. The keys were in it, so I climbed in and left. The joys of private air travel meant nobody checks you when you have the money afford it.

I drove from Verona to Trent without stopping. The cornfields and vineyards gave way to the lake and the Dolomite Mountains. I arrived at Trent and stopped briefly to gather food and drink supplies. As I drove past the old castle there, I remembered crazy events from some centuries ago.

I continued north and left town. The road I was on followed the Adige River and I was on the east or right bank, going upriver. The water ran fast and cold, with that wonderful green color only seen on rivers with a limestone bed. Its water, including glacial melt, went from the mountains to the drier lands to the south. Roman aqueducts still functioned to get to all the places that needed it. Farmers turned some of that water into polenta and wine, which I thought was a good use for water.

The road narrowed as it entered a gorge. Mountains came down to the river, sandwiching the road between the two. Ahead, I saw a bridge over to the other bank. My GPS alerted me to take the turn, but I continued straight. I could see the other end of the bridge ended at a narrow lane that turned sharply right, or north, along the far riverbank. I was now paralleling it on my side of the river. A kilometer upriver, the lane came to a building, then passed it. The building looked like a hotel or residence building cut into the cliff side. I bet that was where most of the Center's employees stayed. I did not see a guard at that building, but I could see that the underground garage was gated and there was a keypad for entry. Probably multiple cameras and sensors scattered around as well. As I continued for another few hundred meters, I saw the lane on the other side came to another building and ended. The second building on the far riverbank was the Center, according to Monk's coordinates. It looked like a smaller manufacturing plant with a parking lot in front, the river on one side, and steep cliffs on the other side and back. There was a gate and guardhouse on the lane going into the parking lot. Only way in or out, at least for most people.

I turned around to drive back by the Center and back to Trent. It gave me a second chance to see everything and think about the layout. There was nothing obvious on the bridge, but I was sure sensors were present. It seemed well guarded and safe, which made me happy that Jo and her colleagues were safe. I was less happy about having to break into that system. Something kept bothering me, then I finally realized something unsettling. A real assault on the buildings would turn them into deathtraps with nowhere to escape unless there were unseen tunnels in the cliff. With all the limestone, that was a possibility. But also, another security threat. That was always the issue with static defenses; attackers could use them against you.

I gave myself a time limit of no more than twelve hours to find Jo and get us back to Verona. Otherwise, the plane would be gone and I'd have one less escape option. Should be easy, I thought sarcastically.

I parked in Trent and walked to a cafe open to the sidewalk. A cappuccino helped me think. I needed a quick decisive plan to grab Jo, and today, if possible. I was getting antsy and drove back to the Center again. There might be cameras on my side of the river, watching for people like me passing by too many times, but I needed to act. As I approached the bridge, I saw Jo jogging down the lane across the river, almost at the bridge. I pulled over on the border of the road on my side of the river, just past the bridge, then got out and stood at the back of the car. Apparently, further planning was unnecessary, and my grandiose ideas for a rescue plan were now undramatic. Even a blind possum finds another possum occasionally.

Jo continued jogging to the bridge, then saw me and stopped before walking over to my side. She was wearing black tights and a melon tank top. She was about as fit as a body could be. I remembered to keep my eyes on her face.

"Imagine finding you here on the side of the road. What are the odds?" I asked.

"Very high odds, I would say. In fact, the odds of you being shot in a couple of minutes by Center security are much better than you being here by coincidence."

"That is why I am on this side of the bridge. The extra fifty feet could mean the difference between getting shot center mass only three times, instead of five."

"Don't bet your life it. So, why do I have the pleasure of your company in a place you are not supposed to know about?"

"Remember that incident a while back, involving a free helicopter ride?"

Her face clouded over. She was about to get angry. Her next words were clipped. "How could I forget?"

I pointed my elbow toward the Center. "Someone in there authorized and paid for that incident. Now it's active again."

She looked surprised. "Are you positive?"

"Enough to risk everything to show up here and convince you to leave with me in the next thirty seconds. Just temporarily, to get this straightened out with Michael. And that thirty seconds might be optimistic." I watched a black SUV pull out of the Center.

"You really think I'm in danger and you came to rescue me, instead of just calling Michael and clearing this up?"

"I'm trying to be gallant, with a touch of the dramatic."

She considered for a few seconds. "Oh, what the hell, things are tedious just now and I could use a break. Do you have a plan?"

"I have an elaborate plan with multiple facets."

"Sure, you do," she said with due sarcasm. "Let's go then." She hurriedly got in the car while I did the same. I spun it around and headed to the south. I lost the black SUV in Trent while moving as fast as possible to get back to the Verona airport. Jo took the bag I gave her and crawled into the backseat to change into the clothes I had brought for her.

"Not exactly my style, but you got the sizes right somehow."

"I remembered your sizes when I cut your clothes off in the Netherlands. I adjusted for your new body."

"Oh, of course. Glad you could keep up with sizes while treating gunshot wounds, stripping me naked, and turning me immortal."

"A guy must multitask to impress the chicks these days. Or use lotions and makeup. But I'm not the metrosexual type."

She stared at me. "We need to work on your banter."

"Apparently, we have plenty of time for that. Both of us being immortal and all." We both winced.

"You just proved my point."

We arrived at the airport in record time. I drove around to the side where the private planes were, and we went through a gate with no issues. I pulled up to the hangar as the main door opened. We jogged inside and went directly up the steps into the plane. The copilot nodded to us, then pulled up the steps and closed the door. The gate guard had notified the pilot when I drove, so he already had the flight plan and departure approved.

Jo and I sat down. "OK, I thought you were joking when you said you had a plan. Now I'm impressed. A private jet?"

"A gift from Thomas."

"Where are we going?"

"Middle of nowhere in Finland. Then to the coast to get a boat. The next step after that depends on how, or when, Michael can treat his internal infestation and bury some embedded baddies."

"Then you don't think he is involved?"

"I have been over this entire scenario dozens of times. I don't know everything, but none of my analyses point toward Michael. Just as importantly, my gut tells me no."

"I don't think so either."

"I also have a strong feeling this whole thing is a setup. Finding the kill order was too easy, as was getting you away from the Center. We are being played by somebody, probably Michael, to help him with internal housecleaning."

"So why go through these motions? Michael stirs the Church pot with us, then skims off the crud when they surface?"

"Seems likely. We just go on a vacation for a few days to accommodate his plans. And if we are completely wrong, at least you don't get killed until next week."

"Always the optimist. Thanks for being so empathetic to the girl with a target on her back. Now, got anything to eat around here?"

"As it so happens, there is a galley. Not much of a selection, but I'll get us something."

"Thanks."

"Oh, look through the other bag. Take anything else you need, including weapons."

"I shall."

Jo and I ate the light snack I had gathered up in the galley. She went through the bags and pulled out one pistol and some ammunition and put it in her pack. I took the rest of the items and stashed them in my backpack. After that, we were both a bit bored. Jo had all her books saved on her phone, but the phone and her clothes were somewhere on the side of the road outside of Trent. I did not want to risk anyone tracking us. I offered her my phone and book library, but our literary tastes were wildly different. Once again, I was reminded that you never know how different people are until you get to know them. We made some small talk but discussed nothing important. I offered her my phone and earbuds, and she accepted. She didn't hate my musical tastes at least.

During the two hours to Tampere, I never saw the pilot or copilot. They probably wanted as much plausible deniability as possible. They were smart enough to know something not entirely legal was underway. The crew, I'm sure, was ready to get rid of us.

The plane turned and started rapidly losing altitude. We landed, and as soon as the plane finished taxiing to the private hangar, the copilot came out of the cockpit and lowered the steps. I nodded at him, then Jo and I stepped off the plane. The steps lifted back up, and the plane kept moving. The pilot was back on the runway five minutes after he had landed.

I pulled out my phone and called for a taxi. It took a few minutes for one to find its way to the hangar, then we rode into town. The airport was some distance from Tampere. We arrived in town, paid the driver, then walked to the bus station. I was trying to minimize potential security camera exposure, so the bus seemed a good choice. Although I saw no cameras in the city itself and only a few old models around the bus station. I doubted they integrated those into the internet and were probably nothing more than theft deterrents, possibly not even active. We were likely undetected so far.

Jo knew that the bus departed in approximately three hours. "Since we have time and there does not seem to be any security risk here, I am going clothes shopping across the street. Want to join me?"

"Sure, I'll fit right in at the ladies' store. Even better if it's a lingerie store."

"You wish. I'd like to grab some things to supplement your choices. Or perhaps replace them altogether."

"I'm hurt. I spent five minutes picking out your wardrobe."

"Probably five minutes longer than needed. Let's go. I feel the need to spend your money."

I offered my arm; she grabbed it and off I went into the nebulous country of women's clothing stores. It took nearly two hours, and three stores, but Jo finished her shopping. All nice but simple shirts, shorts, capris and skirts, and another pair of shoes. Finland was having a late heat wave and was unseasonably hot, and the clothes I had gotten her were heavier than needed.

"Anything else before we leave? Still plenty of time."

"Oh, yes, I will get my own earbuds. And since we have time, a decent meal before the bus. Any ideas?"

I could see down the street on a quiet corner a Greek place, with outdoor seating. "How about a Greek restaurant in Finland? If they are still in business, they must be good."

"Sure. I saw earbuds in the station, so I can get those before we leave. Now escort me to the establishment and ply me with food."

"Yes, my dear. Off we go."

The restaurant was an interesting cultural experience. They did not speak English; we did not speak Finnish, and my ten words of Greek were unintelligible. But somehow, we ordered, sat in the sun, and drank a nice red table wine. The food was excellent. We talked and laughed like we were old friends. Other patrons were looking at us, not in an offended manner, but more friendly, as if they appreciated us enjoying ourselves and the restaurant. Even the owner came by to wish us well. Of course, she may have been telling us something completely different in Greco-Finnish, but there was extra wine given with lots of smiling, so we assumed the best.

We finished our meal and walked back to the bus station. Jo got her earbuds, and we loaded up on the bus. And sat there for a long time. Someone announced something, then everyone got up and began exiting the bus. We did as well, and then discovered the bus was broken and would not be leaving. Next one departed at nine the next morning. We walked back into town and found a decent hotel. We checked in and then left to walk the town to have something to do. The town was a pleasant enough place to visit. We ended up at a bar for a few drinks in the heat, by the river, then back to the hotel after dark to retire to our rooms for the evening.

We met the next morning and walked to the station. Hopefully, the bus was fixed, or another was ready. The bus was there, so we got on and, amazingly, it cranked up and left the station.

CHAPTER EIGHTEEN

We were on the bus for an hour, but talked little, as we were both listening to our own music on earbuds and watching the Finnish countryside pass by. Although the bus was operational, apparently the air conditioning was not. We were both sweating and almost dozing with the heat. Sitting beside her was getting distracting, between the slight pheromone mist and the perfume that kept wafting over. I doubted she was doing it on purpose, but eventually it would not matter. Against my better judgment, I put my left hand on her hand. It was the first time I had touched her with meaning. The heated, almost angry look she gave me somehow seared me.

"I think we should get off the bus for a while," she said.

"I think you are right."

I pressed the stop button above the seat. I could see the driver looking in his mirror back at us, as we were in the middle of nowhere. Then I pressed it again, heard him mutter something, and finally the bus slowed. We stood up and grabbed our backpacks and walked forward to the door. The driver looked at us, shrugged, and opened the door. I said thanks, and we hopped off. The bus lumbered away without delay as there were no other cars were on the road.

West, across the road, were miles of low boreal terrain, a mix of fields and woods. We crossed over and hiked away from the road for a time. We spontaneously began running across the grass, then we sprinted at full speed across the mostly open fields toward the tree line and the hint of blue that suggested a pond or lake hidden somewhere in the trees. It was a beautiful warm day full of green horizon, bookmarked by the blues of the sky and a touch of water. If someone had seen us running at that speed, they probably would have mistaken us for wolves. It felt wonderful, even in the heat.

Once in the trees, we slowed as came to a clearing. The water was another fifty meters past it through more open woods. The clearing was a meadow with grasses waist high and dotted with a few small trees. There was an old fence line on one edge, possibly for cattle or reindeer. We stood and looked around, then at each other. We were breathing hard and sweating. I also knew I was wearing entirely too many clothes.

Pheromones and scents flooded my senses. Beyond that I could sense Jo in my consciousness like I could most humans, but she was blazing in my mind, even brighter than how I remembered Hia. It was an extraordinary sensation. I knew that I was flooding Jo's senses as well, and she probably was not at all ready for the onslaught. Pheromones built upon pheromones. It was much too late to even attempt to stop. And yet, after I sensed her in my mind, something in my brain rebelled and tried to stop everything. I ignored it when she pushed me so hard, I landed on my back.

I jumped up and rushed to grab her, but too hard. We flew back, and she hit the old fencepost and snapped it off with me on top of her. She lay there for a second, then she kicked me back to where we had started. I lay on the ground a second, then before I could get up, she straddled me and then kissed me hard enough to draw blood from both our lips. I ripped her shirt off, then she returned the favor.

The next two plus hours were a blur of flesh, exhilaration, ecstasy, and pain. It was a mixture of physical, mental, and the spiritual, heightened as I also experienced through my extra sense. In my centuries of life, I had never come close to anything like it. It was the most intimate and most violent episode of lovemaking I had ever known. The part of my brain silently screaming to stop was always present, but I kept it at bay.

We experienced the purely physical aspect on an animal level. All the pheromones pouring out of both of us only intensified the experience and pure abandon. And the enhanced physicality of doing things typical humans could never manage. We filled our minds with the searing light of the other, and the light seemed to combine to be brighter, as we blended into each other in a way I had never imagined, and I guess that most humans cannot. We howled, screamed, groaned, and loved like nothing I had imagined or ever read or heard about. Then we both collapsed, completely spent.

I looked around and saw we had badly ripped up the small clearing. All the tall grass was flattened on the ground for ten meters in any direction. All the saplings were bent over or snapped off. Of course, the fence was no longer standing. It looked like a combination of wild hogs and a tornado had landed on this little piece of former paradise. Our clothes were also ripped to shreds and mostly gone. Both of us were dirty, grass stained, and bloody as we both had long scratches, just and multiple bite marks, just clotting up.

Now done, I realized that not only was this new to me, but Jo had certainly experienced nothing like this and probably was hard-pressed to understand it. Normal humans could not have survived what we had just done to each other. I wondered if this was how Bengal tigers or grizzly bears mated. Or if this was what the aftermath would look like if a grizzly tried to mate with a tiger. I also decided that Jo and I should never get a hotel room, at least not in our names. We would make rock stars destroying their rooms look like amateurs. It was both incredibly exhilarating and frightening that we could do so much harm to each other and enjoy it so much.

Now that we were done, it all went completely to hell. Waves of nausea and physical illness hit me, at the same as a psychic assault tore into my mind with the certain and powerful emotion that this was horribly wrong. My brain screamed that I needed to get away from her. It was so strong it overwhelmed me, and I may have blacked out for a minute. I tried to hide it from Jo, but there was no reason to, as when I was finally able to regain my vision, I could tell she was feeling the same way. I started to get up but was still too dizzy and sick.

"I feel incredibly odd, and now deathly sick," Jo said, gritting her teeth with the words. "Despite the overwhelming desire, this now seems a horrible mistake. I really can't be close to you." Not exactly the warm and blissful postcoital purr someone wants to hear from their intimate other, yet I understood completely and agreed. We both rolled away a couple of feet from each other.

"I can't explain it, but I feel the same way. I have never felt this ill after sex, and I can't explain it." We were both too uncomfortable to continue talking for a while.

"You understand how bad I feel? And it never happened before like this?"

"Yes, to both questions, and I hope this goes away soon. Sorry Jo, but two hours ago I wanted you with every cell in my body, but now all I want is to do is forget about it and never do it again. There must be some physiological explanation, but it may take some time to figure out. I'm too spent and ill to even think about it."

"I understand. On the bus and even during everything, it felt so right, and I knew I really wanted it," Jo said. "Maybe it was all the pheromones overloading my system. Whatever it was, I can't do this again." She pulled a dirt clod and sticks from her hair.

"Ugh, I agree. I think it might be wearing off finally." I felt less like hell and more like purgatory.

"What do we do now? I'm a little uncomfortable staying here with you after this, whatever the hell this was."

"Once it wears off, we need to clean up and get out of here. For now, we stick to our plan. And, well, no extracurricular activities."

"No problem there. A good soak in that lake and never seeing you naked again will be a good start."

"Back at you, miss-makes-me vomit." She didn't laugh, but there might have been a slight smile. "OK, I'm going to stand up, pull you up, then we will stagger to the water. I have some soap and a towel in my pack."

"Fantastic, let's do it."

Normally walking down to a lake with a naked woman I'd just spent two hours doing unimaginable things with would have resulted in a second round of doing those things in the water. Now I really didn't want to look at her. Nor did she even glance at me. We went down to the water and plunged into the cold, clear depths. We washed as best we could. During our mating ritual, I had broken my left wrist and sprained my knee. Jo had similar injuries beyond the scratches and bites. We would heal by tomorrow, but probably best to avoid public scrutiny for the next few hours. Or come up with a story about a bear attack. Later this afternoon, we might at least be presentable enough to find a roadhouse for the evening without looking like roadkill.

We slowly dressed in clothes from our backpacks. We were quiet, as there didn't seem to be much to say. We were both spent, and I had never been so tired and injured after making love to someone. All the years prior I had been holding back, always afraid to hurt the one I was with. Today had been too intense and too wonderful, then it had taken a horrible turn. I also realized we could potentially kill each other during a session. Good reasons not to ever repeat today. For Jo to feel the same as me told me something unusual was happening between us but that did not make it any better. I finally found the one I wanted to be with, and now we could barely look at each other.

Dressed, we walked back past the destroyed clearing. I moved closer to her as a test to see if the feeling worsened as I got closer. The ill feeling receded instead. Something strange was still happening to us.

"Did you feel that?"

"Yes, it was strange. As you moved toward me, I was about to tell you to go away, but then I felt much better. What is going on?"

"I do not know. But we have enough intelligence between us to figure it out."

"OK, come back closer." I did, and she looked thoughtful. "Strange, but much better than a half hour ago. What's next?"

"At least we can now tolerate each other. We continue to Turku or somewhere smaller, possibly a village that has a marina," I said. "I want to get us on a boat and completely off the grid, somewhere off the coast in the North Sea. Once there, I plan to contact Michael and try to find out what is going on. I still don't think he is part of this, but even if not, we have to protect ourselves for the next few days. We stay together and stick with the plan. Maybe we can figure out what has just happened to us."

Jo nodded, and we started back toward the road. It took a lot longer to return by walking since we were not running at cheetah speed. At the road, we turned right, the direction the bus had been going, as the next town was ahead a few miles. There were very few cars, and we did not hitchhike. Just as well, since no one seemed inclined to slow down for our disheveled selves. Just two hours of mostly us walking and not talking. As we got closer to the outskirts of town, I asked her about motorcycles.

She laughed and said, "My god, man, you want me to wrap my legs around a throbbing engine and hold myself against you, possibly for hours? How long do you think we would ride before I crushed your spine from desire? Of course, then I'd probably dump your body in a creek because of how sick you would make me afterwards."

"Uh, well, I didn't think about that. But you are right. We should stick to buses or possibly find a car. It would not do for me to float lifeless in the creek and scare the tourists."

"No worries, I'd weight your body down."

At least we were back to joking. We continued talking and kidding each other as we entered town. It was easy and good-natured, almost back to our normal banter.

We needed to find a restaurant or a market to get some food and drink, as that would speed our healing. At least we were no longer limping as much. The bites and bruises on my neck were also less noticeable, but I raised my collar to hide the worst of it. For the first time I also had a fleeting black thought - what a turn of fate if she became pregnant. I banished that vision as quickly as I could. But in this new world we had created between us, we would have to consider it if our fledgling romance ever made it to a second event. But that highly unlikely to ever happen, as even now the thought about sex with Jo brought the nausea back.

There was a small cafe that was open in town. We went in and were the only customers. The menu was limited but perfect. Country pate to start, then roast chicken with vegetables. The owner-server, an thin older lady, seemed a bit surprised when we asked for two pates and two chicken meals, each. A pitcher of water and a bottle of decent red wine finished our meal. Until we realized there was cake. Two slices each. We finished the entire meal fifteen minutes after it hit the table. The lady was confused but seemed impressed. Possibly a new town record for an average guy and a petite woman.

"Do you feel better?" I asked Jo.

"Definitely. A hot shower and a nap will complete my day. Hopefully, I won't get a dickey tummy from all that food."

I just looked at her after that turn of phrase, but kept my mouth shut. "We can ask our proprietor, if we have not scared her off thinking we might eat her too, if there is a roadhouse or inn nearby."

The cafe owner directed us toward the small inn another few hundred meters past the center of town. Not that there was much town, just houses, a small market and a tiny park. The inn was sparsely furnished but welcoming, with a lobby and bar that could sit eight people. We went in and got two rooms on the third floor. Steps, but no elevator, as usual when out of the cities. We went up and entered my room, a slightly triangular-shaped room with bright dormers, a comfortable bed, bathroom, and little else. Just like the cafe, simple and perfect. Jo's room was across the hall, so we walked over to look. Same as mine, without the dormers. She dropped her pack and headed to the bathroom.

"I will head back down to the bar for a couple of glasses of wine."

"I'll join you when I get finished with my hour of hot water," Jo replied.

The day was warm, and the bar area was cool when I went downstairs. I ordered a glass of red wine and a bottle of Vellamo water. There was nothing to do but sit and think, so I thought about getting us a boat. Helsinki was too far away and a bad idea with all the security and cameras. Turku was close and a medium-sized city that should have plenty of boat options. A coastal village, Uusikaupunki, was also close and had a marina. If I was buying a boat, then we should go to Turku. But since we only needed a short time to get off the coast and then contact Michael, I only needed to rent one for a few days. Should be less scrutiny at Uusikaupunki. Besides, with a name like that, how could I pass up the chance to visit? It also had a church built like a boat, according to the brochure I found in the bar. U-sicka-u-punky it was.

I spent another hour with a couple of red refills and another bottle of Vellamo. I was feeling much better and not much was hurting other than my wrist. It should be good by tomorrow. Jo came down the steps, and I sat and stared, wondering whether I was going to feel attraction or repulsion. She stood tentatively before sitting down, and I could tell she was thinking the same thing. She gave a half smile. I felt nothing negative, and it seemed she did not either. I ordered her a glass of wine and water.

"Having fun drinking alone and ogling women?"

"It's Finland. I believe that is the national pastime. Although in my current state, I can barely even ogle. Now that I think about it, I have seen no one else anyway. Oh, the town we are in is Loimaa. I don't think it is anything famous. A great place to blend in and be anonymous. How was the bath?"

"Quite functional. No extras, and I guess no spa attached, but just as well. An hour of hot water cures all ills."

"I think I'll try it a little later. While I was sitting here with my brain in neutral, I think I came up with a simple next step. Take a bus to Uusikaupunki and hire a boat."

"I hope that is not how the town, in reality, is pronounced."

"I don't know. I am just making it up. Small place with a marina. Since no one can pronounce it, I doubt there will be any surveillance there."

"I would agree with that. Now what about dinner? I'm getting hungry again."

I smiled at her. That was an astonishing appetite. But I was getting a little hungry as well. "Let's go to the market and stock up for the night. There is a short menu here we can order later, but better to be stocked than not."

We went to the market and bought enough for a small group of people. We then had an early dinner in the lobby. I walked upstairs and took a warm shower. It was after eight by the time I finished, but there was still lots of daylight left. Jo and I walked around the town and discussed what kind of boat to get. Of course, we didn't have any idea of what boats might be available for hire, but that didn't stop us from dreaming and talking about sailing a schooner to Greece or the Caribbean. We did not specify whether we would be on the same boat.

We went back to the inn, traipsed upstairs, said our goodnights, and ducked into our respective rooms. We were both shy about being too close together for too long.

I woke to sunshine and birds loudly chirping. It was only six am, but days were long this far north. I got up as I had had enough to sleep to finish healing, mostly. I knocked on Jo's door to tell her I was going down for breakfast. She immediately opened the door, already dressed, so we went together. We were both healed and showed no signs of yesterday's ordeal. After breakfast, we packed our backpacks and food and checked out of the inn. We walked to the bus station for a seven am departure to Uusikaupunki.

Chapter Nineteen

The bus ride was uneventful. No pheromones were released, or unscheduled stops made. We both listened to music for most of the two-hour ride to the coastal town. The tiny bus station we arrived at was a few kilometers from the marina, but the sidewalks were good and the terrain flat. There were restaurants along the way, so we started walking. The church I had read about was also on the same road.

The appearance of the church confused me at first. It looked nothing like a boat, but a standard stone and wood building topped with a metal roof. It was when we went inside that I saw they built the entire interior shaped like a large boat hull, upside down. They dedicated the church to all the sailors in the area that had been lost to the sea. There was probably a lesson in that.

We continued and came to the marina. It was more like a lot of boats tied along a narrow channel with some docks further down. A small bridge crossed the water, so we walked across to the restaurant placed right on the water. Fish and chips seemed appropriate, so we sat, ate, and talked.

We needed a boat for a couple of days. Something with a cabin complete with a galley, head, and double bunk, would be ideal. Jo wanted a sailboat, and I was OK with that if it also had a motor. I knew from a few hundred years ago just how many islands and rocks covered the coastline. Even an experienced sailor would occasionally run aground or rip out a bottom in these waters. The restaurant owner gave us a name of someone likely to rent us a boat. We finished our early lunch went to the marina.

We spent some time walking around looking at the boats tied and moored all around, looking for a particular boat on a dock that the potential boat lessor lived on. After a few minutes, we found the right spot, and a man was having coffee on deck. We said our hellos, and I told him what we were looking for. A boat with a cabin, motorized, that we could explore the local islands with for three days as we celebrated our anniversary. He spent some time thinking, some extra time looking at Jo, then finally came up with two options. He just needed an exorbitant amount of money for the rental and a credit card for damages.

It was good that Finland used the euro. I gave him fifty percent of the asking rate and a credit card in the name of Ceryl Vogel. I used that name often and threw it away as needed. The card, a burner like the other five in my pocket, was encrypted and attached to a special account set up by Monk. The man would get the other fifty percent once we saw the two boats, and we made our choice. I mentioned we wanted to leave after lunch, and although he protested a bit at the quick turnaround, the money won out. He walked off to get the boats ready. We went to the market, which was nearly a kilometer away. Good thing we could each carry as much as the average mule.

We bought quite a lot of food and water. I also bought a pull cart used throughout Europe. Might as well use it, plus it made us look more official as part-time sailors heading out for a few days of relaxation. Back at the marina, there were two boats tied to the dock near the petrol station. Both were decent. A runabout with an inboard engine and spacious cabin; the other was more of a traditional sailboat with a diesel motor large enough to hurry it along in case the sails weren't cooperating.

I looked at the sailboat first, as I knew that would be Jo's pick. I checked the engine, tanks, radio, and mechanicals while she went through the galley, head, and berth. We talked and were both OK with the boat. We went topside and told the guy we were taking this one, no need to see the other. He grumbled but visibly brightened when I handed him the other handful of colorful euros. Wasting no time, we took our supplies aboard, stowed them, and left the marina.

"Hey Jo, do you know how to drive a boat? I've never done it before."

She gave me the look used to freeze granite. "About time to learn, I would say. But I guess the credit card you used for the damage deposit was fake, so it really doesn't matter, does it?"

"No, I guess not. But come over and we will learn together. You might need to know how in case you throw me overboard in the middle of the night."

"Can't argue with that logic."

"Push that thingy and turn that thingamajig, and off we go. To go less fast, pull that doohickey." I stopped after the swift elbow that would have cracked another man's ribs.

It was a beautiful day, with sun, mild wind, dark blue where the water was deep, and aquamarine colors along some of the shallower sandy areas. Not much sand around, as the shoreline was mostly rocky. Clouds were sparse but billowy white and non-threatening. As we moved out further, the islands were emerald jewels set in the dark blue water. Gorgeous, but of course my thoughts turned darker as I was wondering how many sunken Viking ships we were skimming over. We sailed, mostly aimlessly, for the rest of the day. As evening approached, we anchored between two islands and prepared an enormous meal. This should be the last large intake of food to finish the healing from our meadow encounter.

Afterward we sat on the deck with the last of the warm breeze of the day, while the stars began appearing. It was late, since the days were so long.

Jo began our necessary conversation. "I wanted you to know that, while I'm not a prude, I don't normally do anything like we did back at the meadow. That just isn't my nature."

"I think I understand. And one of my cardinal rules has been not to get involved with anyone I work with professionally. Since we met, I've been attracted to you, but I had no plans to act on it. I think the pheromones really jumpstarted something that got out of hand."

"Yes, I think that is true. I definitely agree that colleagues should not be romantically involved either. But why did we end up repelling each other strongly afterward?"

"My only idea is that your microbiome basically came from mine. Almost a clone, although I'm sure it has changed to adapt to your body. But they are closely related. After the initial pheromone rush overrode our judgement, the microbiomes rebelled and forced us apart."

"We are like two magnets. We feel attraction to each other, at least through our abundant pheromones, but then we repel each other. Just like two magnets when the poles are reversed."

"That's a good analogy. Once the microbiomes recognized they were closely related, we were done. Which relegates you and I into the sister-brother relationship for the next decade, century, or possibly longer."

We sat silently for a moment. "This is not so bad then," she said. "We can remain colleagues, friends, and even relatives at the microbiome level. But definitely nothing closer."

"Yes, we will be fine. Taking sex off the table, or of the entire continent in our case, will be a good thing. But as your new big brother I now get to choose your boyfriends."

"Not bloody likely. My life in that regard is my own."

"Rightly so. But damn, as I just realized something. If I turn a group of people, they cannot pair up afterward. That is a good thing in my case as it prevents me from turning all the Farm people. Assuming they would even want to get together, after being turned they couldn't. I can't start an empire if nobody can have sex and procreate."

"Yes, your ambitions of empire are well known. A sexless empire would be difficult to populate."

"Hey, don't go spoiling my dreams of conquest. I'll just have to find some other way to dominate the world."

We turned in to our respective bunks not much later. We got up early the next morning, ate, then pulled up the anchor for another day of sailing. I also decided we had been missing long enough and made the call.

"Hi Michael. Thought I would check in and see if there is anything going on in your neck of the woods these days."

"You must enjoy making my life miserable. You could have just asked for some vacation time for you and Jo, rather than eloping to wherever you are."

"Uh, well, no elopement. Just needed to bug out and stir the hornets' nest for you. Did you have any good hunting while all the animals fled the forest fire you started?"

"There were some people in the organization that reacted oddly to your escapade. A couple of days playing whack-a-mole proved most productive in cleansing our system. I believe you wanderers can come home now."

"Sure, would you have a plane or boat handy for a pickup?"

"I am thinking of having a helicopter on standby with your names on it. Not sure if it should be a medical or a military helicopter."

"Both would probably be best, since you know me. We are just off the Finnish coast. Nearest town with an airport is Turku, but we can get to the Aland Islands if needed. But I don't do helicopters, ever."

"Of course, you don't ride in helicopters. That would be too easy. Let me check on what we have available and where. I'll call you back in twenty minutes."

"Sounds lovely."

Michael called back on his personal line. "I have a plane scheduled to pick you both up in Turku. We can't get it there until tomorrow. One thing to know, I believe we have taken care of all the threats in our group. But it was more widespread than we had expected. It is possible that some may have slipped through. To alleviate any further threat, I'm having you both taken to a safe facility in Copenhagen for a few days. It is impregnable, so you both will be safe. Look out for those storms tonight. See you tomorrow."

"Thanks. See you tomorrow." There was no inclement weather in the area, and nothing was forecast. I stepped down to the back of the boat where Jo was waiting. Her hearing was just as good as mine.

"Storms?" She asked. "I see nothing ominous in the sky, nor is there anything on the radar."

"Nope, I think Michael is just giving us a warning. Nor is there any impregnable facility in Copenhagen. He called back on his phone line, even though we could have finished our conversation on the first encrypted call."

"He's setting us up as a target and letting us take down any leftover bandits. They will have to act fast, as they only have tonight or tomorrow."

"Sure looks that way. Let's hope they don't damage the boat, or I won't get the deposit back."

"But you are not worried about me. Such a romantic."

"You can more than take care of yourself. But if they come in shooting, I'm willing to take at least one bullet for you."

"Ah, there's the man I destroyed a meadow for. What if there are multiple bullets incoming?"

"I feel it's my duty as a feminist to step aside and let you share in the moment."

"Arse."

"Yep. But from what we just heard from Michael, it's obvious this scenario was part of his play. Our prediction was accurate. My dumbass hero routine was a useless act. No rescuing the damsel, just two people on the weirdest vacation ever."

"Yes, you certainly didn't rescue me from impending death. More evidence was the lack of response from the Center sniper positions, or even much of a car chase."

"The good guys have set us up. Glad they trust us this much."

"How's that?"

"They let us get away, then during the chaos the double agents get fried, and now they let us take out any remaining garbage. We are part of the team, operating on our own with no specific orders. They trust us."

"Well, then tonight or tomorrow, let us kick some bad boy arse."

"Hmm, you need to work on your bad-girl jargon." Yes, she hit me for that.

Jo and I sailed on, and I plotted a course through the islands to arrive at Turku the next day. That night we moored just off an island, and after a light dinner, we had drinks on deck and watched the stars. We retired below, acting as if everything was normal. Neither of us slept as we expected unwelcome company.

I felt more than heard something that seemed to be a bump. Since I was not asleep, I rolled over, got to my feet, and padded out of the cabin toward the stern hatch and waited in the shadows. I sensed Jo was up and crouched near the bow hatch.

The first commando, dressed in black, entered the hatch. He was silent, but that didn't save him when I punched his neck, my knuckles finding his spine. He went limp without a sound, and I held him up in the doorway. The second commando bumped into the body and impatiently pushed forward. He got the same throat punch, as I eased the first down and held up the second body. The third in line realized something was wrong and tossed in a flash bang. In an instant, I picked up and threw it back behind him. It went off, but the third goon, although disoriented, started firing his weapon. The body of the second commando absorbed the rounds, then I threw the body into the third guy. While that tangled him up, I shattered his temple with my fist. I assumed they were all in body armor and I was not risking any injury to Jo or me since we were on such a small boat.

Jo was at the bow handling her end of the boat. During the excitement, the other three commandos would have taken us out from behind. They were not prepared for Jo to spring up the bow hatch and punch their faces into mush.

"You OK up there?"

"Yes, love, got all these before they shot you in the back. How are you?" Meanwhile, she was trussing her three survivors up with their own zip ties.

"Only got a light bullet wound, a stray that passed through the body I was holding up. I'm hoot owl holler and half together, as they say in North Carolina. So, I didn't really take a bullet for you, exactly."

"Close enough." She was standing beside me by then. "And you need to work on your he-man jargon. Whoever would say owls and hollows?"

The six commandos in black had arrived on two black rubber dinghies that were tied to our boat. Each body had a silenced pistol, but all carried tasers, dart guns, stun grenades, and zip ties. And each of their boats both had the capacity for four. Seems they were more interested in capturing us than killing us. If they had wanted us dead, it would have been much simpler to just blow up the boat. The three still alive got dumped in the tiny engine compartment after stripping them of all equipment and retying them. The Church could have them tomorrow, along with the three dead that I tied together and put in the water as a makeshift cooler.

We gathered our few supplies and hopped into the other dinghy. I sunk the other dinghy by putting a knife in the major bladders. We then motored over to the island and pulled the rubber boat up just inside the tree line. We would spend the rest of the night in the trees just in case the handlers for these guys got itchy after not getting a report and employed more lethal means.

At dawn, we were up and about to go down to the shore when the boat exploded. We were far enough away to feel the blast but not get hurt. A few hundred yards away, a sleek speedboat sped off. An RPG or two, most likely, had taken out the boat. They didn't even bother to check who was on the boat. Very amateurish.

"Damn, there goes my deposit. And prisoners for Michael."

"Nice of them to leave us another boat, though."

"Yes, glad I grabbed the gas can from the other rubber dinghy. May not get us to Turku but will get us close enough to find another boat."

We tossed our stuff in the boat, carried it to the water, and continued our journey. I was going to charge Michael for the boat deposit. My minor wound had already healed, so I probably would not charge any hazard pay. It was a good morning as we ended up with enough gas to get to the island of Satava. A bridge connected the island to Turku, so we walked to the nearest village and got a taxi.

We arrived at the airport an hour later at the private plane hangar portion of the airport. A small jet touched down, and after a few minutes, pulled up to the hangar. Two commandos trotted down the lowered steps and entered the hangar, while another two took off down the outside of the hangar, checking the perimeter. They finished and formed up near us, so I guess not all the loose ends were tied up yet. Then Michael came down and welcomed us back to the fold.

"Good afternoon, my children. Hope you had a wonderful vacation in sunny Finland."

Jo looked a little bashful. I joined the banter until she recovered. "It was a beautiful evening until the assassins arrived. Then a gorgeous morning until another group blew up the boat."

"Awfully sorry about the boat. I suppose you will lose your deposit."

"Yep. But luckily, I'll recover it in the expense report. Guess you figured not all the roaches got exterminated in the latest purge."

"No, we knew there were more, even after we discovered and dealt with quite a few. Many had been in place for years. But they had gotten complacent until your antics shook them up and they got sloppy."

"Always glad to help."

"Good to hear that. Oh, and I need you in America immediately. And Jo, I need you to complete your training as fast as possible. I now have even more open positions to replace, including the head of our European team. Seems that was one of the infiltrated roles."

"No rest for the weary," I said. "Rinse and repeat."

"Quite right. Now let us get on the plane and you can tell me about your adventure."

Michael had already turned toward the plane and did not notice Jo's silence. But she needed to talk soon, or Michael was going to get suspicious. The four commandos trotted past us and into the plane. As we went up the steps, with me in the rear, I whispered to Jo, low enough so Michael would not hear, "You still have twigs in your hair." She flinched and looked at me with murder in her eyes, but I was smiling so sweetly that by the time she got to the top step, she was also trying not to smile. We might get through this after all.

CHAPTER TWENTY

The Uya, a bad type of Wendigo, were moving north. A few reports from western Texas and New Mexico confirmed gruesome murders as they left Mexico. What we did not know is where they were ultimately heading. They could turn east toward Oklahoma, north toward Colorado, or west to Albuquerque and on to Phoenix. The worst-case scenario was Phoenix, with five million people. The Uya could hide there and harvest hundreds of humans in a short time. I would start in Phoenix and would work backwards as needed, whether south or east, to head them off. It was such a vast, unpopulated country of desert and mountains I knew it would be very unlikely to find them quickly, but I had friends to help. Michael's group was covering the other cities, and I had my ace, my extended family from Oklahoma, ready to travel. I wanted to keep my people and Michael's folks apart in the early stages to prevent any disagreements, since my people were not formally trained. But then I wanted my people involved to get them some experience and observe the Church teams in action.

I stepped off the plane at the Phoenix airport to get a whiff of still-hot air breezing through the jetway. I stumbled and had to stop for a second. The undeniable essence of Uya, a stench of death, was in the air, and close. Or if not close, then recent. Damn, they were already here, and Phoenix was not prepared. I fiddled with my carry-on bag to mask my stall-out on the jetway.

I started walking again to keep from getting run over by the passengers that were eager to leave the plane.

So much for planning to intercept them away from the city. Urban hunting was not much fun when there were groups chasing groups in a city much larger than Amsterdam. By the time I got to the end of the jetway and entered the terminal, I had my cell phone out. I called Michael's lieutenant for this operation, Elias Martinez. Elias and I had not met, but we got along well during phone and internet meetings. He was a Cambridge-trained anthropologist and had gone through Michael's program, including combat training with Simon. Now in charge of the Church teams in North America, I thought he was smart, funny, and probably a natural killer. He did not know Jo but knew about her work.

"Hey Elias, I'm in the Phoenix airport and smelling Uya, or Wens, as you guys like to call them out here. I guess they are already here in the Valley of the Sun. Or should I say all that in Latin to make you feel at home?"

"Ah yes, my Roman friend, no need for Latin this early. It makes my head hurt. The stench you speak of comes from two advance Wen's that flew in a short time ago. They are young and have adapted to modern ways, luckily for the rest of the passengers on that flight. We have them under surveillance as they traveled into the city and are now looking for large houses to rent. We think the primary group is moving this way from the east. The latest report is they killed and ate a family in New Mexico and took their van."

"OK, since you know all that, I assume your people are on the move."

"Yes, as you know, we had placed teams in all the regional cities, covering their possible destinations. Of course, the teams are now traveling to Phoenix, except for the one already here and tailing the two advance Wens."

"Good. Any idea of the van's route yet?"

"The two Wens here are looking at houses in north Mesa and east Phoenix. We know the incoming won't be traveling on I-40. That does not leave many other road choices."

"Nope, just highways 87 and 60. Let me think. Can you blockade 60 for a day and announce the road is closed? That should force them to use 87. Less populated and hopefully fewer collateral casualties around our ambush."

"Great minds think alike. We have a total closure of 60 set to begin in an hour. What's your play?"

I told him my general plan, and he told me his people would be ready to go. I hung up, left the airport, and called my gang and got them on a charter flight out of Tulsa. They should be in Phoenix in three hours since they were ready and waiting.

It was still hot here. Not the asphalt melting, tires-sticking-to-the-driveway midsummer hot, but still hot. Especially compared to Amsterdam or Asheville. The alien landscape always surprised me when I first saw it again after years away. Flat and beige, with odd mesas popping up randomly, even amid subdivisions, lots of cactus, and high brown mountains in the distance. A pang of remembrance for a time long ago in the Mediterranean region passed through me. Not sure where that came from.

I found my car, a four-wheel-drive SUV I originally thought I'd need to cross through rough country. Now I might only need to drive down to the nearest suburb to kill some Uya, hopefully without collateral human casualties. If things went badly, the next few days would be gruesome.

The two major routes running east of Phoenix were Highways 87 or 60, and with 60 about to close, I would head towards 87 to intercept the vanload of cannibals. I pulled out my Mac and quickly scanned the satellite maps. I saw some interesting landmarks and started driving rather than waiting for backup. Most of the rest of the crew were hours away, and meanwhile, I could set up a suitable site for an ambush.

Each time I came to Phoenix over the years it surprised me how many more people were here than the last visit. A sleepy desert town now a thriving city of five million souls. More people and much greener here than I remembered, which meant more golf courses for all those new arrivals. A thousand miles of desert in nearly every direction and humans were squandering water on lawns and golf courses. Courses that many people living here would never get to play or even walk on. The current hundred-year drought, which could last another five hundred years, was likely to have a say about that kind of water usage soon.

The subdivisions seemed endless as I drove. The land along the road I was traveling was recently desert and scruffy sand lots on the outskirts of Phoenix. Now large homes on tiny lots, many of the neighborhoods gated, stretched on for miles. Those gates would not be any good to keep the Uya out and would only help keep the people in once the Uya began their gruesome harvest. I suppose that was a version of irony. I finally got to the end of the sea of shingles and concrete and the first signs of real desert.

There was a large new casino and resort on the left that did not exist the last time I was here, at least not in its latest form. Obviously, it had had a golf course. I needed to immerse myself in American culture and study the anthropological question of what kind of human plays golf on grass in the desert. Also, the resort was on the west bank of the Verde River, fronting Highway 87, the same route the Uya van was taking into Phoenix. I pulled up to the lobby parking area and went in and got a room. I also reserved enough rooms for my folks. Not sure they would need them for sleeping, but they might need the showers the following days.

The rooms were decent and reasonably priced, and the resort was obviously geared to make their money with the gamblers and golfers. I threw my bag in the room and then went for a walk. Like in most of America, walking here was frowned upon, and openly discouraged, as none of the roads had sidewalks or safe places to walk. I went across the bridge and turned right, going south and downriver. It was reservation land, but I wanted privacy; although I was trespassing, there did not seem to be anybody around. On the digital map, I saw a small mesa that was downriver, and had old ruins on top. A cross-hatched pattern was etched in the soil at eight-foot intervals, along with a forty-foot diameter double circle of rocks, indicating ancient town.

I crossed a dry creek bed just past an old rodeo area, then scaled a short cliff to reach the top of the mesa. I walked around and confirmed there had been a village here. The old adobe walls had long since returned to the dirt, but the stone circle was easy to find. There were pleasant views in almost every direction. I decided this would be the spot we would do battle.

Now I just had to let my crews know that, then entice the Uya to cooperate. I hop-jumped down the cliff and returned to the casino. I got on the phone with Elias to give directions to the kill zone. After that, I called Nan, who was less than happy about being left out of the action. I had already explained many times that she was not expendable. Not for any reason, ever, but she still did not like it.

"Hey Nan, baking any cookies today?" Sometimes I could not resist poking the bear.

She responded with a series of words not suitable for television. Some of them were in Cherokee. If I had been someone else, I would feel insulted.

Once she finished, I laughed. "I suppose that is a no. I was hoping Henry was bringing me a batch of chocolate chip cookies, though."

"If I sent anything to you, it would be undercooked possum. Greasy, smelly, and full of bacteria."

"That's the spirit. Let's save that for Thanksgiving dinner, though. What can you tell me about how to lure a group of Uya across a quarter mile of desert to an ambush site?"

That got her attention, and she was now all business. "The best lure is human blood. We know they also track human prey by following wood smoke. There are also a few other things that attract them. I can text you a list, although you may not have time to find everything."

"That is alright, I will do what I can. I can get my colleague to get a couple of gallons of blood from the Catholic hospital nearby. Wood smoke I can easily do and the rest I'll improvise from your list."

"OK, the text is coming your way. You have all the surprises set? I assume Henry is bringing those?"

"Yep, will be a good time to test everything. Hope it will be a brief but interesting interlude with our favorite enemies."

"Just don't underestimate them if they are in a group. A pack can take out an entire fortified village in less than an hour."

"I'm counting on that type of aggression. Timid Uya won't trigger the trap."

"Don't get eaten."

"Don't plan to, and anyway, I'm much too tough for their old teeth."

"Good luck. And I caught that cheap shot about Thanksgiving."

"Thanks Nan, see you back at the Farm, hopefully in a few days. Goodbye."

I called Elias again and got my blood delivery arranged. Also, a load of old smelly clothes from a local homeless mission. Wonderful stuff for putting out a load of human scent. Some of the other items from Nan's list just would not happen. I didn't even know where to get large quantities of used tampons or feces or cornbread, nor did I plan to find out. I guess those were all things associated with scents from a human village.

I went outside to continue planning while walking. I also thought about the area, and that it was about to become a battleground again. US soldiers had battled the Apache and Yavapai for years in the area. A few miles away was

Skeleton Cave, where less than a hundred and fifty years ago, a portion of the Yavapai tribe was massacred. They did not want to move to the reservation, so George Crook slaughtered them. He left the bodies lying under the rock overhang, as any good Christian man would do. Thirty years later, the few remains were collected and buried at Fort McDowell, just north of the casino. Some of those bones were from children. Now the casino I was staying at was ostensibly owned by the descendants of the tribe. The circle turns, but I doubt the tribe would ever recover from the previous deprivations of massacres, forced reservations, and the infamous boarding schools for children.

I left those dark thoughts behind and walked back toward the low mesa where the ambush would occur. I stayed on the side of the main road, dodging cars. Once I got back on the mesa, I unwrapped my axe I had brought and began cutting small trees and mesquite scrub. I needed a giant pile for a bonfire, and it took me an hour. I needed to remember to get matches, or it would lead to an embarrassing moment later tonight. Once I had a large enough pile, I walked back to the casino hotel.

As I arrived, a van pulled in the parking lot. The driver, one of Elias' men, hailed me. He parked and opened the back to pull out two boxes containing the supplies I'd asked for. I picked up both boxes to load in my SUV and he took off. One box was full of bags of blood from the hospital. The other was full of very lived-in and odorous clothes from a local shelter. Fire, blood, and human sweat should be enough bait for the Uya.

Cars, trucks, and vans began pulling up. All very nondescript, but the men and women were not. They had a hard look, efficient movements, and seemed hyper-alert, very much of what I would expect from Elias' people. Some were clean cut and looked like college students, others passed for cowboys or bikers. A good mix of looks and unlikely to draw attention in Arizona. A guy my size full of ropy muscle, wearing black pants and tee shirt, sporting a gold chain with a crucifix, walked up.

"I have a good idea that you are Senecus."

"I now have an even better idea that you are Elias."

"Your powers of deduction are outstanding, especially since we have seen each other on video calls."

"Maybe I should call you Father Obvious?"

"Just don't call me asshole."

"Pretty sure we are both assholes. By the way, what do you call two assholes?"

"No idea."

"Two assholes."

"It's going to be a long night."

"Yep. Reel in some bad Wens and tell bad jokes. Only way it could be worse is if one of them eats my liver."

"You could just grow another one."

"Partial to the one I got. Besides, never tried to regenerate anything before. Could grow back as asparagus."

"Then your pee would always stink."

"Yep, but I would always have something to cut off and put on the grill."

"Any chance we will have a serious conversation?"

"We could slip up and fall into one. You have all your team and their supplies here?"

"I think we have everything. You should already have the clothes and blood."

"In my car. We should probably round up your folks and go over the map, then walk the site and unload everything. My team should be here soon. Got a few special boxes for your shooters."

"My guys may not like that, as they are partial to their own stuff."

"I think they will make an exception tonight. Hand loaded to a hundredth of a gram, plus a little something that guarantees a takedown with one shot, even if it's a near miss."

"Damn, if that works on a Wen, I believe we'd all like to get some of that."

"Must be your birthday then, cause everybody gets some of that cake."

"Michael said you were strange, but the best operative around. He got the strange part right."

"Yep. Find out the rest tonight."

I liked Elias. I liked the gold cross because it announced who he was without being flashy. And more so because we were talking crap just before meeting the most dangerous group of things in North America.

Chapter Twenty-One

My team pulled up in the parking lot. Henry was driving, of course, and he had brought his hunting buddies. At the Farm, they had been giving lessons on multi-day hunts in groups. It might sound simple, but it really is not. Group dynamics can significantly affect readiness and overall teamwork. I trusted the Church team, but I was quite glad that Henry and his group were here. I did not allow the kids here because if it went bad tonight, then some of those on the mesa would be dead and eaten in a few hours. I hated not giving them the experience they desperately needed, but in this case, the risk was not worth it.

I shook hands with Henry and the group. One of his guys took a heavy bag over to Elias. "Hey Elias, there's your birthday cake," I yelled over. "Tell your guys not to touch the tips, though, or they will wake up with a terrible hangover three days from now." He nodded and started handing out boxes to each of his group. I chatted with Henry and his group about the plan. It was a brief conversation since I did not like elaborate talks and there was an elegance in simplicity. Mainly because I could remember it easier.

Five minutes later, the two groups coalesced around the back of my SUV. I did a few seconds of introductions of my people, then Elias did the same. Then I gave the group my two minutes of planning. We all looked at the map and discussed a few points. Everyone here was experienced and efficient, so ten minutes later, we were all in vehicles heading over to the old rodeo spot just north of the mesa. We parked, unloaded lots of gun boxes and a few other items, and carried everything up the mesa. Luckily, the Uya would not even recognize all this traffic might be a trap. They enjoyed being insane and chasing human dinners; abstract thinking was not their strong point. They were clever, though, when threatened, so if the trap timing was not right, then all bets were off.

As they brought the guns out, I told Elias' people that the bullets were sealed after treatment, but to still take extra precautions to handle the tips as carefully as possible. I just needed to mention the word neurotoxin to get their full attention. I told them head shots were fine, but body mass shots were just as good. One hit would work, but several hits should put the Uya down for days. They seemed impressed. The only thing worse than an Uya chasing you at night was a gut-shot Uya chasing you. Even headshots with regular bullets were no guarantee they would go down, so everyone appreciated the special bullets.

I set up some bright lanterns near the bonfire site where I would wait for the Uya. Elias set up his teams around the bonfire at least thirty meters out. The first critical shot would likely be through my position and into the Uya. I didn't want that shot to be through me with one of those special bullets, so I set Henry up directly behind me.

I unboxed the smelly clothes and started hanging them around the far edges of the clearing. Then I took out a few dozen blood bags and dropped them all around. I would cut them open after dark. Once the teams set up, I walked around to check on positions. We had to move one team as they were too close to where our best guess of where the Uya would come up the mesa. We were setting up a funnel leading to me. Everything looked good, and the teams had their spots ready. I just hoped, like they did, that the plan would work. Since everyone was a professional here, we all knew it was unlikely to be glitch-free.

Elias and I took one of his teams back over to the main road. This team would take out the Uya van and set up the trap.

"Looks like a good and simple plan. If the timing is right, then it should be easy," Elias said.

"You are saying it is likely to be a cluster you-know-what, and has no chance of success?"

"Nope, you said that. I'm just agreeing with it."

"Was Smartass 101 a class in the seminary?"

"No idea. I was over at the all-girls school."

"That just sounds wrong. But I guess there was less competition there."

We had time to kill as the sun went down. Michael's estimate, based on watching some real-time satellite tracking, gave us between one and three hours to wait. I asked Elias if he wanted to go with me to the casino and gamble, but he declined. It was going to be a clear night with not much moon. Perfect for stargazing and trying to not get eaten.

I placed the lanterns pointing toward where the Uya were expected to ascend the mesa. I wanted them well-illuminated rather than relying on the dancing light from the bonfire. Plus, the Uya needed to keep their attention on me, not on their surroundings. I hung more stinky clothes behind me to spread scent after checking with Henry to make sure I was not blocking any of his sight lines. I went around and cut open all the blood bags, then picked some up and poured them on some clothes to help get the scent on the air. Most of the brush in the immediate area I had cut to feed the fire and clear the probable kill zone. I would wait to start the fire until I got confirmation that the Uya's car was closer. Elias had hooked up with Michael's team and was on a pad watching the satellite feed. They wired all his guys up to talk to each other. All Henry's guys were wired as well, but on a different channel.

There was also a common band for everyone, but if that was needed, it would be because things had gone severely sideways. With that rosy thought, I sat and waited. Lots of preparation, lots of waiting, and probably a couple of minutes of chaos and terror. Good times in Arizona.

An hour and a half later, Elias yelled, "Target is inbound, ten miles out." That was the signal to light the fire. I got it going, and the wood and brush were dry enough to catch quickly. In two minutes, the flames were six feet tall. I sat down on my little camp stool and concentrated on something special I had been practicing and would likely need tonight. Now it was time to wait for the Uya to do their thing, and to trust all the people surrounding me to do their thing.

Elias provided a running commentary of events on the highway. The shooter on the team by the road took out the front passenger-side tire of the minivan the Uya had liberated from their earlier human meal. The car swerved and pulled off the road. Two of them got out, looked at the tire, then the rear door opened and four more got out. Crap, six was going to be a handful tonight. With the two advance goons already in Phoenix, we were expecting only two or three in the van. Two of them began efforts to change the tire as the rest milled around. The Uya were good at some things, but less so at menial human tasks.

The fire was burning, the clothes and blood scents were wafting, but if they didn't notice then all this would collapse, and we'd move on to Plan B. Which was follow these six on to the reunion with the other two, then take out all eight in a suburb where collateral damage was likely. But I don't think anyone had ever taken on eight Uya successfully.

I had one last trick. At a store in the casino, I had bought a variety pack of fireworks. I pulled out a few whistling bottle rockets, some flashy silver fountains, and, of course, Roman candles. I went over to the edge of the mesa, pulled out a lighter and started the show. Elias spoke over the network that I had gotten their attention. A moment later, Elias said the pack was moving toward the mesa. They probably needed a little fast food after the long ride. Showtime, so I turned on the lanterns and went back to the fire and my stool. Elias said they were moving fast and at the bottom of the mesa. Then he went to radio silence.

The first one that came over the top was young. He raced straight toward me at inhuman speed. I stood and waited. As he reached me with his hands toward my throat, I stepped in and slammed my fist into his face. Said fist was holding solid silver knuckles imbued with binder syrup. He went limp as his back slammed into the ground, his face a bloody mess. The rest of the pack had appeared over the edge and saw the brief encounter. Probably not what they expected, as they slowed and spread out on both sides of the alpha on the other side of the fire from me. I expected a sneak attack, with one or two trying to flank me and come at me from both sides.

The alpha started talking to distract me. "You have injured one of mine. It will upset him, so when he wakes up in a moment, he'll take his revenge." He wanted me to be afraid and to look down, but I would not play along.

"He will not wake up." I smiled. So did the alpha Wen. I'm sure he was thinking in another moment his colleague would eat my leg, then they would finish me off. After a minute, his smile wavered.

"We were the gods of the Maya and the Aztec. Now the cartels worship us and pay homage. Whatever you are, we will show you our power and consume you."

"Wait just a second. You mean it was you guys that caused all those humans down there to wear that crazy shit and cut hearts out? To mimic you bunch of useless, shapeshifting dumbasses? And now you work for drug lords and drive minivans? What's your next gig, a neon carwash buffet in Vegas?"

He looked enraged. Meanwhile, I pulled out my pistol and fired several rounds into the one lying on the ground as I kept smiling. One Uya, to the right of the alpha, made a move. The dagger flew fast and straight at my chest, but I had been preparing for that move for the past few moments. The dagger hit my little window of conjured nothingness just in front of me and disappeared. To make it happen, I had been concentrating to slow time and open that window to elsewhere. It was the limit of what I could do so far, and that was only with a lot of mental preparation. Not a real-time street fight sort of move, but it looked impressive.

The thrower and the alpha looked shocked and hesitated for a second. I brought up my left hand in a wave. Dozens of suppressed rounds filled the air and into the Uya. All five went down in a heap. They were spasming as they had been on the cusp of turning into their animal forms on their way to eat me.

A hand on one of the Uya kept turning into a bear's paw, then back to a hand. I walked over and put a couple more rounds in his head. Others were partially turning into other creatures as well. Elias and his people put more rounds into them. I had supplied them with plenty of ammunition, with .308 rounds for the sniper rifles and 9 mm for their pistols, all coated with binder syrup, and then sealed. They were obviously effective. Elias and Henry walked up beside me at the fire.

"They were gods to the Aztec and Maya, huh? No wonder those civilizations went bat shit crazy." Henry had a point there.

"Crazy is not a suitable business model," I added. "No wonder the cartels went so bad. They had all the money in the world and still had to kill everyone, bringing down the wrath of governments."

"Well, thanks to you guys, we bagged a nasty bunch tonight with no casualties," Elias said. "I'll let Michael know. Meanwhile, our guys are now taking down the other two since we know these bullets are so effective."

"I'm hurt that you didn't trust me."

"Trust but verify. I think one saint said that."

"Saint Obvious?"

"Close enough, for religious work."

"Close counts in horseshoes and God, I guess."

Elias walked off to supervise his people with cleanup. I did not know what they were going to do with six messed up Uya, which was about to be eight, but I was glad it was not my problem.

"You heading back to the Farm next?" Henry asked.

"Yep, still got stuff to do, and definitely need to get the kids ready."

"Part of that is going to be teaching us how to make knives disappear?"

"I had hoped not to, but I don't think there is much choice anymore. We will need all the special tools we can get."

"You been hanging out with some interesting people to pick up magic like that."

"Nothing magical about it. I couldn't even buy a magic trick. This is just some weird physics."

"So, where did the knife go?"

"I think somewhere out near the asteroid belt. Might make a nice shooting star in a few thousand years."

"Hmm, maybe so. Be a mighty handy trick, especially to throw some other things way out there."

"Yeah, I can think of some people worthy of that trip, but I'll have to work up to it."

Elias' team was making quick work of the bodies on the mesa top. They pulled out something that looked like a zip tie, but was wider and darker, to bind the arms and legs of the six Uya. The material resembled something like carbon fiber. I asked the nearest woman, with a mean haircut and great tattoo, what they were using.

"These are Smart Cuffs. Can't be cut and rated for well over ten thousand pounds of breaking strength. See this little box on them? If there is any change in electrical potential or resistance, such as the shifters changing form and the limbs shrink, the cuff automatically shrinks until substantial resistance is engaged. They can't get small enough to escape."

"What happens if they change the other way and get bigger?"

"That is when things get messy. Impromptu full or partial amputations happen. The cuffs are also impregnated with silver to handle special types of detainees. They work well in the field."

"Huh, I need to get some of those. Will they work as dog collars around politicians' necks?"

She smiled. "Technically, I'm sure they would work. Good luck getting volunteers."

"Who said anything about volunteers?" I made a mental note about getting a box of those from Michael. Would be a good trade for the bullets we had brought. "Your accent makes me think you are from Boston."

"Close. Went to Harvard on a Church scholarship. Most boring four years of my life. But it paid off when I got to join Elias' team."

"Thanks for your help tonight. Good luck out there."

"You too. Based on the crazy stories, I'll probably see you again."

"Hope so, but maybe at a party instead of a shootout. What's your evaluation of tonight's operation?

"It was fun. But the staging was too elaborate."

"How's that?"

"Could have just closed the road, stopped the van, then gone full Bonnie and Clyde on them with those bullets you brought while they were still in the van. Pulled the bodies out after."

"Huh. That's good, a lot simpler and more elegant."

"But I'm just a shooter, not paid to think."

"What's your name? I'm Sen."

"Zena. That's with a 'z', so not spelled like the TV show."

"Nice to meet you, Z. See you in the funny papers."

She just smiled and kept working. Smart, proficient, mean, and funny. A powerful an aphrodisiac in my case and the tattoo just topped it off. I put that nonsense away and made a mental note to get Elias to send her to the Farm as a strategy and tactics trainer. I had once again found someone better than me, and I needed to utilize her talents to keep us alive.

Twenty minutes later, we were all back at the casino. The clothes, blood bags, and the minivan had disappeared, and the fire was out. A van favoring an armored car was hauling the Uya to somewhere. I shook hands with Elias as we traded a few more insults. He was good people. They all left, including Zena, dammit, before I could enlist her. I went with Henry and his people to have one drink, as that was the limit for all of us. Then we all went to our rooms as we had an early flight out in the morning, back to Atlanta and then Asheville.

I thought about calling Michael, or Jo, or Nan, but did not make any calls. I sat in the room, then on the balcony. Then I walked outside and back to the top of the mesa. I dropped on my back, lying on the sand` of an ancient village, and looked at the stars. It was going to be another sleepless night for me.

CHAPTER TWENTY-TWO

Lying in the cool air on the warm sand, under a sky filled with thousands of stars, was both relaxing and frightening. Contemplating the sheer size of just this tiny portion of the galaxy full of countless suns, and even more planets, was scary. Kind of like an intelligent ant sitting on a bench in Central Park. I was overthinking life, probably because I and all my colleagues and friends had survived the evening, when things could have gone badly.

I rarely visited the desert anymore, as it reminded me of loss. But that story began when, for reasons I had mostly forgotten, I embarked on a crusade. Although that portion of the adventure ended before it began, it led to a wonderful time of my life with the best friend I ever had. That adventure ended tragically in the desert; therefore, my longtime aversion to visiting deserts around the world. Since I was in the desert alone this evening, I thought back to that time. Best of times, worst of times, like Dickens said.

For many reasons, most of them not good, a trip to the Holy Land became something for Europeans to do, starting around 1000 AD. Small, unofficial groups had been going there for pilgrimages long before that. Once the larger, official Crusades began, they were not numbered, not organized, and not successful most of the time. Most began as a vague, word-of-mouth, edict from a Pope that a monarch was going to the Holy Land in the next few months. Would you like to come, fight the infidels, and possibly get rich?

Although no one really knew anyone that had gone, gotten rich, and come back. Much later in history, the Crusades received categories and numbers according to various popes and kings that put together armies to conquer or secure Jerusalem and surrounding areas. But most went because they got to pillage and plunder for profit and fun along the way.

I made the trip, more for the travel to a place I'd never been, than any conquest. Perhaps my wanderlust from Viking days had not been sated, or I just wanted to escape another dreary winter. I grabbed some weapons and started on my way from Utrecht, early in the twelfth century, on one of the many paths leading to the Holy Land. First was a boat down the Rhine, then a walk over to the Danube to get another boat. I could have stayed on it all the way to the Black Sea, changed boats and sailed south. That seemed the long way, even though it would be easy if the weather and pirates cooperated. But there was not much in that direction I wanted to see, so I ended my boat trip on the Danube at Bratislava. The river was acting odd anyway, with lots of eerie fluorescent creatures following the boat at night. Time to get back on land.

I decided to walk the few days' journey to the Adriatic Sea since there was a good road to Trieste dating from Roman times, and it skirted most of the mountains. I met lots of others along the road that were traveling to the coast to find passage to the Holy Land. Most of the travelers were poor farmers or warrior wannabes that had no affiliation to a knight or noble. I had the means to remain independent and not need an affiliation, so I was a rarity. But I still walked with those people as the few nobles along the way were boorish. The nobles saw no difference between me, the poor walkers, or livestock. To them, we were all barely human. They had a penchant for mistreating anyone they considered below them, including raping the women and occasionally killing any man that protested. Two most egregious nobles that I encountered along that stretch of road did not make it to the Holy Land. Very unlucky accidents befell them, but I did not think anyone would miss them.

When I arrived at Trieste, I spent a few days perusing the array of boats and crews offering passage to various ports in the Mediterranean and the Holy Land. I tried one of the less dubious boats. Two other contingents signed on later for the trip. One group was fine, the other wasn't. They had arrived and chartered passage after I had, so I needed to make the most of it. We were only traveling for two weeks, so I thought it would be bearable. I had already offed a couple of nobles along the road, so I was trying to behave myself. But by the third night, a clumsy noble fell overboard without a sound. His group really did not settle down much even after that, but at least they were now only fighting among themselves.

We had a day off the boat in Dubrovnik, also called Ragusa, while dodging a storm and picking up supplies. I decided while there to find another boat to continue the trip. There was plenty of traffic moving south, so I hopped another vessel that had mostly mercenaries that were sailing south to search for that elusive treasure. They seemed well behaved, for mercenaries.

The last leg of the trip was a long ten days. My boat was part of a contingent heading to Tartus to land and fight the infidels. Or maybe we were the infidels, as it kind of worked both ways. As we approached the coast, sails appeared. A lot of sails, and not shaped like ours, so apparently, we would fight before landing. The slow-motion dance of the two small fleets began. I took a nap, as I knew it would take a long time before anything happened. I don't think my fellow passengers appreciated my lack of concern, but it was a warm sunny day with easy swells.

When I woke up two hours later, I saw an enemy boat close enough to send arrows our way. Taunts and jeers followed from both boats. After more arrows and then a round of sling stones, the boats got closer, then we exchanged ropes with grapples. The boats quickly became entangled, and things were about to get serious. Swordsmen formed ragged lines on each side, readying for when the boats touched. Nobody wanted to dive across open water or swing across on a rope. That scene might be depicted in a movie, but most men preferred a lower risk activity, or at least death by combat rather than drowning. Then the boat hulls slammed into each other as the wood groaned. Men immediately began jumping over, and the melee was on. An enemy I had not met yet swung a sword at my head, so I joined the fracas.

I quickly dispatched a couple of men that took swipes at me. I did not jump across but held my ground on my boat. Several more men on both sides went down. A worthy-looking opponent appeared opposite me, and we dueled. We were both standing and balancing on our respective hull top rails. He was better than anyone else I had battled to this point. My strikes were not touching him, and neither were his taking any of my blood. His sword was a light scimitar, longer than my gladius. He had a dagger in the other hand, where I carried a light Viking axe fashioned with a crazy-looking hand guard. Ugly but effective. His longer sword gave him reach advantage, but my axe kept him off. I doubt he had seen anyone use it the way I did, as more of a shield than an offensive weapon. We both got earnest, then even more intent, yet neither of us could land a blow. Then I geared it up a notch, slightly above the human level. Then he did too. I halted but kept my guard up. He did too, and we both stepped back. I had stopped because of the unnatural noise around us. All the other men from both sides had quit fighting each other and were cheering and betting on the two of us. Perhaps a third of the crew from each side was still standing.

My opponent bowed and said something that sounded like it honored him to meet a worthy opponent. I bowed and repeated something similar. Then we went back to it, again at a speed above normal human motion. I stopped again after five minutes. We were both finally breathing hard, but neither of us could harm the other. I stood a moment, then jammed my blade tip into the hull, did the same with the axe, and bowed toward him. He did the same. I offered him my hand, and we clasped forearms. I did not know it, but I had just found my best friend and traveling companion for more than a decade.

We greeted each other, at first in Latin. I gave him my name, Senecus, and he replied he was Asif al-Safi, of Egypt. We agreed to an immediate truce. I looked around and told my men to give up the fight. They already had. Asif said the same in his language to his crew. That was when I noticed my boat listing a few degrees. The hulls grinding together in the waves had taken a toll on our older vessel.

I told Asif I needed to take stock of our boat and care for the wounded. He nodded assent and said he would do the same. I evaluated the men on my boat and the count came out to about a third alive and unwounded. Several others wounded, a few mortally; the rest were dead. Our captain was alive, but none of his officers survived. Our boat was leaking badly, and I did not think we had enough men to sail and bail or pump enough to save the boat. The captain agreed. I made some plans and decisions in my head, but we did not have many choices.

The flotillas had canceled each other out. All the other boats had sunk during the fight, minus several that fled as soon as it looked like it might be a fair fight. Strategic disengagement and retreat sounded better than abject cowardice. I did not have a problem with cowardice in this case. Better alive than dying from a septic sword wound, drowning, or adrift eating rotten ship food.

The sun was moving down closer to the water when I went to the other side of the boat and spotted Asif. He walked over to me. "Our boat seems in worse shape than yours. I ask if you can deliver us to land before we must swim there."

"I believe we could make such accommodations," he said. "But we have lost our sailing crew during the fight and even our captain is wounded, perhaps mortally. Most of us have little knowledge of sailing, as we were hired in Tartus as mercenaries to protect the coast. We may not easily sail to land unless the currents push us in that direction."

"Our captain still lives, and some of our men not wounded are sailors. I believe we could at least sail your boat in the right direction to deposit both our crews to land."

"Your sailors and our boat. That seems like a natural compromise. However, I am sure you would not be welcome should we go to Tartus. I don't believe they would welcome us there either, as my employer only needed us to man the fleet. It no longer exists, and he is said to punish his troops for military defeats."

"Is there a nearby port where both our crews are welcome?"

"Due west is the island of Cyprus. At the moment, the port is neutral territory. Also, our best opportunity for both crews to either find work or another boat for passage. Is that acceptable?"

"I think so. I don't know of another possibility. So, do we have a deal?"

"Yes, we do. You will be guests aboard our ship until we reach port at Famagosta. Then the men can go about as they wish."

"Good. Any idea how far to port?"

"Should be about a day if the winds are kind."

"I believe we will finish taking care of our dead, then move to your boat. May as well move west, since the sun will lead us in the right direction."

We both took care of our respective boats, then everyone on my boat gathered their belongings, plus quite a few items that I believe they liberated from the newest dearly departed. We moved aboard the other boat. Everyone was too tired, and too grateful to be alive, to cause any problems. Luckily, the voyage should end before the men returned to belligerency.

We untied from the badly listing boat and turned our new floater toward the sun. We raised sails, and the captain and a few men started their duties to get us to Cyprus. When I told the men about our new destination and travel mode, they were happy. Not dying or being enslaved was a good thing. A couple of them had been to Famagosta and told the others it was a decent place. Easy to get hired on another crew to get to the Holy Land or take a boat back home.

Asif and I sat together as the voyage began. "You are quite a fighter," I told him.

"And you as well. The first I have not bested. That should make quite a tale among the men."

"I have not met my match before today either. And yes, by the end of the voyage, they will have us as two war gods fighting to a draw."

"Yes, and perhaps they have some notion of the truth."

I laughed. "I am very sure that I'm not a god."

Asif laughed as well. "Understood, but then not even the gods are gods," he said with an odd look on his face. We never discussed it again, but we had a relationship that was highly respectful of each other that began as soon as we fought.

Asif went to pray as I waited for the first of the stars to appear. The night was uneventful, although two of the wounded died, and we respectfully passed them overboard. No storms troubled us that night. As the sun rose directly behind us, I knew the captain had kept us on the right course.

Asif was praying again as I had a light breakfast and some wine, which was a testament to the poor water quality. I was glad we had brought it over from our boat. We sat and talked through the morning as our ride continued. The wind was not cooperative, so we were still a few hours away. We discussed his religion, my lack of religion, our homes in a general sense, and some past adventures. We also discussed what would happen when we arrived in port. Perhaps the Tartus ruler would want his ship back. None of Asif's men on the boat wanted to return to Tartus or work for the ruler again, so they would either stay with Asif or make their own way. Asif was not their leader officially, but the remaining men would naturally follow him. The men from my boat were mostly undecided about what they would do next.

"Asif, what if we kept some of this crew and the boat and started up a merchant trade? I am already tired of the crusader's life and prefer to see the ports as a trader rather than a fighter."

"My friend, I have similar thoughts. As traders, we would be welcome in most ports, and could see the entire sea without too many fights. Of course, there are always pirates to fend off, so we could still have some fun. I'll ask my men for volunteers."

"I'll do the same. I assume we can find more men in port if needed."

"That should not be a problem as busy as the port is. And sailors are always looking for opportunities."

We saw land that afternoon. Cyprus may have been an island, but it was a big one. The port was ahead, so the captain was better than I thought. We sailed closer, then dropped the sails and rowed in. It was slow, as there were a lot of other boats, but we eventually found an open berth. We got some odd looks from others, as we were obviously a mixed crew of Muslims and Christians, and mostly soldiers.

We carried the wounded to the hospital, then Asif and I talked again to our men. They were free to do whatever they wanted, but we intended to use the boat, or trade it for another, and set up as merchants, traders, or transporters. But we were not interested in hiring out to any martial entities, nor joining in further hostilities on either side. Some men from both groups exited the crew for various reasons, but about two-thirds stayed on. A few days later, we hired a few extra sailors and began a decade of trade, travel, and adventure.

The merchant boat we sailed called at multiple ports between Venice and Constantinople. I saw the Black Sea for the first time. We also did rounds of the Eastern Mediterranean, depending on the cargo being delivered or picked up.

Ports changed constantly from welcoming to menacingly off-limits. Literally in a day's time on some occasions. The politics were rampant, opaque, and constantly changing. Throw in lots of money and trade, dozens of combinations of different nationalities, religions, and races, and it was both a time of great excitement and great confusion. Better to stay sober, stay alert, and adaptable at all times. At least the weather was much better than the North Sea. But storms were storms, and boats here were not much better than the Viking longboats I had sailed a couple of centuries prior.

We encountered many races and religions. I saw descendants of Vikings around the Black Sea area, Italians, Egyptians, Lebanese, Cretes, Turks, Franks, especially in their Outremer countries, sometimes a lone Chinese, and lots of North Africans. When in Muslim-controlled waters and ports, I relied on Asif to get me through any difficulties we encountered, and I did the same for him in Christian-controlled areas.

When we had to fight, which was only once or twice a year over a dozen year span, we fought back-to-back, and let our superior speed and strength win over the attackers, either by straight superiority or by attrition. I did not have to do anything above the level of a highly skilled human, so I did not have to reveal my superhuman abilities. But Asif was easily my match. I never asked him if he was holding back as well, but sometimes I wondered, especially after our first fight. But it was not a conversation I wanted to have, so I let it remain unspoken. We had more fights at sea than on land. Merchant ships at the time could resort to pirating anytime the right opportunity showed up, but over the years, most learned to leave us alone.

Asif and I matched up well. We were about the same size physically. We had a remarkably similar outlook on life. And for whatever reason, we got along well. We had the same interests when traveling; we kept drinking to a minimum, neither of us were interested in prostitutes, and we would rather avoid fighting than start or take part in any violence. This was both resident in our nature and good for business. If a fight resulted in a death or reflected poorly on a local noble, we might be banished from that port for years.

Since we did not go whoring, we found more creative and expensive ways to satisfy our interests in female companionship. We had to cultivate the affections of local women of a certain class, rank, and occupation, over time, and ended up spending both time and money on gifts to continue those relationships. Luckily, we had found two sisters in Sicily that liked us, so that was always a good stopover, especially as we were there several times a year. I also had cultivated a friendship and more with a Frankish widow in Crete, and Asif had found a similar scenario in Tunis, and another in Alexandria. The women in Venice were also lovely, but deadly. Dalliances would almost always result in a glass dagger in the kidneys, a slit throat, and a lifeless swim in a canal that night for those offending the honor of Venetian men. That would not happen to Asif or me, as we'd win those encounters. But because of our natures, we didn't need or want to fight over such petty reasons.

CHAPTER TWENTY-THREE

M ost of our adventures were drama-free since we stayed away from the more problematic romantic entanglements, but we still had fun when we could. In one port, I pulled a good prank on Asif when he got carried away one evening with a beautiful woman. He and I attended a party at a large house in town. Uncharacteristically, we arrived there by transport wagon as we were moving and loading supplies all day before a trip. We both enjoyed the party, but I was becoming bored as the night wore on. As it got late, I went out to the wagon and climbed in back as Asif was still at the party, wooing a lady, and the surroundings seemed safe enough. The two horses received feed bags and had already received water. They seemed content as I pulled some blankets around me and fell asleep. We had been working hard the previous three days getting ready for the trip. Plus the first night out on the water, I usually could not rest, so now was my chance.

I awoke as the wagon was moving and jerking. I peered up through the blankets to see how many robbers I needed to persuade to turn the reins back over to me, but it surprised me to see Asif driving the wagon with one arm, while the other arm held a lady. A particular lady from the party, that because of marriage and local society rules, should not have been in that situation. I sighed and pulled the covers back over my eyes. The wagon stopped sometime later, and I heard Asif and his friend depart. I peeked out and saw he had stopped at the side of a large house, completely dark. Asif and the lady went into the house and did not come out. Once again, I pulled up the covers and fell asleep.

Dawn was breaking when I felt the wagon moving again. Asif was driving the wagon back to the port and was humming happily to himself. After a few minutes, I jumped up behind him and yelled, "Good morning!" He shrieked and jumped forward and off the wagon onto the back of one horse. "Good thing your lady friend wasn't around to hear you shriek like a little girl."

"What? Senecus, what the hell are you doing here?"

"Just along for the joyride. I left the party early to get some rest. Imagine my surprise to find you and the Mrs. driving off to find a love nest."

"Did you see her, who I was with?"

"But of course. Good thing it was me, since anybody else would extort you for money. I'm just going to tease you about how high pitched your voice is in the morning."

"You ass. My voice is not high, it is very manly, all the women remark about its deep timbre."

"Yeah, well, get your squeaky timbre off that horse. We have work to do before leaving port."

I teased him about that episode when the men were not around. I also saw him checking the wagons when we were in other ports of call before driving anyone home after any parties.

Our time on the boat and in the ports passed well, and too quickly. Both Asif and I enjoyed life; it was perhaps the most enjoyable time I had until I met Hia. Travel was good, and we had plenty of trade to keep things busy and profitable. We had loyal customers and a great and experienced crew. Of course, it could not last.

The storm that caught us was ugly. Gale winds from the east blew us well off course. These storms were not that unusual, and it should have dissipated in a couple of hours. It lasted a day and a night instead, and we lost two crew overboard during the storm. The rest of us hung on to whatever we could, while the captain and helmsman, with the help of others to spell them, manned the rudder to minimize taking waves broadside. Lightning was all around, but the boat was never hit. It was a miserable experience for everyone. The men were not doing well due to fear of drowning, being constantly wet, and the inability to eat or drink. Then it got worse as the storm flung us against the coastline and we could not avoid the rocky shore, where the ship broke apart. Asif was at the bow, trying to help the sailors on that end of the boat, and I was on the stern. There was not much we could do but try to keep them together in a group as the boat foundered. The bow exploded into wooden pieces as we hit a major rock dead center. That flung me and all the crew in the back forward onto our faces, then the water took us.

I grabbed the two men nearest me and started swimming toward the shore. Once I got them on the beach, I headed back out toward the larger pieces of the boat. I grabbed two more sailors and hauled them to the beach. After that, I found no one else or the remains of the boat. The ship, now a small raft of broken wood, had moved on. I was not sure whether to stay with the men on the beach or start walking and possibly rescue others as they floated in from the sea. I put the four men together, gave them part of a sail for shelter, and told them to stay and wait for me to get back as I would try to find the others. The wind was with me as I walked down the beach, stopping occasionally to see if anything was floating in. I found pieces of the boat and an occasional body. As I walked, the storm lessened, yet there were no signs of Asif or any survivors. It was now lighter, so the sun was somewhere above the clouds. I estimated I was a few hours away from where I had first come ashore so I turned back.

More bodies had washed ashore; I knew them all, but there was no Asif. Some hours later, I was back to where I had started and could see the rocks further down the coastline where the boat had foundered. The men I had left were not on the beach and there was no sign of them. I could see footprints in places, and they were leading in the opposite direction I had just arrived from. I followed them toward a large rock outcrop ahead. It was roughly in line with the offshore rocks we had smashed into. I climbed the rocks and about ten meters up, I scrambled over the top. I saw a small bay cut into the coastline ahead with several boats at anchor along the shore, more than a kilometer away. I wished we had known about the bay and could have reached it before hitting the rocks. Wishes were not doing me any good, however. There seemed to be a disturbance just inland from the boats. I had a feeling these were slavers or pirates, and the crewmen I had rescued were part of the disturbance. Based on the number of boats, they highly outnumbered me, and I would have to be careful.

As I began climbing down, I saw a familiar color, as Asif's headscarf was an unusual shade of blue. He was being mobbed by the pirates. There were probably twenty dead or wounded around him, and the mob had learned to stay out of sword range. But a hundred more were shooting arrows, slinging stones, and throwing short spears at him. Asif went down, and the mob swarmed him, hacking with swords. I was too far away to help. My rage told me to run and attack the mob and kill as many as possible before getting killed. My survival instinct told me that was a bad idea. I realized with brutal reality that Asif was already dead, and that I would go down there later and kill every pirate on that beach. I doubted the pirates would sail off before dark, as they had lots of comrades to bury. After dark, I would sneak into the camp and start my vengeance.

The mob dispersed and began dragging bodies inland and hastily digging graves in the sand. They piled Asif's body and our shipmates just outside of camp without a burial. I counted six bodies besides Asif. He must have rescued two men, and while I was searching in the opposite direction, found the four other men and then gotten caught by the pirates. Or they had gone to the camp hoping to negotiate passage with the pirates.

Once dark, I began walking toward camp. There were a few sentries, but most of the camp was having a meal. An hour later I began killing sentries. I moved in a semicircle around the camp, slitting throats along the way. The rest of the camp began bedding down in tents. I went to each tent and quietly killed the inhabitants. The sand under tent after tent turned red in the darkness until the whole place stank of blood. I only had a few tents left to go before I got sloppy. Or maybe I was looking for a fight. I killed one man rather loudly and the remaining tents began stirring and shouts rang out. When nobody answered, I guess they knew something was wrong. Men came out of the tents with weapons, and they died rather quickly.

The entire camp was now dead, except for a few much younger men still on the boats; I assume they were sentries to keep a rival from stealing their boats at night. I thought about killing them as well, but decided I was tired of blood. Plus, I could use them to crew a boat to get me away from this place.

I called out to them to surrender. They jumped down into a small group. Several wanted to fight when they saw only me. They made a mistake by betting their life against mine. Six I left alive and tied up, then I ransacked the camp and took everything of value. I did not need it but did not want to leave anything behind for other pirates. Asif had a few important possessions on him before his murder, so I searched for and found those in tent that likely belonged to one of the pirate captains.

I went to my six captives, untied them, and forced them to bury our six men in the sand. They then carried Asif's body to the boat that I had picked out to sail away from the cursed place. We boarded, then I tied them back up for a while. I went back into camp and gathered firebrands, to set fires on all the other boats. Then I jumped on my new boat, and we pushed off to get away from the boats just catching fire. I wondered what the first people to stumble upon the camp would think. A hundred bodies, mostly killed in their tents, and five boats burned. They might attribute it to a rival pirate or something supernatural. I would not think of it further for many centuries.

Not far down the coast, I saw three islands that should be easy to sail to. In an hour, we arrived, and I needed to decide which island to land on. The westernmost was a tall island, and the central and eastern islands were much lower and flatter. There were signs of habitation on the center island, with small boats, probably fishing vessels, anchored on the eastern island. The western island was difficult to land on because of its rocky coastline, but it was the choice for my task. I gave my new sailors orders and to the western island we went. The small island group is now called the Chafarinas Islands, very close to the Moroccan shore at the Algerian border, and the westernmost island now bears the name of Isle del Congreso. Shortly, we arrived and waded ashore. I tied them up once again, not taking any chances they would take the boat.

I carried Asif's body wrapped in a shroud made of sailcloth. Up we went to the rocky ridge at the highest point of the island, on the western side. There was a hollow spot in the rock near the base of the ridge. I enlarged the hollow as best I could with the tools I had brought from the boat. I placed Asif's body in the makeshift tomb, then dragged a large flat rock from a hundred feet away. It made a decent cover for the tomb.

I knew some Roman and Christian lines of prayer, but my heart was not in either of those places any longer. I paused and thought about prayers I had heard Asif recite over the years. I remembered a few lines he had interpreted for me, and while insufficient, they would have to do. I said them out loud as I pushed the cover stone in place. I put a few more rocks to cover the spot to make it look more like a natural rockfall.

Asif had to be buried as soon as possible, according to his religion. But I planned to return after contacting his family and turn over his remains to them, since it was the right thing to do. He rarely talked about them, but he came from means, and occasionally wrote letters that he dropped off when we were in Alexandria. I was certain they would like to recover and rebury him in his home country according to their customs.

I climbed back down, untied my sailors, and we pushed off the island. I set the course for the northeast. It should take a few days, depending on the wind, but my next planned stop was Barcelona. I stayed off the coast of southern Spain as I did not want to get too close to land. Muslims controlled the coast, but the real problem was the slavers. The slavers were nondenominational in Spain; south they were more associated with the Muslims, north they were more associated with the Christians. I needed to stay away from all of them.

We reached the area near Barcelona without incident. I grounded the boat at night onto a small sandy beach west of the town. The sailors looked nervous, as I suppose they thought I would now kill them. I tied their hands and sent them off the boat. They could wander wherever they wanted to go. Of course, their options were limited. To the right was the Christian city sacked by Muslims, with many people killed or carried off as slaves. They would not be welcome there as Muslims, and even worse as pirates. To the left were lots of slaver operations. Even as Muslims, they would be enslaved. Straight ahead was the interior, with little habitation, high heat, and little water. But their lot was to make their own choice now, and I would not directly add six more young men to my tally of death.

After I sent them off, I damaged the boat enough to make it unusable so they could not use it to escape, then began walking toward Barcelona. I did not know the town well, but I knew enough that I could find shelter and supplies there. My cover story was that I was a crusader shipwrecked while returning home. That would explain the loot I needed to exchange for supplies. From Barcelona, I could sail further north and east along the coast to Marseille, then walk home. Or I could ride a horse across the Pyrenees and then France for home. I would get news in Barcelona and decide the route from there, based on who was raiding and killing at present, and in which direction any active armies were traveling.

Barcelona looked better than the last time I had been in port, but it had not yet recovered from the attack by Almanzor. I had brought in a large sack the most valuable of the items from the pirate camp. I always kept gold and jewels sewn into my clothing but did not want to use them yet. It was going to be a long way back home and I might need those resources. I went to the market and began bartering and got all the supplies and clothes I would need. I converted the leftover loot, such as silver chalices, into more manageable gold coins. Based on my story, all the merchants thought they were cheating a dumb and desperate crusader. But I didn't care that they fleeced me for the value of my goods. I just wanted to get rid of the pirate spoils as quickly as possible.

I also bought some quills, ink, vellum, and candles, as I wanted to write Asif's family a letter. With what must have been foresight, I wrote a brief letter to the family describing what had happened before leaving Barcelona. I did not know the name of the burial island at the time, so I couldn't direct them to his makeshift tomb. I addressed the letter to his family name and the city where Asif had told me they lived near Alexandria. Several gold pieces I gave to the most reputable trader in town. I hoped that would get the letter to its destination.

The land route between Barcelona and Toulouse seemed free of conflict. I decided to make the journey and see the Pyrenees for the first time in many years. I went to the stables and bought a horse and tack, then loaded up and started north the next morning. The remains of the Roman roads looked familiar, and I was looking forward to mountains and clear streams during my week of travel to Toulouse. My time was mostly horse-dependent, as I could travel long distances without stopping even in poor weather, but the horse could not. The towns along the way were small and sparse, but I should be able to get lodging most nights. It was more important for the horse than me.

The early part of the trip was easy. A decent road followed the river and was level. Then the road started climbing into the mountains. As I approached the town of Puigcerda, a familiar sensation began creeping into my body. The usual sweating, pain, and headaches. I would not be going to Toulouse after all. I had in my supplies a waterproof leather bag, and everything I would need to protect my assets during my long sleep, so I just needed a likely place to spend my multi-decade nap. There were caves about, and the larger towns had crypts at the larger churches, but I was not sure I had time to find an acceptable one on such short notice.

To my favor, there were a few new crypts that would work for my hibernation. I ate a last meal, then sold the horse and supplies I did not need. Later that night, I found a likely crypt among those available, opened it, and crawled inside with my bag of valuables. If my luck held, I would lie undisturbed and wake up in a few decades. At least Asif's family had been notified, assuming the letter had gotten through. Unfortunately, by the time I awoke, his family would have passed away. I could not guide them to recover his body, but at least I had given him a proper burial.

I woke up in my normal state with my clothes ruined. From a crack in the crypt's corner, I could tell it was still daylight. As soon as it was dark, I kicked the slab loose and rolled out with my bag. I pulled a shirt and pants from the bag and got dressed. The weather was nice and felt like early summer. No idea what year it was. But I still had plenty of funds to get a horse and finish my trip to Toulouse.

I ended up there just over a week later. I took a slight detour on the next northern leg of the journey and arrived at Tours. Then Paris, but I did not stay there as it was too populated for my tastes. I finally crossed Belgium and made it to Holland, then visited one of my caches of wealth I had secreted in several spots. A behavior as old as humankind based on the many buried caches discovered over the years.

I planned to purchase my way into a new identity and profession. After the past dozen years, I felt much more comfortable as a merchant or trader. And I had finally learned to sail, but I would not visit the Mediterranean again for many years.

The sun was rising over the Arizona mesa as I finished my remembrances. I went back to the casino hotel to get my bag and check out, then drove back to the airport by myself, as everyone else had already departed. I really enjoyed thinking about those early years before the pirates killed Asif and the crew, but now I just felt a pervasive sense of loss settling in again.

Chapter Twenty-Four

F inding Odin was something I had been thinking about for a while. I spent some time looking up how others had tried to locate or summon him, using everything from the internet to old texts from the late Middle Ages. Who was he, where did he appear, and was there any pattern? A god of war and a god of poetry, possibly a god of healing. And he occasionally helped humans, not only easing the passing of dying soldiers but also providing them a heaven. Complicated fellow. An entity worshipped by much of Northern Europe at one time, centuries before Rome came to Gaul. All the evidence pointed to Wodin, now called Odin, as a creature that was ancient, complex, and powerful. Likely making him narcissistic and dangerous, but then the label of god implied that.

My experience dealing with a being on that level was essentially nil. I had personal misgivings of finding and dealing with Odin. I decided I should talk to Kal for advice before contacting Odin, so I drove out to the nearest private forest, walked into the dark, and kept going until I could not hear any traffic or other human noise. I sat and concentrated until I felt a presence nearby. A very large presence with a familiar aura.

"Hey Kal, thanks for coming on such short notice."

"Not a problem. I appreciate you considering the time zones and not bringing me over at an inconvenient time. Also appreciate the location. Woods at night are good, although these trees and land are very young."

"This new polder land was the closest forest I could get to. So not that many years ago, were we here, we would be standing on the bottom of a shallow sea."

"Yes, it was quite a transformation. We watched this undertaking and appreciated how the hairless in this region were doing something positive and working together. It does not happen very often."

"Destruction is more our thing."

"Yes. Now, how can we proceed to your business?"

"Ah, to the point. I am beginning my efforts to contact Odin per your suggestion. But I feel that I'm competing above my normal weight class. I would like to get some background before proceeding."

Kal thought for a moment. "I believe this concerns whether you feel fully competent to converse with a nearly omnipotent being and succeed?"

"Uh, something like that."

"He may be more relatable than you expect. But wisely, you have misgivings about dealing with him. Know that he will be civil to a fault unless you give offense. If you act as a proper gentleman, then you should not have any problems. Do not be afraid to show humor, or even be brash, but he'll brook neither insults nor fawning."

"I can do that. There might be some smartass slip though, but I'll try to control it. Is there any general background I should know?"

"Odin has a long and varied history. However, for your purpose I can give you some background that will be useful for asking him the right questions. It may also give you a better understanding of what you are dealing with."

"Thanks, I'll be taking notes in my head."

"Odin can travel the links. Huginn and Muninn, typically seen as ravens, assist in time and place travel by guiding him or others through the layers. They can't get lost because they are entangled with each other. Odin opens the way, and one raven enters and travels. It remembers the journey, and can always return to its entangled companion, so they never lose their way. Thus, by sending them through the links, Odin can know most anything he strives for in any place-time. Or he can travel to a place-time himself. As all three are gifted shape shifters, they blend in well regardless of their destination. Very successful at spying, and a most dangerous opponent, or gifted ally. Those powers have given rise to powerful myths of his abilities, and most of them are true."

"What are his interests? Anything there I can use for a conversation?"

"Odin is always Odin's primary allegiance. You may know the stories and myths of who he is, but you will need to dig deeper. He may be directly involved in wars and conflict, but he also champions healing and poetry."

"Sounds like he is a complicated being."

"Yes, like most of the old beings. His is a vast history, and he has been involved in everything that has happened in the area between the Mediterranean and the North Pole for the past twenty thousand years. If what you want coincides with his interests, then you may have an ally."

"Does he have a place where he spends most of his time, or is it possible he lives in the links?"

"A most interesting question. We have associated Odin with sites mostly in Northern Europe, but it is possible he could dwell mostly in the links. Even in the links, however, he would be readily available to enter our place-time whenever he sees fit."

"That does not narrow it down much. Could take a while to find him unless he wants to be found."

"If it was easy, anyone could do it."

"Then I will concentrate on finding Odin. Once I pass the leprechaun, I turn left at the unicorn, then knock three times on the enchanted door?"

"You could try that. But the unicorn is insolent and will not let you pass. I believe you can find the way, regardless."

"I thank you for your time and help."

"You are welcome. But it was not my time spent, as I chose not to use time for this visit. This was your time."

"Someday we need to have a long talk about what time really is."

"I look forward to it. If only there was time." He gave a strange sound that passed for laughter. Then he disappeared.

I thought about all that Kal said. It wasn't terribly helpful for the initial contact, but it gave me some great background. Time to stop procrastinating, since finding Odin would require careful thought and planning. After further contemplation, plus chasing a few squirrels around in my head, I concluded I would not find Odin. I would have to put myself in a likely place and let him find me. There were lots of places scattered around Europe that were associated with him, so I needed to find one satisfying several criteria important to him and set up camp until he showed.

Since he was the god of war, an existing conflict would be ideal. Except there wasn't an ongoing battle in the area, and if there was, I didn't like the idea of getting blown up. But there were lots of old battlefields. Odin oversaw half of Valhalla, so dead and dying soldiers were in his purview. Several large battlefield cemeteries were within driving distance, thanks to WWI and WWII. Oak trees were an important symbol for Odin; some cemeteries were mostly treeless, but others had oak trees on site. The relationship between Odin and poetry was interesting, and there was a famous poem about the poppies in the Flanders fields in WWI. Estimates of casualties listed a million men killed, wounded, or gone missing there. Perhaps one of the few positives produced from that battlefield was a memorable poem. Cemeteries with oak trees in that vicinity seemed a likely place to start.

I decided the best option was to research some sites, then drive down and see which place felt right. A map of potential sites revealed once again how bad WWI had been. Cemeteries with forty to fifty thousand graves each. Many, many smaller cemeteries, and even one for the Chinese. I did not realize the British had brought in that many to help with the war effort. The sheer numbers of dead soldiers and civilians were staggering. But as morbid as it felt, I needed to go there and try to find Odin.

I drove south among the immense flow of truck traffic, now filling the highways to Belgium. It was a cold and miserable night when I found the cemetery. The wind was pushing the heavy clouds off the ocean, which were then mean-spiritedly shedding mist on all things below, including me. I was sitting in a portable camp chair with a jacket and hat on. Not at all suspicious, since I was in a cemetery after midnight. The ugly wind was whipping at the last of the leaves gamely clinging to the large oak trees.

Military cemetery, oak trees, crappy night weather, and the site of a famous poem; it seemed an excellent combination to find an ornery god. I didn't know my chances, but I hoped he would show up sooner rather than later. I did not have that many nights left before I needed to head back to America. The wind finally did something right and blew away all the dark clouds, bellies laden with sleet. A three-quarter moon showed up and quickly illuminated the headstones with a dim glow.

I had a large bottle of mead. Figured it couldn't hurt, and better than bringing a ratty old noose and hanging it in the nearby oak tree. Or a bag of corn for the ravens. In America, I would have started a fire and burned some cedar, sage, or wax myrtle, depending on which region I was in, since those were supposed to bring in the spirits. With Odin, I didn't know what would work or why. But I still had faith that he would find me and an hour later, he did.

In front of me, a strange line of dusky white appeared about six feet horizontal to the ground. Then two slashes of the same color light to the ground, parallel to each other and attached to the ends of the first line. Another line at the bottom by the ground created a door frame made of nothing but light. The rectangle of night vanished, and from the open door stepped a man.

"You looking for me?" he asked gruffly as he peered around the cemetery. "Damn, it's a beautiful night. You gonna share that bottle?"

I just nodded and stood up, then picked up the bottle. He gestured toward the door of light and I stepped through. He followed, and the door popped out of existence. Now we were standing in what looked like a small village with stone houses. The house directly in front of us was large, but not opulent. Smoke was rising from several chimneys. He opened the door of the house and gestured for me to enter. There was a nice but plain wooden table with nothing on it, and no chairs. He went to the other side of the table and stood facing me. I sat the bottle on the table between us.

Odin was not what I imagined. A large man with long reddish hair with grey streaks. Jeans, leather boots, and a short, leather vest. A leather eyepatch that also helped hold his long hair back. His other eye was a piercing blue, but also changed to green or grey. Maybe it depended on his mood, or was a distraction, so you didn't notice the large knife in his hand hanging down his side, almost out of sight. Basically, he looked like a member of a biker gang I had seen in Finland. I also thought I did not know what he really looked like, since he likely had more physical appearances than taste buds.

"Hah, this isn't up to your expectations of a god, is it?"

"Not really. But when I finally meet one, I'll let him know."

"Hah again. You are an impertinent shit. How did you live so long with that mouth?"

"I usually keep it closed. But I surmise there are some people I'd do better to go straight at. Subservience is for dogs."

"Quite right. And well met. Just don't piss me off too much. I have a bad habit of setting my wolves on people that get too mouthy."

"Well met and I'll behave. But I do like wolf meat. Shame it takes so long to marinate it to get it tender."

He took a long swig of the mead as he looked at me with that eye that continued to change colors. I kept an eye on his knife, too. I felt like he was looking at me and through me until he finally nodded. "You'll do." I didn't know what that meant. I guess I had passed the first test.

"Now to business," he said. "Would you rather be Thor or Loki?"

"Well, I have never been asked that before. Seems they might want to keep their own selves, rather than me taking one of them."

"There is no Thor or Loki. Or rather, there have been several of each. Most that journey here choose to be one or the other."

He held out his hands. The knife became a hammer. In his other hand was a large milky crystal, swirling with blues, greens, and greys, oddly like those in his eye.

"This is Thor, the hammer. Actually, it is Mjollnir, and the one who wields it becomes Thor for a time. Men like you come to take it and use its strength, typically to beat down their problems or enemies. Loki, the crystal, is for other kinds of men that want to outsmart and confuse their enemies, then psychically beat them down. Which is it for you?"

"Thanks, but I'll pass on both. I think the cost for either might be more than I'm willing to pay."

"Ah, a smart one, finally. Few think to even ask about the costs. Even fewer decline the offers."

"If I had taken one, would it have bound me to you?"

"No, you'd keep your free will. But both always come back to me, in time. The hammer to make you a Thor would have given you great physical powers to defeat your enemies, but in your case, it would have shortened your life by centuries. The crystal to make you Loki would have given you unique powers to outwit your enemies. You'd be a shapeshifter, invisible, or whatever form you'd want, while planting thoughts in the minds around you. But the price there is early onset dementia, again by several centuries."

"Anybody ever want both?"

"Nobody ever had the balls to ask. Most men are so greedy that they would take one as quickly as they saw it and head back to be a hero."

"Never had much desire to be a hero. All that fame, power, women, ad campaigns, television appearances. None of which I want."

CHAPTER TWENTY-FIVE

"What do you want, now that you have refused my deadly gifts?" Odin asked.

"I'd like to have a conversation with you."

"Now that is a request I've never had before. You want nothing other than words? Or do you want to talk me into helping you or your people?"

"I don't think I could talk you into anything you did not want to do. This is more of a conversation about what ifs. If I move against my enemies, what counter moves might I expect? When they move against me, what would they expect me to do? Without becoming Thor or Loki, I need to be both strong enough to take them on, but smart enough to know when and how to battle without telegraphing it."

"You need a strategy consultation, then. And you think I can help with that?"

"I believe so. Since you travel the links, and Huginn and Muninn can go anywhere and anywhen, I think you would be the best to consult about logical strategies. And more important, the sideways moves."

"I see you are well informed. And wise, since sideways usually wins."

"Before I ask more, what is the price of my consult?"

He thought for a moment. "This is a most unusual request. I think the price should be high. You will dine with me and tell me your story. As we finish the meal, we will discuss the how and when of your plans and countermeasures. Is that acceptable?"

"Yes. I thank you for your hospitality and for welcoming me as a guest."

"Hah! Making sure you can leave unharmed by invoking the guest right. Good. You will be one worth watching. Let us eat."

He picked up the bottle, turned and walked through the doorway that was behind him, and I followed. As he walked, he shortened nearly a foot and his clothes turned into business casual. His hair shortened and turned a steel grey. His face did not change. A feast hall was before us. He tossed Thor and Loki on the dining table and set the bottle down. The table was already set up with plenty of food for two.

We sat across from each other. Two ravens flew in and perched on the back of his chair on either side of his head. Their eyes had the same swirling colors as Odin's eye, while the eyepatch on the other side had disappeared and the socket contained a solid white crystal. He spoke a few words to each bird and tossed them a chicken leg. They both flew away.

"The famous raven twins?"

"Yes. They go to look for your past paths, and your most likely path in the now. I will hear of both, then I will have a better idea of how to counsel you. They will also follow several of the most likely, and several less likely, future streams. Those I won't tell you about, as it's not my place. I have standards, plus that pisses off Fate and Destiny. I don't want to get those girls riled up again. They hold a grudge."

We ate as I told him my story. He did not ask many questions. I assumed the H&M raven twins would give him what he needed, anyway. I think the talking and eating was part of the social contract. He provided the food, and I provided the entertainment. After half an hour, the ravens flew back in. Each got another chicken leg. No wonder they were so big. Lots of eye color swirling going on amongst the three of them, but no talking. He looked at me and laughed out loud. Not sure what that was about. The strange conversation continued another thirty seconds.

"Damn, son, you really have some balls."

Again, no idea what he was referring to.

He grew somber. Then he jerked his head up at me and slammed his drink on the table. He did not look angry, just surprised. He settled back. The birds finished, then hopped onto the table. They had picked the chicken legs clean, so they started on the grapes. These guys were going to be the size of turkeys at the rate they were eating.

"Well, this has been the most interesting dinner I have had in a while. My colleagues have told quite a tale. None of which I can tell you, of course. Other than you have some surprises coming."

"Surprises are always good. They keep you thinking and moving."

"Be careful what you wish for. Some of these you might come to regret. The other finding is what I have suspected lately: the gods are moving again. You have made and will make some powerful friends and terrible enemies. Hmm, I need to make some preparations myself."

"I heard something else that may be of interest. Just a vague rumor, but that something is moving on a larger scale than just Earth. And I know things are moving in the future of humans that are affecting the present."

He looked at me sharply. Both birds immediately flew off.

"I have already heard some of these rumors and I will find out more shortly. If this is a regional space issue, rather than just planetary, we will all need to prepare to give the best odds of survival. Meanwhile, you need to practice more on your slant and traveling through the links. Might be the only path that saves you." He winked, or maybe not. It was hard to tell, since he only had one eye. But I took his message seriously. "Now, let us discuss strategy, as well as how to protect your people. Always take care of them better than you take care of yourself. After all, you are dragging them into the storm."

"Good, I need to establish their safety so I can concentrate on the battle."

He nodded. "And you need to know how to move sideways, and through other dimensions. Always keep them guessing. How do you feel about becoming female?"

"What?"

He laughed. "Never stop considering alternatives to current reality. If turning female and becoming pregnant helps your cause, you must do it. Kick reality in the balls and swerve sideways, keep moving, and you stand a much better chance of surviving. Survive, and you may get to protect your people. Become adept at slant and traveling the linkages, as that will keep you ahead of your enemies. That is the strategy I counsel."

"I think I get it."

"Get it or get dead. And maybe get your people dead too. Of course, you will need to move so fast and so oddly across time and space, you may not know the difference. But it will be a hell of a ride."

The ravens flew back in and landed on his chair back. They all shared that weird eye thing again. They finished, and Odin leaned back in his chair and sighed. He stared at me for half a minute.

"The linkage network is like a four-dimensional infinite spider web. The more movement and the larger the traveler or number of travelers, the more it resonates with a song as old as the universe. You need millennia of experience to interpret even a part of that song. Right now, the song is both warning us of the 'what might be' and resonating with a call to gather among our enemies. And not just on this planet. We had best get to your inquiries quickly, as you need preparation."

"OK, what is the best strategy to protect my people?"

"You should already know that no physical place is impregnable. Thousands of years of mistakes should have taught that lesson by now. You can defend a place, but it is better not to be at that place when the enemy arrives.

Keep moving and go everywhere sideways and through illogical paths. Not if, but when, they catch up to you, have multiple exit options. Running is better than fighting if done properly. But a people need their home. So eventually you need a place, or better yet, several places, for them to be. Again, defend it through both space and time, and keep everyone flexible enough to drop everything at a moment's notice and run."

"Seems like a good plan."

"Usually is. Last thing. In your reality, always think three dimensionally. Most of you have enough trouble with two dimensions. Add in time for another dimension, then you can really set up defenses and escape routes that don't end up ambushes."

"Thanks. It makes sense except for the time defense, and I got a guy, or well, a Kal, to help with that."

"Use him well, there is not a better defensive mind on the planet."

"I had an unrelated question, though. How do you gain knowledge by hanging yourself?"

"Hanging solves nothing, gives no insight. You just get dead unless you are truly immortal. Not much good unless your enemy thinks it is some magical portal and does it to gain an edge. Works for me as I then have one less dumb bastard to worry about, which is always a good thing. But to your question, hanging does not kill me, but it forces me to focus. Also gives the twins some time off to do their own research. Mostly a win-win, except for the tree. It almost always dies after I hang myself on it."

"OK, thanks, I will refrain from swinging in the trees."

"That would be best. And goodnight to you," he said, while moving his hands oddly. Then he kicked me in the chest, and I went falling backwards into the door he had just conjured. And fell right into my chair in the cemetery. Audition was over, I guess.

I grabbed my things and walked to the car as I had a long drive back to Amsterdam. At least the truck traffic would be light at this time of the morning. That is when I realized it was still the same time as before Odin had showed up. Our little talk had not used up any time in my reality. Another neat trick, and perhaps one perk of being a god.

I drove back to Amsterdam, stopping only to get coffee. My music was pleasant and helped pass the time. The rolling hills and hedgerows gradually gave way to flatter green fields, especially as I traveled north and crossed the rivers. I was just happy to have gotten past my first god meeting. And I only got kicked once.

I was feeling chipper for the rest of the evening. Then morning came and threw my optimism in the toilet. Michael called and asked if I could join a conference call with Elias. A minute later, I was on the line with them both.

"Sen, glad you could make it. We received more information on our wayward Wendigos, and it looks like trouble." Elias said.

"Good morning, or afternoon, to you too, Elias. What kind of trouble?" I asked.

"The pack we took down wasn't out on a random ramble. They were sent, or goaded, into leaving Mexico and settling in Phoenix."

"My questions are, who and why?"

"The who seems to be the same amorphous enemy stirring up things all over, like your recent issues in the Netherlands. The why is that the Uya were to hit Phoenix and kill and eat as many as possible and be real public while doing so. Imagine what would happen if they were openly eating their way through the white suburbs."

"Man, that would set off the gun toters and they would shoot just about anything."

"Not just anything. Specifically, any Hispanics in town, especially Mexican immigrants, not that the gun toters would stop to ask."

"So, the Uya attack wealthy whites, provoking the fifty percent of the virally affected into open violence. Race Wars 101."

"What virus?" Elias and Michael asked at the same time.

"Uh, well, I suppose with all the excitement lately, I forgot to tell you about a new friend. He's highly placed but doesn't really exist. The Sky Lords, the future humans meddling with us, slipped us a virus a few millennia back. Not the microbiome vampire one, but something different that they are using to manipulate humans into tribalism and violence, including using white nationalism as a motivator."

The phone was quiet for a moment. I decided to get ahead of the accusatory silence.

"Obviously, the Uya would have set off a race war in Arizona, likely spreading it elsewhere. It was a setup for a beta war. Michael, I owe you an explanation, which we can start in a few minutes. But shoot, I just realized those Uya disappeared without a trace. That could get a lot of attention from the other side if they wonder what happened to their pet monsters."

Elias came back on. "That was the other part we have heard. They have attributed the Uya takedown to you. The other side is about to issue an all-points bulletin to eliminate you."

"No good deed stays good, I guess. I'll need to work on Farm security."

For the first time, Michael spoke up. "We can assist with that, as we had already begun discussions on that topic before calling you. Now, we probably should discuss the background you just mentioned. Elias, you can sign off."

"Actually, Michael, might be better to have Elias stay on, since this falls in his jurisdiction in North America."

"OK, Elias, stay with us. Sen, please begin. This should be good."

I told them the basic story of meeting Kal and summarized our conversations. I didn't give them all the details, nor my slant efforts or meeting Odin. When I finished, the phone stayed silent.

"You guys still there?"

"Yes, I was sending text orders to all my people regarding the new threat pattern. I hope we can recognize it as it begins, and perhaps negate it before it explodes, at least in the places we monitor. I believe we are now seeing the first salvo in attempts at open war. Sen, anything else we need to know?"

"Not that I can think of on that topic. Just for fun, though, I also got to meet Odin. I'm using him as a consultant on Farm security."

I thought I heard Elias swear in Spanish. Michael finally chuckled. "Of course, you are. He is the best, so I can support your choice. However, Sen, please take extra precautions for yourself. I believe the other side will act swiftly to revenge their loss in America."

"I'll try. I still think the best plan is to get Caius, as he's likely the source of problems in Europe, and the most likely party to execute any contracts on my head."

"I agree with that. Let's all keep alert. Good day, gentlemen."

CHAPTER TWENTY-SIX

Caius

I was a monster and had been one for a long time. However, I thoroughly loved and embraced my monsterhood. I was the most benevolent and compassionate vampire that I knew, as I did more good than harm through the centuries. And now, with modern technology and a willingness to meet the needs of the community, I have increased my good deeds. I, or rather my shell companies, operate homeless shelters, support youth groups, sponsor community sports teams, and give out scholarships to deserving students. Each year, I improve thousands of young lives.

Follow up surveys I commission show these improvements last through the years and even into later generations. The young people in my organizations average higher secondary school retention rates, higher college attendance rates, and better pay through age thirty, as compared to similar control groups. Yes, I make a positive impact on those young lives. I use my computer programs to keep track of everyone's progress through the system. An added benefit for me is that I can carefully vet and choose the children in these programs that have no close family. That results in less risk to me when I eat the ones that seem the tastiest.

My only price, and such a small one in comparison for all the benefits I provide, is that a few of them each year become my dinner. Their sacrifice ensures that thousands of others have better lives. That was how it had to be in this society we live in, as it is all about balance in the world. Thousands of better lives traded for a few dozen walking dinners. Anyone will agree that proves my good deeds far outweigh my appetite. Overall, I am quite proud of my system.

The old days were easier. The Nazi school at Vogelsang, especially, had allowed me to feed on young ones at will. I never felt bad about that, as I considered that for every Hitler youth I ate there would be one less Nazi officer in the war. Plus, I knew that many of them would soon be dead because of Hitler's insatiable need for cannon fodder. In a way I was doing them a favor, as poaching them at school kept them from enduring the horrors of war.

I smiled as I remembered those WWII years also provided nearly unlimited hunting opportunities everywhere in Europe. Free-range young humans were abundant, with little to no oversight by the authorities. I have evolved since but hunting those young innocents through the streets and fields before catching and devouring them was simply divine.

Oh, I easily lose track of my thoughts when thinking of my lovely dinners over the years. Typically, when I have a young person as a meal, their whole body is trying to jerk away from my teeth, while usually emanating those cute little mewling noises. Then, biting into that live muscle is so exhilarating. It is still quivering as I chew into it, spasming in my mouth and shooting out tiny spurts of blood. I could sometimes feel those muscle convulsions all the way down my esophagus. Utterly thrilling, especially as it still jumps and contracts in my stomach. Perhaps that is as close as I'll ever get to what a pregnant woman feels when her baby kicks.

I'm sure my current therapist would make something sexual out of that statement. Perhaps I would ask her before I ate her. I only keep them for two years before killing them and hiring another. That was one way they had almost caught me. Too many missing therapists associated with one local client. I realized I had to break that pattern, so I always choose the next one at least a hundred kilometers away from the last one. The same type of tracking technology that made it easier to find my young meals also worked against me, aiding the authorities searching for the missing therapists. But I had adjusted, as one must, to survive.

I lay back down with my new partner. There was so much nonsense put out from Hollywood about vampires, and the one truth they missed was that our sex drive was extremely low. We truly only lusted after power, wealth, and raw bloody meat. Blood as well, but only when we were newly turned and needed a quick fix. We take lovers rarely, as we rarely need nor desire sex. Procreation in the traditional manner is not possible, and the virus completely rewired all our pleasure centers in the brain. Nor did I understand the human obsession with gender as related to sex. A body was a body, whether you had sex with it, killed and ate it, or both. But the "both" was a real treat, and in that case, it is truly hard to separate sex and food.

I had only recently taken Adriaan after a hundred-year hiatus just to have someone for a time, possibly as an outlet for my increased stress. Once-a-century lovers were interchangeable and rarely lasted long. I could think of a dozen over the past thousand years, half of them men and half women. Their shelf life was limited, as I always killed them after a few weeks. I turned them, enjoyed them, then reveled in their suffering during the excruciating torture inflicted. I even enjoyed the bittersweet pain in my head when I finally killed them. The best of them I ate to death.

Yes, it was likely that Adriaan was helping to relieve my stress. Losing all the Church contacts was a terrible setback. Ninety percent of our assets were gone, eliminated by Michael. The few left were worthless, as they were more frightened of Michael than me. Centuries of work were now undone, and here we were with no Church assets.

My opinion, which I kept to myself, was the Sky Lords had gotten sloppy by ordering us to throw obscene amounts of money at new recruits to buy their loyalty. In my experience, all that money without the proper threat basis just feeds the narcissism of the recruit. That's bad because a narcissist without restraints will never believe they will be caught or punished, including by us, so they get stupid and take risks. All master vampires are narcissists, so I am sure I am right about that. The only bright spot was Russia and its Church that we had been diligently working on the past three decades. Highly malleable and under our influence in so short a time. But again, I worried about the amount of money flowing there without threats or blackmail backups. Too much money, and not nearly enough killing, could lead to problems; yet so far it was working, but only in that country.

I preferred the tried-and-true methods, which was mainly scaring them nearly to death with threats and random actions. Such as killing one of them at random; having videotape of them practicing their vices; or kidnapping and torturing their mistresses. Those were useful ways to keep them in line. I even had my people occasionally torture a high-level Church operative or one of their children in front of the rest of them, just as a reminder of what we could do. I considered all these methods to be good business practices. Perhaps someday, after my ascension to world emperor, I would write a business management self-help book.

Infiltrating the Church used to be so much easier in the early days. When I first started the process fifteen hundred years ago, we tried several ways to gain influence. You could turn a Pope into a vampire like us, although that was dangerous and had only been done once. It was easier to keep them human, find their multiple weak spots and twist their wills to ours through tried-and-true blackmail. The golden days were back when the position was hereditary. Imagine, the head of the Church that professed to be celibate and the ultimate Christian, passing the position down to his son. Of course, the younger man was always referred to as a nephew. Yes, in those days, it was easy to get things done. The excesses of generations of popes and the monarchs that supported them made for easy machinations.

Then Michael showed up. We spent a century determining who he was and where he came from. We never found out the details of either question, but it did not matter ultimately. All that mattered was his success against us. It took him a long time, but he was able to change things, including getting slightly better cardinals nominated for the papacy. But his genuine talent was ferreting out the many blackmail chains and then disappearing our agents that yanked those chains. We found some of our people quite dead, but most just disappeared. We had to quit the obvious tactics before Michael could trace those back to us. Our strategy changed to working more slowly and at lower levels, through priests that showed enough potential to become cardinals, and hope that one would eventually get picked to be Pope. It rarely happened, but we always had at least two cardinals turned in our favor, and others under them, whether bishops, powerful priests, or those on their staffs. Although it took us much longer to get things done, those people on the inside could pass us useful be useful information. It also kept Michael from finding those of us running the operation.

The only positive outcome of all the recent Church losses was that I had convinced the Sky Lords that Senecus was their primary problem. It took little effort to convince them he stopped the shapeshifter war in the US. They had given me orders and resources to ferret him out. But instead of killing him like I wanted, they instructed me to capture him and provide his torso mostly intact, with intestines undisturbed, and head attached. Preferably still slightly alive. Limbs and major pieces of the exterior torso were unnecessary, so I could have some fun before putting the remaining body on life support and shipping it off. I was already considering all the most painful ways to reduce his body to a minimum husk. I could not decide whether to give all my servants a bite, or to enjoy the process all by myself.

I needed to decide soon as I had intentionally leaked information back to the few remaining Church contacts about my operations in Prague. I believed Michael had probably left a couple of our former agents alive after agreeing to be his double agent. It is what I would have done. I also had a person keeping tabs on Senecus' computer usage, and we knew the information he searched for. I had my person put a few nuggets out where Senecus was likely to find it. Not too much, just enough to arouse his curiosity. That would lead him to me and result in joyous dismemberment. Then the husk sent off to the future, where I hoped they had horrible things planned for him. This operation should also cement my relations with the Sky Lords and lead to more opportunities with them.

Luckily for me, the Sky Lords had not blamed me for the survival of the second target they had recently ordered me to kill at the Church's new Center. The two lowlifes under contract had shot her but not killed her. My servant had killed those two before they could talk, but Michael's team had killed my servant afterward. Since there was no follow up by the Sky Lords, the genuine threat must have been the Center researcher that my other team killed in Italy.

But just in case, I had set up a new contract with the best team in Italy. They had to go to Finland to track the target, but Senecus had gotten involved and provided protection. That would be the last time he would meddle in my business. Meanwhile I kept everything about the affair quiet, as I had no intention of alerting the Sky Lords to yet another failure of eliminating that original target. All they knew, and would ever know, was that everything was fine. I needed to consider another try once Senecus was removed, but I would hold that thought for another day.

Soon I should be well along the way to capturing Senecus and ending his existence in my timeline. I hoped to earn enough goodwill to gain more assets, allowing me to kill off more of my colleagues and reduce competition in my quest to rule the world. A vampire of my status must dream big.

CHAPTER TWENTY-SEVEN

P rague was a great place, so I was happy to visit whenever I got the chance. I walked down to the old town, past the clock tower, and to the Charles Bridge, but there were too many tourists for me. I headed to more secluded locations that were quieter. The grotto gardens of General Wallenstein's palace grounds were worth another trip. The dripstone wall was quite odd and interesting. Like most that saw it, I always felt there was more to the wall than the obvious. Either the grotesque melted semi-faces were speaking some unknown language, or there were secret tunnels hidden behind them.

The oldest site in town that I liked to visit was the Vysehrad area. It was once the fort and palace of Prague, long since destroyed, with a few parts identified and partially rebuilt. The bluff over the river now held a basilica and graveyard, haunted by generations of citizens and soldiers, now ghosts. The area was rumored to have ancient caves and even old underground WWII bunkers. Large trees, ruins, and sunken sidewalks dotted the area, adding to its aura of mystery. But I would save that visit for later, when the shadows made it eerie.

For now, I walked towards the hotel, past various shops and museums. And lots of beer halls since the area was famed as the birthplace of beer. I passed those up, as I had no interest in that beverage any longer. The food in Prague, however, was quite good. Typically, very hearty but simple, it was comfort food perfected by an ancient people. I stopped and had a plate before the long walk down to Vysehrad. I could take the subway, but sometimes I felt cities were best walked and inhaled, smelling the town at its best and worst. Each city and town had its own scent, and I could usually tell which city I was in by its smell.

I was in the city, and specifically this area, not as a tourist, but doing some detective work. Monk had alerted me to some odd chatter originating in a Prague neighborhood, specifically around the Vysehrad and the Basilica of St. Peter and St. Paul. I discussed what I heard with Michael, and he told me the Center had also gotten a ping for the area, possibly indicating master vampire activity. He was readying a team, but I told him I could come down and take a quick look, and he could send his team if I found anything. He agreed, as his teams were stretched thin anyway, looking into a half dozen other places for master vampires. All I had to do was to check in with him twice a day. I was basically on vacation but getting Church consulting pay, so it was a good gig. And like most things too good to be true, it was about to break bad.

When I got to Vysehrad, I strolled around and reacquainted myself with the grounds. As I walked through the basilica cemetery, I saw Caius, or someone that looked like him. Of course, I followed him as morons like me always do the obvious. He left the cemetery, passed behind the basilica, and was going downhill toward the river. I was following distantly enough to not give away my pursuit. The paved path I was on sank between stone walls on either side until it was almost a tunnel. The pavement turned into a metal drainage grate at the lowest part of the walkway. As I walked, the grate turned into nothing but air. My dumb ass had walked, then fallen, right into the trap.

When the metal grate disappeared, I had immediately thrown myself toward the nearest wall, but I was not fast enough. I fell vertically about ten meters, while the open space above closed back. I landed hard on smooth concrete, resulting in bruises and a sprained ankle. In a short time, I would get over those issues, but as I stood, I realized there was not going to be any recovery time. There were others in the semi-dark space, and I doubted they were friendly.

The first team came at me with blades. It made no sense, unless they were just trying to bleed me enough to slow me down and capture me. As I backed up defensively, I could tell they were nearly my match in speed and strength. They looked human, but moved so quickly they must be enhanced, but also had that jerky movement, like the vampire I had killed in Rotterdam. I now had the pleasure of entering Caius' pit of vampires without backup.

There were five of them, three actively attacking, with two backups ready to step in for any attrition in the front line. It was an excellent strategy for most conflicts, as we had used similar tactics in the Legion. What it did not account for was catastrophic failure. I pulled out my concealed pistol and shot all of them in the head in just over a second. I was feeling cocky, just like an Indiana Jones, when two more groups of six each showed up with blades. And with many guns. My small pistol only had ten bullets to begin with, so I had five shots left to persuade those twelve heavily armed vampires to surrender.

I started shooting at them, but they were ready for it. Only three of them went down from my gunshots, so it was nine on one. I dropped the empty gun and went to using a blade I picked up from one of dead vampires. Time to go old-school, but they did too. They were whirling and getting into my guard with their blades, slicing me up as I could not defend all the attacks.

Curiously, they pulled back to give me a few feet of space. Then, behind them, I saw another figure walk up, with two guards on either side. He looked familiar; Caius was in the house.

"Finish bleeding him and take him down," he said. "Preserve the torso. You have five minutes to get him downstairs."

He said nothing else, just turned and hurried out with his two goons. Maybe he was smarter than the average television supervillain, who spouted his plans while the hero recovers and conquers. But if I was the hero, I still had nine minions to wade through. If they did not use their guns, then I might have a chance. Yeah, they were not that dumb.

The ones in front attacked with blades, the ones behind them pulled their guns and started shooting at my arms and legs. I needed a different approach to survive this and tried to drop into slant. But the shots were quite painful and then something slammed my face on the right side. I had taken a bullet in the cheek and could not see from my right eye or hear from my right ear. My left side collapsed as my arm and leg were not working correctly and went numb. The only positive was that the pain from the wounds in those limbs went away as well. The gunfire ceased, as I was not much of a target anymore.

They warily approached and stood in a semicircle with guns out and blades ready. One bent down to grab my blade. I had just enough left to slide it forward and rip out the inside of his thigh. Unless he could heal quickly, he would be dead in thirty seconds. The fellow beside him immediately stepped on my right arm and kicked my blade away with his other foot. Two of them moved forward to stab me a few more times in my right arm and leg. I figured they were about finished as my torso was the only thing mostly intact. Other than the stab or bullet wound I had in my right lung. They were too good at following Caius' orders to kill me now. I had a few seconds to ponder which hurt worse, the lung or the face wound, as they slowed their stabs.

I was slipping in and out of consciousness as I heard rapid gunfire, but curiously, I felt no more bullets ripping through me. I got my head up enough to see the vampires farthest from me were already dropping. By the time the ones that were still stabbing the rest of me realized their fate, it was too late. They died quickly too. The last one was turning with his gun raised when his head exploded. I looked up with my left eye and saw Jo standing above me with a bloody sword and a machine pistol.

"Well dear, you are a right bloody mess. Good thing I was around to save your arse."

I had a peppy riposte on the tip of my tongue, but it came out as a bloody gurgle.

"OK, time to mop you up and take you home. Can you walk?"

One leg tried to obey, but the left one doth protested too much. A wet noodle had more spunk.

"Oh, you lollygagger, guess I'll have to carry you. You owe me an ice cream for this. Perhaps a double cone."

"Done," I finally sputtered.

She picked me up easily and carried me across her shoulders. It hurt like hell, at least on one side, but also allowed me to breathe a little easier as the lung that was grazed could drain. I drooled a steady stream of bright blood down Jo's back, plus a few dozen other trickles, realizing I might have to pay for a dry cleaning. Along the way, I saw several Church commandos, including Elias and Zena. I knew they were in Europe for training, so Michael must have called out the big team, expecting major trouble. As usual, he was smarter than I was.

Jo carried me through the building that had several vampire bodies lying around. We got to an elevator and floated up several levels until the doors opened. There was a gurney there and Jo dropped me on it. She looked at the right side of my head and started speaking, probably for the medic's benefit. "Shot through the upper cheek, with shattered bone. Looks like a deflection down the side of the head. Exit past the ear. OK, Sen, I doubt you will see or hear much for a couple of days on that side. Any issues with your left side?"

I gurgled something resembling an affirmative answer. I was about to pass out and was only catching snapshots of what was happening by then. They rolled me toward a van, and it looked like a nice evening outside. I was contemplating what type of eye patch to get when the world went white, then went away from a massive dose of anesthetic they had just injected into me.

I woke up disoriented, in an unfamiliar hospital room. I slowly regained my senses and recognized it as the private Church facility that Jo had been in after the shooting. Getting me here must have taken hours, so I had been asleep for a while. I spent a couple of hours in bed while slowly regaining feeling on my left side. Unfortunately, the return of feeling brought with it the pain from multiple bullet and stab wounds not yet healed. Nurses were in every hour checking some things hooked up to me that lit up and beeped constantly.

After sliding in and out of consciousness several times, with no idea if I had been there for several hours or days, the nurse brought me several high calorie milkshakes. I drained them quickly, and was considering getting out of bed to move to the bathroom when Michael walked in. I waved a hello without speaking as my face still did not feel right.

"You appear to be in somewhat worn shape for a Prague vacation. I hope you continue to heal quickly."

I waved again. It might be a new way to communicate.

"It was your good luck that we had scrambled a team and sent them to Prague. Mainly on intuition, but my gut told me it was too much of a coincidence that such activity was appearing, and that you were there alone."

"Thanks." That was the word I intended, anyway. It came out as more of 'tinks'.

"We have been able to get close to Caius and damage him significantly these past two days. The information on the vehicle from the night you were shot in Woerden, the facility where you were just attacked, and one other business location we recently discovered led us to him and his organization. We triangulated and discovered his shell companies, financial holdings, homes, and businesses. We have not caught him yet, but we have destroyed or confiscated everything we can find."

"Won't that leave him desperate? Or do you think he has backup plans?" My words were not quite right, but Michael understood me.

"Yes, it should leave him desperate enough to make mistakes, even if he has other resources or plans. That investigation also led us to some other potential masters. Even if we don't catch them, we can damage them. And we left enough clues for them to determine that Caius was the one that led us to them. Perhaps even if we don't capture him, they will take care of him first."

"I doubt you are that lucky. That cockroach will show back up. But maybe he's hurt enough he won't be able to wait a few years before he surfaces again."

"That is what we also think. We will continue to trace and track down everything we can to force him back up."

There was a knock at the door. Jo came in and shut the door behind her. She looked at Michael and said, "You, out. He needs more rest to heal up. Time for you to go." He just nodded with a half-smile, and then left, closing the door.

She looked at me with her hands on her hips. "You, move over. As your 'microbiome sister', I am going to sit here and bore you to sleep." I moved over, as otherwise was not an option with that voice. She sat on the bed, and I noticed she was warm and smelled nice. "I wanted you to know that you are an arse. You almost got killed, or worse. Apparently, I can't leave you alone for a moment, as you don't make good decisions without me."

"I must agree. That was entirely too close, and if I wasn't lucky and had you guys around, I'd be dead."

"Probably the only you have gotten right this week."

"Changing subjects, I'm glad we can be this close without us getting nauseous. Not sure if this bed is big enough for you to be comfortable, but you are welcome to stay as long as you want."

We said nothing for a while.

"You are leaving, aren't you?" she asked.

"Yes. Too much, and yet too little, is going on here right now to stay, and I owe too many debts to my people. I have neglected my family for too long."

"Does your decision have anything to do with your near-death experience?"

"Of course. I realize I should get some things done before I get myself killed."

"I'm not surprised to hear that. I just did not think you would say it."

"It is the truth. I need to be smarter, or perhaps harder, or both. Regardless, I think the people at home need me, at least for a while."

I nodded off after that. Eating ten thousand calories earlier to regain strength, and having a warm body sitting next to me, did the trick. Even before I opened my eyes, I knew she was gone since there was no bright comet in my mind. My brain must have glitched anyway, because when she was on the bed with me, I had been seeing double comets. I reached over, grabbed my cell phone, and got a reservation on a flight to Atlanta. As of tomorrow, I was finished with Europe.

Later that evening, after I had woken up, I realized I would not be going back to sleep again. I got up and gathered what very few things I had in the room. All my clothes were unwearable - getting them cut off me, after being shot through a few dozen times and soaking in a gallon of blood, ruins cotton and wool. I was standing in my newly issued sweatpants and tee shirt when Michael opened the door after knocking.

"You are up and looking better. Anything to do with a previous visitor?"

"Actually, no. But she got me to sleep within five minutes, so maybe she helped. We've said our goodbyes and I don't think I'll see her again. And with that, I guess I need to tell you, too. Michael, I'm out. I don't want to do this anymore, at least not here, not now."

"I understand, and I want you to stay. But you will need time to sort this out and find your way forward. When you do, please remember that we need you. Jo really needs you as a friend as well. This, of course, is your decision, and one you must feel comfortable with. I hope you will return soon."

"It's possible, but I just can't see that happening right now. With these threats and rumors of more trouble to come, I need to go to America and continue preparing my people, my family. I have lost too much of my family already because of my poor decisions."

Michael sighed and then sat down. "If this is goodbye, at least for the knowable future, then I would like you to indulge an old man. I have a story to tell, one of family and loss. Perhaps it will help, I don't know."

"Michael, you don't look or move like an old man. But I'll hear your story. I have too much respect for you to not listen." It was very unusual for Michael to tell a personal story, so it must be important to him.

"Thank you. And I am far older than you. But that doesn't make what I'm about to tell you any easier."

Damn, he had me there. How could he possibly be far older than me? But I always knew he was more than he seemed.

"My story tonight, and one of my greatest regrets, is about my son. My wife and I had a son and two daughters together. The girls were beautiful, intelligent, and have been a blessing to us. Our son was handsome and intelligent. I was very blessed to have such a family. For many years, I felt I had the perfect family. But daughters grow up and find their own way and look for their own families. And sons must do that as well. But in the way of sons, he was also more rebellious on his journey to become a man. He wanted to go into the world and find his own way, more interested in fame or fortune than family." Michael paused. I'm sure we were thinking about our own impetuous youths.

"He left home and his university posting and became a wanderer. Not really doing anything wrong, but always searching for something and getting by as best he could. He also became more martial than we would have liked. He became a warrior, and sometimes mercenary, for various factions that were fighting. Because of his gifts, he was very skilled and in demand for the sheiks and rulers that had need of armed protectors. At some point, during an epic sea battle, he found his match. Instead of a duel to the death, however, he and his nemesis became great friends. They left the business of war and traveled together, spawning stories of adventure and action. We were very glad to hear later that he had turned to pursuits of travel and trade, rather than war.

"His letters to us were sparse, but when he wrote, he told captivating tales of what he and his friend had done, the ports and countries they visited, the humorous situations they found themselves in. Even beyond that, I heard from many sources in and around the Mediterranean of his exploits. He was becoming famous in a way we had never considered. And he seemed to enjoy his incredible life.

"After a time, the letters ceased, and the stories had gone quiet. I then received a letter from his friend and accomplice. They had shipwrecked off the coast of Morocco, where dozens of pirates surrounded him and eventually killed him, after he killed many of them. Of course, the news devastated my family and me."

"He fought bravely and killed many," I interrupted. "By the time I got to him, it was too late. That night, I went into the pirate camp and slaughtered them where they sat or lay. Almost every one of the nearly hundred there. I captured a few of the youngest to sail me away from that wretched place, then buried Asif in the traditional way, as his Muslim faith required, on an island just off the coast. I sailed on to Spain and sent that letter from Barcelona."

We sat quietly, both with tears in our eyes as we remembered Asif.

"How long have you known it was me?" I asked.

"I suspected, but only truly knew just now. The world is a wonderful place, and God works in mysterious ways."

"He definitely works the long game. But the bastard really bungled it when he let Asif die."

We paused again, lost in our thoughts. I had just blasphemed, but I felt justified in my anger even after all the years gone past.

"I am sorry for not saving your son when he needed me the most."

"I am sure you did everything you could. But it was his fate, regardless of what you did or wanted to do."

"What happened after you received my letter?"

"I was heartbroken for my son. I tried to find you, but you had disappeared. My elders spoke nonsense that my son received his just punishment from God for abandoning his family, his scholarly life, and befriending an infidel. We had a significant argument. I left that place and took my family with me. I put my faith of that time behind me, and I changed employers in a manner of speaking."

"Damn, I'd say you did. I'd think they would have had a hard time getting over that."

"Yes. They still hold a grudge. But my assassins are better than theirs, so they nurse their grievances in private and no longer stalk me."

"I fell into a coma shortly after writing that letter, so there is no way you could have found me. I assumed all Asif's family was dead by the time I woke up, so I didn't even try to find any of you. If I had any idea that his family was still alive, I would have found you and told the story in person. My apologies for not doing so. But I would like to take you to his grave sometime."

"I would like that as well."

"You obviously know how hard it is to lose family."

"Yes."

"That is why I now need to go to America and complete what I have started there. I have abandoned them for too long, and now must return to finish preparing them for what I think is coming. Perhaps then I can rectify my mistakes and maybe even pay it forward for a change."

"I really understand. And we will see each other again someday. Meanwhile, go with God, and go in peace. And when the troubles come, kick their collective ass."

"That is mostly what I do best. And after my latest experience, next time I'll do it smarter. Before we part, I would like to tell you of some of Asif's happier days. We got into unusual situations that mostly had happy endings. It is the only way I have left to honor him."

Michael listened entranced for nearly two hours, occasionally asking questions or telling me that Asif had written something of a particular tale in one of his letters. To me, random stories of brief moments of Asif's and my life together were the best way of remembering him. Michael seemed genuinely touched by my tales. Finally, I finished the stories.

I stood up, as did Michael. We shook hands and then Michael embraced me.

"I thank you, more than you know," he said.

"You are most welcome."

Michael left. I put my personal items in my pocket, turned off the light, and left the room. I had a few hours to get home and pack for my flight to America. As usual, I had a lot to think about. Life continued to get stranger.

CHAPTER TWENTY-EIGHT

Jo

I thought back to meeting Sen at the cottage for the first time since my change and time away from him. It had been bittersweet as I realized I liked and respected him and felt an attraction for him. But I also felt a certain revulsion for his casual attitude toward killing others. I was still working through the complexity of feeling gratitude for his act of saving me, versus the anger I felt of having such a major change imposed on me without consent. I realized that knot of emotion needed time to resolve. But my first minute with him betrayed my true, subconscious feelings, as my unknown pheromone machine spoke up. I quickly hid that once I realized what was happening. It was another aspect of me I would need to understand and control.

Later, when we were sparring, I enjoyed it immensely. It was a much better workout than with Simon because I wasn't worried about hurting Sen. In fact, I was doing my best to hurt him, at least a little. His technique and speed were excellent, and he was still stronger than I was. I thought I was making headway with my speed, but he was so sneaky, or experienced, he used it against me and took me down. He explained about a wily old boxer I had heard of, but had never seen box, used subterfuge when he fought a stronger opponent. A whole new side of fighting opened up for me. Simon was so good at what he did in training me, but we had not gotten to the psychology of fighting and feinting yet. But I would bring it up at our next session and insist on working it in into our matches.

The sparring was also the first time we had gotten so close and physical with each other for an extended time. I think, from my side at least, that my aggression was anchored in working out some of the negative feelings I had towards him. And perhaps it was that deeper feeling, almost like a physical ritual before, well, other things happened. I knew that the earlier episode of where I soaked him with pheromones was not completely accidental. But it was a slip I needed to control. However, if we had not finished sparring when we did, I would have hosed him down again, and god only knows what the security cameras would have witnessed. I knew I needed to get a better control of this aspect of my new life.

It also was not lost on me that some things I held against Sen, for example, violence and fighting, I was now training for as a new profession. A job that may require killing sometimes. I needed some time to consider all these additional aspects of my life, on top of all the other issues.

Afterwards, Sen left for America, and I continued intensive training in many areas. When the order came, I did not understand Michael's reasons for sending me to America. It felt like exile after I was doing so well here. One day I brought it to him directly, telling him that assigning this trip was hindering my progress and training. Then I asked if he was throwing me out there to Senecus. He apologized for not telling me his reasons but clarified that neither of my assumptions was correct. He was quiet for a moment to compose an answer, but all he said was, "the future is there, not here." I had been wondering about that remark ever since. I could not decide whether it was supposed to be ominous or reassuring. With Michael, it could be both.

When I arrived in America, Sen greeted me, and we spent a first awkward night at his home. We were both aloof, but I think we needed to keep a distance from each other. At the Farm, however, it was much different.

His friends, or perhaps more appropriately, his extended family, teasing him about me, were cute and not mean-spirited. They were all good people, and I really enjoyed being there. I still wondered at Michael's intentions, but I had a great time, even if it was slightly rustic. The other women were nice to me, and the teenagers actually listened to my lessons. The scenery was wonderful, as was the weather. Senecus was again a perfect gentleman.

Sparring with him at the Farm was fun yet difficult. My skills had drastically increased to match my physical capability. But Sen was still cagey and taught me how strategy could sometimes overcome physical prowess. The last match where I caught him by surprise was great. Simon and I had planned it for two days. I was a little worried Sen may not appreciate the ambush, but not only he did he take it well, he made sure everyone knew what happened and how it was a good lesson. Watching him as he talked made me feel much more than I should have for a colleague, especially one that was off-limits in my mind. I knew Sen was thinking the same way, and I appreciated him giving me space and time to work through these recent changes. By the time we were sparring at the Farm, I no longer had those powerful feelings that I had at the cottage, proving I was getting better control of my physical urges. What was worrisome were some deeper emotions that I probably should not be feeling. Yet those I could manage, or repress, and I was already feeling more in control of myself.

By the time my brief stay was done, I felt myself pulled to stay longer, yet also felt I needed to go back to finish training and begin my new career. So many new things were happening I was extremely grateful, but I also felt a little overwhelmed. Going back and settling in seemed like the thing to do. Michael would probably send me back here anyway, and next time, I would willingly agree. Perhaps he knew that would happen, as he seemed so aware of both the present and the future.

I went back and spent most of my time at the Center. There were a thousand administrative things to do, plus all the physical training. Most of my days were twenty hours long, and Michael had to assign two shifts of people to keep training me. It was hectic but exciting and was just getting boring when it all changed.

Seeing Sen standing across the bridge one day should have surprised me, but it did not. Whisking us away on a half-baked escape plan because of an unlikely threat seemed surreal, yet I went along willingly. He had that way of making things make sense, and even if they did not, there was always an adventure to be had. The private plane was a nice touch, as was our short sailing adventure. For me, it was a silly vacation, and I never believed there was a genuine threat until they attacked us on the boat, and then blew it up the next day. I was never frightened, but excited by the violence, including beating down the men sent to capture us.

Of course, the real excitement came during the first bus ride and our meadow experience. I still cannot process all the feelings and emotions that came from that encounter. One of the best days and one of the worst days in my life? That is a poor summary, but an entirely appropriate description. Unforgettable may be the best word. The best sex of my life, easily by a magnitude or greater, followed by debilitating sickness and disgust. Ouch, that still brings back such a whirlpool of conflicting memories. I don't think my mind will ever fully process it, so I'll do what everyone else does and just tamp it down and ignore it as much as possible.

One positive since Finland is that Michael seems more confident about my new role. I believe Senecus was correct about Michael throwing us into the middle of one of his schemes with no warning, then observing how we reacted. Michael could scoop up and eliminate his Church traitors and put Sen and I into a situation that would test us. Of course, he knew how Sen would react, so it was likely a test for me. And perhaps also a test of Sen and me acting together as a team. Looking back, we had handled a volatile situation easily. I must have passed Michael's test as my training sped up afterward, and I was now assigned to a strike team.

They had sent my team on two assignments where we surveilled possible master vampires. The first was outside Barcelona. We were not there to take down a target, but to act as backup for the primary surveillance team. Interesting at first, it quickly devolved to boring. We repeated the same experience in a small city in Hungary. Again, unexciting, but necessary as a good live training exercise.

I understood that the life of a strike team was one hour of adrenaline rush and a month of boredom. The team had to be ready for both, and the personalities had to mesh whether counting on each other for our very lives or spending two weeks staring into binoculars and playing cards. The team, as expected, was professional, but leery of me, their new member. But I did what I was told, caused no trouble, then asked questions after the first assignment was over. I employed some of those answers in the next assignment. That appeared to win over the team's confidence. Well, that and a few examples of my physical capabilities. I felt I was on my way to a new profession, and one that I looked forward to. It heartened me to overhear one of my Norwegian teammates refer to me as "doctor shield maiden" to our team sniper. When I first heard it, I thought it an insult, but when I thought about it for a moment, I decided it was a compliment. And the Norwegian's action had been very positive toward me. Being referred to as an intelligent warrior, even with the implied gender bias, still made me feel good. But I hoped soon it would be "doctor berserker" instead.

When I returned from those assignments, Michael put me on as a leader of a strike team. It wasn't as odd as it sounded, as new members were often given a leadership position quickly, then rotated back into the team or to another team. It was a quick learning experience in becoming a leader, then back to follower, and accelerated how must learn to work with other teams. There was no room or time to be arrogant or complacent in such a system.

I was the team leader when we went into Prague. Michael had a gut feeling something was wrong, so we were sent to locate Sen and provide backup if needed. I don't think any of us expected a firefight and a rescue mission. I was professional in my duties, but an almost overwhelming fear of losing Sen was in the back of my mind as we breached the old bunker system under the Vysehrad ruins and realized what was happening. We cleared the area of vampires and found Sen, or what they left of him. I had never seen anyone wounded that severely and survive. My emotions almost got the best of me, but I pulled it together quickly as I realized how fast Sen would heal. The best cover for my fear was humor, so I began the banter and Sen responded. We joked while I picked up and carried his nearly lifeless body out of that place. While carrying him, I thought about how I had nearly lost him and how bad that felt, but in a different way, how good it felt knowing I was the strong one and rescuing him. My thoughts remained jumbled as I thought this was someone worth waiting for, someone very special, yet well above my league when we first met. Now we were equals, both in intelligence and physical attributes. And I knew how good the sex could be. But now we could never be together, and that was devastating. Fate was a rubbish bitch. Meanwhile, I should have been keeping my situational awareness and not running through all those thoughts while on this mission. Not very professional of me, but no one noticed.

Now Sen was back in America and seemed likely to stay for some time. Michael was keeping me busy in Europe and so far, showed no inclination to send me back over to America. I appreciated the time to work through all my thoughts, but sometimes I had to admit I missed Sen.

Meanwhile, my odd dreams continued, but the original one had changed. I was still in the 'river' when the large rainbow figure approached, and all the phosphorescent bubbles began glowing in a blinding glare. But now I spread my arms out into the 'water' and slowly gathered them all together. As all the glowing bubbles came together between my hands, they merged into a beautiful ball of rainbow light directly in front of me. A deep sense of wonder and serenity emanated through my body. Then the large entity shot into the sky, fading in brilliance until it was just another star in the night. My rainbow ball stayed, and I felt it wanted to speak to me. At that point, I'd wake up with an incredibly refreshed and warm feeling. It was still a strange dream, but something I would only worry about if it turned dark or violent. For now, I rather enjoyed it.

A few nights a month, I had an alternate, repeating dream. I was running through a field of grass barefoot in the early evening. Dew had fallen, but the grass was still warm and wonderful under my feet. As I ran, a million fireflies began rising from the grass in the meadow, and their flashing colors were all rainbow hues. They were everywhere, surrounding me, then above me as they continued rising. One, however, came to rest on my shoulder and began speaking to me. I could not quite understand what it was saying, but I knew it was important. The rest of the fireflies kept moving upward until they became the stars. Then I fell onto my back in the grass, and I as I lay there, the firefly landed on my stomach. It began singing an old song I had not heard in years that my mother used to hum. Then I woke up each time as soon as I recognized the tune. Again, it was a comforting dream and not in any way a warning of threats or harbinger of bad things to come.

Although I thought my mental health was good, I needed to fly down to the Center to check on some physical concerns. After my initial transition and body changes, I felt wonderful and full of energy all the time. But lately I had felt slightly off, not like Sen had described before his blackouts, but strange enough that I wanted to determine if such an episode was coming, or if there was a delayed allergic reaction. I still had a voracious appetite but could feel slightly ill after a meal. With my new position, I could not afford to have any complications if I was on active assignment. Better to be safe than sorry.

Chapter Twenty-Nine

The flight back was long as I lost myself in thoughts that were mostly dark. Across the aisle from me, a woman traveling by herself sat weeping softly. She had a couple of drinks, but that didn't seem to help. Obviously, something was wrong, but I had enough sense to keep my thoughts to myself. I only intervened when she was trying to buy something from the steward but did not have the right currency. It seemed to upset her even more. Since I always carried a supply of euros, dollars, pounds, and bahts, I offered her the right currency for a straight up trade with the advantage to her. Since I was losing a grand total of two dollars, I thought I could float the loss. She gratefully accepted and thanked me in heavily accented English. I smiled, nodded, and settled back in with my dark thoughts.

Two hours later, I was wide awake with my mind running over new thoughts for the Farm and training. I had realized that feeling sorry for myself and brooding about what I couldn't change no longer had a place in my life. I had to get my group ready as quickly as possible. Wasting time was no longer an option. I also needed to get my slant on, so I'd be prepared for my next shot at Caius. Next time, I would bring the surprises. I felt he would try again soon, since he had almost gotten me last time, and I was going to give him that opportunity. His underestimation of me was going to get him dead.

The woman across the aisle had stopped crying and dozed off. I knew nothing about her, but I hoped she was having pleasant dreams. Then the plane was descending into my familiar part of America. I was ready to get out of this aluminum tube and start a new chapter of life.

I opened the door to my house in Asheville, then did all the things I normally do when coming back after a time away. How many more airline miles had I racked up over the past few months? I would have to ask Monk about transferring them to other people. I knew he could just hack and add miles to any account, but I felt it was more legitimate to just transfer my miles.

I was developing a strange sense of having a conscious. Other than killing people, of course. I still needed to do some more of that, especially Caius, but he might not count as human. Some of his minions might be, but they also might be from the future. What happened when you killed someone that will not even be born or cloned for another few hundred years? Those types of questions made me leery of anything to do with time travel.

I sent Henry a text to see where he and the kids were. They had probably gone back west for Thanksgiving, now that it was late November, but I wanted to know about the winter schedule. My phone rang.

"You back on our soil, kemosabe?" Henry asked.

"Isn't that cultural appropriation?"

"Who knows? It's a made-up word from television, so what culture is being appropriated?"

"I guess it is like reality TV, so it is fake American culture. Which is currently much in fashion."

"Sure is. Now that we have solved that issue for the betterment of humankind, we need to get together."

"That is what I was thinking. I need to crank up some new training sessions at the Farm. While we are at it, I want to increase security."

"We can do that. That because of the rumor you mostly died recently? You back up and running?"

"How the hell did you know that? Never mind, I'm sure there is some kind of telepathic mind meld with a raccoon or something."

"Nope. Talked to Michael."

"What the hell? You are talking to Michael since when?"

"We talk since that gig in Arizona. Elias put us together. Been getting along real well. We trade lots of hunting stories. Interesting guy."

"Yep. So, trading hunting stories and gossip about me."

"Not much about you. Until last week. He's also sending Simon back over, along with a couple of others, to train in espionage tactics. I thought we needed some beefing up on that business. And more explosives. Looking forward to that."

My mouth was hanging open, preventing my further momentary participation in the conversation.

"You still there, hound dog?"

"Uh yeah, just surprised. That is what I wanted to do at the Farm."

"Great minds think alike. Glad you eventually caught up. Maybe getting shot thirty times, including the head, slowed you down some."

"Apparently so. But I am catching up. I also have a whole new training topic I want to get started. Wanted you, Nan, Jennifer and Seth to be first up."

"Hmm, is that the crazy stuff you been learning from the Tsul Kalu? Like that disappearing knife trick?"

"Damn, Henry, are you always a step ahead of me?"

"Mostly, but I know you Europeans are touchy, so I try to not get too far ahead."

"Thanks. And yes, Kal has been giving me some training in some crazy stuff. With it, you can change perceptions, shape shift into anything alive or dead, teleport yourself anywhere, and maybe time travel."

"Oh cool, been wanting to try something new."

"Your ability to understate all that impresses me greatly."

"Guess it takes little to impress you. Still thinking about turning the kids into immortals?"

"I really hope that is a last-ditch necessity. Maybe this slant can give us enough of an edge to keep that from happening."

"Maybe. You find it coincidental that the Kal fellow suddenly shows up, imparting all this new knowledge to you? Like maybe he knows something big is coming?"

"Damn, you are right. There are no coincidences."

"Didn't think so. We will all be back east in three days. You be ready to go. I feel the need to turn into a fly, and then go back to see Custer get taken out."

"Sure, you can do that, right after we take out a few gods and demons, get the world back on the right track."

"Sounds good. Better hurry, though. Seems like the other side is rushing climate change along, and we ain't ready."

"I think you are right. Maybe when Kal's folks locked the Sky Lords out of their time travel portal, other entities upped the stakes."

"Sounds like a good story you can finish telling us. Be there three days from now."

"Good, see you then. Don't take any wooden nickels on the way over."

"Ass."

"Yep."

We hung up. More stuff to think about and prepare for. If the other side was accelerating climate change as part of battle, then this global war had already started. Great, now we get to fight beings capable of throwing hurricanes and glacial melt at us for fun.

The days passed like lead weights holding me underwater. Then everyone was back at the Farm, and I finally had something to do again. The Farm training sessions were going well. Simon had flown back over and continued improving his adaptive fighting style and teaching it to the kids. My letting him break my bones had the result of making him irresistible to most of them. Most of the girls still seemed to have a crush on him, despite Nan's warnings. I'd have to watch that, or he might end up becoming a permanent fixture here, which might be a good thing. He was a traditional guy, so I expected nothing untoward to happen, but any day now I expected him to come ask me about courting Jen as they had developed a close relationship. Zena had also shown up to start us on espionage tactics. I got a thrill knowing she was in camp and teaching us things that might save our lives.

Of course, everyone loved explosives training. We had to make up a story about blasting some test holes for mining to tell the distant neighbors so they would not get too suspicious. I knew the entire region contained emerald, ruby, and sapphire mines, so it was not too far-fetched.

When you blew something up, I just assumed you lit something or wired something, made a spark, and it went bang. But there was an entire science behind the different explosives, from how much to use, to pairing types of explosives with the material to be exploded, and what detonators to use. It also got expensive as few materials survived more than one lesson.

The spy stuff was going slower. It was so subtle it was going to take months or years for most of them to get up to speed to be world class spies. Although that probably was not the prime aim, anyway. I was not sure how much good espionage training would do in the short term, but perhaps it made sense in the longer term, as it trained them to think a little differently. Zena was excellent at going slow enough to keep everyone interested in the complexities needed to build an espionage program. I was also figuring out she was a genius housed inside a commando body.

Right now, I was working with the entire group for two hours a day on trying slant. Some were catching on to the basics, others were not following at all. At some point, I might have to consult Kal to get some advice on ways to explain better those that did not understand it. I was feeling the pressure to get this group trained as fast as possible and get the next year's class started. And not take any shortcuts and turn anybody. After the experience with Jo, that thought made me even more squeamish than before.

One day after dinner, Simon asked me to walk out into the dark for a talk. The only thing I did not like about this time of year in the mountains was that it got dark too early. We ambled out past the barns into the fields where no one was likely around.

"Sen, I know this may sound old-fashioned, but I'd like to ask your advice about seeing Jen."

"I think you see her every day, but if she's fading from your vision, have you thought about getting glasses?"

"You must be teasing, as you can't be that dense."

"Hah, never underestimate my stupidity, especially regarding female relationships. Now, with that warning, how can I help?"

"We seem to have feelings for each other. Based on us being citizens of different continents, and both in this crazy business, do you think there is a future for us? If there is, how do we manage it?"

"Well, spend this training cycle getting to know her even better. After Christmas, when the next training cycle begins, if you both still feel the same, then it's time for a serious chat and then deciding."

"Are you telling me that because it is the safe thing, or is it something you would do yourself?"

"It is the safe thing. But, hell no, I would not go that slow. Full speed ahead and damn the torpedoes has been my motto. Not that I have had much success. But I knew when I met Hia that I was not going to even take five minutes to think about it. So, now that I'm finally telling the truth, I'll support whatever you two decide. Or I'll stay the hell out of it, whichever you prefer. But if she's for it, then full speed ahead and spend Christmas together."

"I think she would prefer that you be OK with anything we decide, since you are her distant family. You don't mind us being together?"

"Nope, that business is only between you and her. Might be difficult operationally, but you guys can figure it out. A few billion people do that every day."

"Thanks, that makes things easier, I think."

"You don't mind that she is a shifter? That freaks some people out."

"No. I find it really interesting she can mold and control both energy and matter to change forms."

I started laughing instead of responding to his comment.

"What is so funny?"

"Some guys would like it because it is kinky, and some would like it because when she returns, she is naked. You like it because of the physics."

"Well, the naked part is a pleasant bonus."

"Not that you've ever noticed, of course."

"Right, not that I've noticed."

"You guys should be OK. Move forward to where you both feel things are right. But treat her well or I'll have to get Jo to kick your ass."

Everyone was gone by mid-December. Jen went to spend a week with Simon. They were flying into Amsterdam, then driving to several of the better Christmas markets. It sounded like fun, as I had done that a few times, but I just did not feel like going back to Europe. I called and had conversations with

Thomas, Kate, and Anna. They already knew about my extended absence and Thomas was keeping an eye on my house and apartment. Anna was on her second round of trying to get pregnant, and I wished her and Kate luck. She thought this one would take, and I assured them I would come visit when the baby was born.

Early winter in Asheville was cool, ranging from cold and ugly to pleasant and sunny. Often within the same week. Thankfully, most days lately were clear, with brilliant blue skies and a few clouds. And the night skies were wonderfully clear, with multitudes of ice-cold stars. Trees were all bare, but that let the skin of the land show through. The afternoon sun turned the mountains into various shades of muted oranges and purples.

An early snow came in with all of two inches on the ground. The time around Christmas, in Asheville, could often be beautiful when there was a real snowfall of a foot or more. Those snows were now more of a rarity, but still happened every few years. I got the Land Cruiser running to brave that light snow, as I would take several trips the next few days to escape the tourist hordes descending on Asheville. I would rather stay away from the crowds and spend my holidays either alone or rekindling family ties.

This year was different to an extent. I had spent a day and evening with my distant relatives near Waynesville for the first time. It was awkward at first, but I enjoyed getting to know the people. The North Carolina contingent from the Farm was there, minus Jen, so that helped with the social aspect. I left feeling better having gotten to know their families, but it also made me feel really old, thinking about how many deceased family members were nearby. All my children and grandchildren were now dead. Just too many dead populated my thoughts.

CHAPTER THIRTY

Yesterday I had driven over to Franklin, North Carolina. Just north of town, I pulled off the road and parked. I waded through the frigid river and crossed the overgrown field, then up the side of what used to be the central mound. Two hundred years of plowing by the uncaring settlers had reduced it substantially. I sat and watched the sunset over the river valley from what used to be Cowee Town, where I once lived with my family, but was now just pasture. I was thinking about all that had happened there, all I had gained, all I had lost. In the cold, I wanted to remember all those things and relive them in my mind, but I just couldn't grasp those threads. I went back to the car in the dark and drove home.

This morning I drove most of the way to the area's highest peak, then walked to the top, to where the grove of flame azaleas would bloom in a few months. Hia's bones were here at one time, and the azaleas were the only markers. I left when I still could not get any answers or clear memories. Perhaps my past was finally my past. Luckily, my brain was buzzing with so much that I wasn't giving in to depression. I thought about many topics, including Christmas. Its pagan origins overlain with Christian concepts and meanings. But it was still all the same in some ways, all about birth, gifts, pilgrimages, family, life, faith, new sunrises, and death. People living life and trying to make sense of it, bettering themselves and others. That was my new purpose after so much lost time just existing.

Events had turbocharged my life for the last ten months, events speeding by so fast I rarely had time to reflect and digest, also preventing or deflecting depression. Maybe the decision to pause killing had also helped. I needed to put aside some significant time in the next few months to consider all that had happened, put it into context, and decide how to continue. And practice slant and what came with it. Nearly dying at Caius' lair was entirely my fault, as I was arrogant, reacting in old ways out of habit rather than using new skills that could have prevented me from walking into the trap, or gotten me out of there before getting shot in the head. Those were mistakes I could no longer afford, or I would not survive the next round. My old ways worked on my old enemies and hunts, but these new threats were going to kill me if I did not up my game. Worse, I could get others killed, and now that included my family.

It was Christmas Eve, and I was sitting in front of my fire and processing those thoughts to prepare for the new year. I had expected a lonely and depressing evening like previous years, but my mind was just too busy tonight. Those thoughts should have had a negative effect on me, but now they were stimulating me to do more and do better. Thoughts pushing me to meet the next challenge that I would damn sure be ready for. I was having a premonition that the next year would be quite something.

I was wondering what normal people with families were doing right now. Baking cookies, filling stockings, wrapping presents, going to candlelight services, sitting by a fire with a loved one? Doing things that I would not be doing tonight. But what I was doing by steeling my attitude was going to pay dividends, just of a different sort.

A knock sounded on my door. What the hell, what happened to my security systems? Nobody should have been able to get within a hundred feet of my door without multiple warnings to me and serious injury to them. I picked up my gladius. Even if it was the ghost of Christmas Present, I was going to cut his guts out. I carefully opened the door to find Michael standing there.

"What the hell are you doing here?" My people skills had apparently gotten rusty. I made a mental note to sign up for a social etiquette course after the holidays.

"Is that how you greet all your Christmas guests from overseas? Or have I found myself at the house of Scrooge, perhaps in his Christmas past?"

"Sorry, come in. This is quite a surprise. But a good one, assuming you are not one of the Christmas ghosts. Do you come to America often?"

"Rarely, and it has been a very long time. This is not a natural journey for me over the years. I normally stay within Europe, or the Middle and Near East."

"Welcome to my home in America. Can I get you anything?" I took Michael's coat and scarf while he considered.

"Whatever you are having, assuming it is not bear blood or some other rural American concoction."

"We save that for the New Year's human sacrifice ceremony. I'm having a cranberry cocktail in honor of the season. Not much alcohol, but I can add extra to yours."

"That would be fine, and no additional alcohol needed. I partake little anymore, and I suspect the same for you."

"True, I don't. Unnecessary at this point in my life."

I poured Michael a glass of vibrant red drink, and we sat on the sofa facing the fire.

"Are you over here traveling for business, or are you traveling for pleasure over the holidays?"

"Actually neither. I flew over for more of a hybrid reason. I've only been in Asheville about half an hour. My driver dropped me, and I spent a few moments outside trying to sneak up on your door without setting off the surprises you planted. Excellent system, by the way."

"Well, obviously not good enough. I'll update a few things. But I'm glad you made it through."

"Me as well. Otherwise, you would have had a real mess to clean up outside. That would have both disturbed your evening and mussed my attire."

"It would not have been much of a disturbance. Since the temperature is below freezing, I'd have waiting until tomorrow before going out to pick up the frozen chunks."

"Almost sounds as if you have faced that scenario before."

"Yes, a few times. There are a few less deer around than there used to be. I've also had to make the traps much quieter so as not to disturb the neighbors. So, Michael, now that we have danced a bit, what brings you to my neck of the woods?"

"Hmm; neck, woods, there must be some meaning there. But I am here to visit you."

"No business? Not here to talk me into coming back?"

"Mostly no business. I needed to see you since you left so quickly after your recovery. But I'm not here to talk you into coming back. Your operations here can be most helpful, and we have much of the Old World covered with other operatives for now. Your unfortunate encounter with Caius has given us a bonus, as we have greatly culled his operation. As difficult as it was for you, it was most appreciated."

"Always happy to lend a hand and kill off a few bad guys. Just not the one I need to, at least not yet."

"Plenty of time for that, I assume. We are working diligently to put in place some things that will provide the proper information to ferret out your nemesis and his few remaining thugs. I hope to have news for you in the spring."

"Good enough. I can always fly over for a day to finish that off. And I'll still be available to travel to other places for that type of business occasionally. But you said 'mostly not' when I asked you if you were here on business. Before we have seconds on drinks, what is the business?"

Michael got up and went over to where I had hung up his coat. He pulled two small packages from his pockets and handed me both. "This delivery will complete my business for the evening."

I looked at the two packages with a resigned grin, as I never knew what was coming with this guy. I opened the flatter, slightly larger one first. It was a small photo of Jo in an expensive frame. She was wearing a dress and standing in front of greenery, perhaps with a hill or mountain in the background. I was happy to have it, but a deep pang went through my body, like losing a best friend.

"She wanted you to have it. Taken in England at one of her favorite places this past fall. That is all I know, and I'll leave any other interpretation unspoken."

I kept looking at it. I really did not know what to say. Not to Michael, and definitely not to myself. I got up and placed it on the mantle. I thought it looked good there and Michael looked like he approved. I picked up the other small package. I opened it and found a box containing a silver ring. It looked ancient and had a small gem embedded in it. I looked at Michael questioningly.

"It is a ring that has been in my family for some time. I thought you should have it because the last person to wear it was Asif. It seems fitting."

Jo's picture had nearly gotten to me, but I had tamped down the emotion. I did not this time. My eyes were watering as I turned to Michael.

"Thank you. This means a great deal to me."

"You are most welcome. You gave me a splendid gift telling me about your time with Asif. Those tales recreated his life for me in a way his letters did not. I will treasure that all my days."

I sat on the sofa until I made an important decision. "I apologize I don't have a proper gift in return. But perhaps I have something that needs to be given. I will be back in a minute."

I got up and went down the hall and then into the basement. I had set the vault in the house's foundation itself, with layers of security. Even I needed to do this slowly. Otherwise, I'd be a pepperoni pizza sailing across the sky somewhere over northern Asheville. I opened the metal door finally and took a very special item from a wooden box. I closed the vault and reset the security features. Slowly and carefully. Then I trotted upstairs and back to the sofa.

In my hand was a dagger. When I pulled it from the sheath, it was obviously ancient but exquisitely wrought. The blade was some type of unusual metal and the hilt had small jewels inset, plus Arabic script. Etched on the blade itself was a type of writing that was completely unfamiliar. It vaguely reminded me of proto-Egyptian characters I had once seen in an archaeology course.

I held it out so Michael could see it. I had never seen him so surprised. He could not speak at first, so I talked instead.

"This is the dagger that Asif carried. When the pirates killed him, they took it with all his other possessions. After I killed all of them, I searched the camp until I found this. He revered this more than anything he had, so I knew it was important to him."

I handed it to Michael, hilt first. When he touched it and I still had it by the blade, a blue light flashed from it.

"Damn, never seen it do that before."

"Mijn God," Michael said. "This is an omen."

"I always had a feeling that I needed to keep this blade, and keep it safe, since Asif's death. Almost like it was speaking to me. But now it seems right to give it to you."

Michael continued to look at the blade in astonishment. "We believed this blade to be lost forever. Or worse, taken by our enemies. But when it did not reveal itself, we assumed it was indeed lost. This is priceless, not just for having been Asif's, but for other reasons. Asif took it with him when he left, as his personal dagger, as he thought it was mine. But no one can own a blade such as this. I did not seek Asif out to retrieve this, as it has a destiny of its own, and has always found its way to where it was needed."

"It is a special artifact?"

"Oh yes, more than I can even explain. The blade is metal from a meteorite found in Egypt and originally forged there, but not by men. We refashioned the hilt much later. It has properties and talents beyond the understanding of most. Also, a holy relic, yet very much older than the Church. It is both a most useful tool, and one of our greatest weapons."

"I'm glad that it is back where it belongs."

"This is a gift beyond any thanks or reciprocation. Thank you for holding it safely for so many centuries, and for giving it to me. You do not know how important this event is."

"You can tell me when you come back for Easter brunch."

He laughed and carefully placed the dagger back in its ancient leather sheath that I had kept preserved over the years. He stood and put it in his jacket pocket.

"I'm afraid I have nothing to give you to take back to Jo, however."

"I don't think she would want anything. But what she really needs is…" He stopped and never finished the sentence.

"What were you going to say?"

"Nothing. There are some things I can't say, as it is not my place to speak. But I counsel you to speak to her, and soon. Preferably in person. Important things are happening."

"I will talk to her eventually, but just not yet. She has her family and her life, and her work. Right now, I just don't fit into that. But someday I will, probably when I finally feel ready to go back to Europe."

"Is it because of the strange attraction-repulsion that you two have between you?"

"Partly. It is just tough for us. But I think we will figure that out in time. We should have plenty of that unless I get stupid again and die."

Michael looked as if there was much more to say, but he remained silent. The silence stretched. Tectonic plates were probably moving somewhere, and it looked like Michael knew all about it.

"You have a delightful house here in America," he finally said. He spent little finesse on changing the subject.

"I like it OK. Had it a while and still working on it. Would you like to stay for dinner? I'm having roast guinea fowl and potatoes, plus some fresh green vegetables. Starting off with a pumpkin soup that Hia, my Cherokee wife, used to make. And some sort of dessert to be named later, assuming I get around to making it. I have a hankering for persimmons, and I'll put them in either ice cream or custard, but not sure if it will appear tonight."

"Sounds wonderful. I just need to leave before too late to catch the flight to DC, so I can get back home tomorrow."

"Great. Now, how about ditching these fruity drinks for something home-grown with some alcohol?"

"Certainly. What do you have in mind?"

"How about some syllabub? The southern US version of the drink, heavily fortified with bourbon."

He looked doubtful but nodded a yes.

He didn't know how awful the stuff really was. After I made him drink one of the terrible things, I'd find something decent that both of us might like.

"A toast, to the friends and family absent tonight, but not forgotten," I said as I clinked glasses with Michael.

"Salute," Michael said. He winced heavily when downed the viscous sugary cream fortified to 140 proof.

"Welcome to the South," I laughed, as I took his glass and went to get us something better. I raised my glass to Jo's picture as I walked past.

EPILOGUE

Jo arrived at Schiphol Airport and parked her car. It was not busy, probably because it was Christmas Day. As she waited patiently for Michael to move through passport control, she wondered what her family was doing today. Not being there was more difficult than she had imagined. She tried not to show it, but she also was eager for news of Michael's trip. It did not surprise Michael to see her waiting for him.

"Hello Jo. Nice of you to come down to meet me."

"It is the least I could do. You need a ride anyway."

"I suppose you also wish news of my trip? The wayward son that has moved on to America?"

"He really is gone then, and not coming back?"

"Yes. He thinks he has no choice."

"Should I have tried to persuade him to stay?"

"No, that would have driven him away even faster. He keeps his own course and counsel. When he feels he is doing the right thing, he won't be swayed."

"Is it the right thing?"

"Yes. For now. His destiny will bring him back. But not yet."

"How do you know so much about what he will do?"

"Because I turned him all those years ago, and in a twist of fate, did not even know for certain until last night. Even stranger, he was my son's greatest friend for many years. Through that connection, he came into possession of one of our most important tools and weapons, thought to be lost, and kept it safe for a millennium. Something higher has bound us together in unusual ways. The only stronger binding I have witnessed is between the two of you. I don't know to what end this course will take us, but you two will probably end up there together."

She looked thoughtful. "But that does not mean it will end well, does it?"

"No. Destiny has no interest in whether endings are good or bad."

They stood without talking for a moment.

"How is the child?"

Jo looked down for a second, then said, "She is fine. But I believe she will miss having a father."

AUTHOR'S NOTES

All the physical places described in the book are real. At least all the ones described in the current century. And most of the more ancient places exist as well and can be visited today. All characters in this book are fictitious. Any references to actual historical figures were also fictionalized to fit the story.

This book was originally published as *Resurgent* in 2021. This new version has substantial revisions, including new material, deletions, and chapter organization compared to the old version. Although the story is similar, it had to be rewritten and improved as the old version was not good enough.

If you like this version, please consider leaving a review, or at least a rating. That information is priceless, and what led to this current rewrite. Thank you for buying this book, and thanks in advance for any reviews you make.

Read on for an excerpt from the next book in the Fisher of Time series, *Danu Valley*.

ABOUT THE AUTHOR

Doug Smith, PhD, is a former scientist, professor, and non-fiction author. He is now recovering from those distractions and writing stories in the world of fantasy fiction.

Formerly a resident of The Netherlands, he is now living near Asheville, North Carolina. Visit his website at for more information, including books, short stories and excerpts.

Danu Valley Preview

Chapter One

The four warriors, carrying a hodgepodge of lethal weapons and proficient with them all, circled me and moved in for the kill. Unlike television battles, they all moved in at once, rendering a solid defense impossible. I could not dodge everything as they cut and gouged chunks from me. Lucky for me, their guns had already run out of ammunition. I needed to go on offense, but these guys had been practicing this for a thousand years. I was down a few pounds of meat and a quart of blood when Jen saved me by shooting two of them in the back with her last bullets. The third moved from me to deal with her, leaving me just one to tangle with. I roused myself and broke both of his collarbones, popped his knee backwards, and swept the legs. He grunted hard, but at least he stayed down. I watched Jen work on the last one. But he dealt her a killing blow just before I got there to assist.

The knife he had thrust at her was touching her neck when he froze it there. Her eyes got big as she knew she had just died. I hobbled back over and pulled my last opponent up from the floor. He was already healing and clapped me on the back, yelling something vaguely Scandinavian. Not clear if it was a taunt or a compliment, but he was kind of smiling. He and the guy that tapped Jen said something to her as well. The two on the floor Jen had shoot began moving, so the two talking to Jen went over and helped them up.

I was rethinking my strategy of asking these guys to attack us every day. I was glad we were all wearing the rune amulets that protected us from lethal blows during these "games" with Odin's einherjar. We needed the practice and improved weekly, but the barn and side building we had set up for the training attacks would not last much longer. I congratulated Jen on saving my ass, then we walked outside.

The two dozen attackers gathered together outside with what sounded like loud taunting and kidding among themselves. As the Farm people filtered out, most looking somewhat battered, they joined the attack group and grasped forearms, while a few traded high-fives. It was strange watching a hulking warrior killed two thousand years ago high-fiving a petite shapeshifting woman. A moment later, the good-natured attackers ambled off to their portal. I realized they were heading back to Valhalla to drink and carouse, and probably fight some more. I was proud that my far down-the-line descendants, most of them shapeshifters or friends, were adapting so well to the training sessions we had here at the "Farm," preparing for worse days ahead.

This craziness had started right after the New Year, after I had talked to both Michael and Henry about all the new threats we could be facing. Michael was my friend, sometimes mentor and employer, and one of the highest placed members of the Church no one had heard of, since he was the chief assassin and head of security. Henry was on old acquaintance and shapeshifter. Emphasis on the old as he was the oldest being I had met yet at somewhere around twenty-thousand years.

Henry and I had started sessions with the other Farm adults on the best way to improve defenses. I knew there were two people I needed to contact to up our security, although neither was exactly human. I made a "call" to Kal, my mentor and West Coast Bigfoot, and when he arrived, I gave him the thoughts and plans the group had come up with. He understood my ask and had some of his local "security representatives" join us the following day. It was like having the strangest board meeting ever, me and my people with six Bigfoots standing in the mountain woods in North Carolina. Or was that Bigfeet? I did not ask. They dwarfed me and the Farm adults, but we had a good meeting.

Since their telepathic communication was so fast, plus with their linkages to their network of their entire species, they came up with a defensive plan in a few minutes. They would have a few of their own on a nearby patrol to start, while setting up a network of organic sensors. I asked what those were, but did not get a satisfactory answer. Apparently, they have some sort of passive communication with trees and large underground networks of fungi. The other part of the plan was a passive portal that they activated in our camp. The portal, once activated, would transport us to one of two safe spots elsewhere. I asked where, but only got "out west" for an explanation. After everyone else had left, Kal and I had some time together.

"I am a little unsure how this system works, specifically the sensors," I told him.

"The organic sensors are acutely attuned to their surroundings, and have been here, in or on the ground, for years or centuries. Your activity here is registering now to produce a baseline. Any future unusual vibration, pressure, metallic presence, or one of a few dozen other criteria will immediately alert my people. If there is a threat, it will notify you and yours in seconds. It will also activate the portal in case you need to escape. In case the worst happens, take everyone through, including the injured and dead."

"OK, that sounds reasonable. If something or someone odd shows up, we will know in less than ten seconds, right?"

"Yes. I suggest your people have drills to form defenses and lines of retreat. We can assist by timing false incursions most inconveniently, such as the middle of the night."

"We start that later today. What about the escape locations?"

"The first location will be somewhere near the Pacific coast. I cannot tell you where exactly, as the location changes. I tied it to one of my groups of people. As they move, the location moves. The idea is to get you to a group of my people to provide more extensive protection. Since the enemy cannot predict the location, it also helps prevent detection, unless one of their people gets through the portal.

"If that initial portal destination is compromised, once you arrive, my people will immediately teleport you away, or escort you to other portals. Any of those will take you to a sheltered valley under multiple layers of protection, including time barriers. I won't tell you where it is, as it is a closely guarded secret. If you don't know, you can't tell, regardless of the interrogation methods that the enemy might employ."

"I appreciate your thoroughness. I believe that should keep us safer by having both better defenses and escape routes."

"Yes, these measures should enhance your longevity. I trust you can also prepare your people to last long enough to repel the attackers or ensure enough time to escape."

"That is next on my list of calls. Thanks for your help, Kal."

Kal's people were absolute geniuses at setting up passive defenses. They were, however, completely non-aggressive, so the more I thought about our situation, the more I felt we needed more teeth in the system. I knew just the guy, or rather the god, to call and set that up both in place and in time, so he was my second "call." I just had to find Odin and figure out what he would want for payment, assuming I could convince him to set up a system.

While I pondered how to contact Odin, I thought about the past few months, and how everyone at the Farm had progressed through the winter. Everything had gone better than I had imagined, which always worried me. The kids had progressed, and the adults were sharper than ever, while the borrowed Church operatives had also blended in seamlessly. Even a few romances were moving along without issue. In a few months we would have to recruit in new members, and even Michael had suggested bringing in a group from the Church to train with us. I stayed for as much of the training as possible, and since I wasn't in Europe, it was most of the time. Michael did not have any major projects for me, but would occasionally ask about coming over for a visit, which I always declined.

I really did not need to since my house and apartment were being managed by a service. Thomas, my best friend in Amsterdam, also visited each place once a month to monitor them. He leaked that Anna may be pregnant, so I was waiting to hear confirmation, and I would plan to fly over after confirmation for a planned celebration. The one odd omission in my life was Jo. My mythology researcher, sort-of-wannabe girlfriend that could never be my girlfriend, colleague, and commando that had recently saved my life after I saved hers. I knew our relationship was complicated, but she had gone quiet, and even when I asked Michael about her, he just said she was being kept very busy. I quit asking after it was apparent by her actions that she was not interested in keeping in contact with me.

I ended my procrastination and made plans to find Odin, first by putting together a list of places in the US that might offer the best chance of contacting him. I asked Kal one evening, but his suggestions were mostly those I had already considered. And those were not likely to work, as I didn't think that hanging out in Arlington National Cemetery at night to meet a god would go over well with the guards.

The next evening I was at my desk working on supply lists, the budget, and searching for other locations of battlefield cemeteries with no guards. As Odin walked in, I looked up. I jumped up with a gun as I did not recognize him at first, since he was wearing a long cloak and hat, and carrying a large walking stick. I quickly remembered that was one of his "wandering" outfits.

"Hello Odin, and welcome. I'm surprised to see you here, but also glad since I have been working on a plan to contact you."

"Obviously you were, and that is why I'm here. That and to see what you have been up to since last we talked. I am always interested in new shapeshifters, especially since we have so few in Europe now."

"Would you like a tour while I prepare my ask?"

"I already know what you need, and I have made those preparations. My visit is to determine if there are any modifications needed."

"Thank you in advance, then. Will I be able to afford your offer?"

"The only payment I need is your assurance that you will keep these shapeshifters alive."

"That is my primary objective. Protecting them for now and preparing them for when they will need to wreak havoc. Ensuring that they and their families are safe afterwards; those are my objectives."

"And good ones at that, for those must be priorities when you lead a people. Now let us see what you have built here."

We walked out and went through the building and around the grounds. One group was in the classroom with Zena, the Church tactician and spook here on loan, learning something sneaky. Another group was in the field, training with Henry and Simon. Simon was also from the Church, a field operative and martial arts expert. Odin and I got a few odd looks, but nobody looked very impressed. We moved away from the buildings and toward the outside group. Odin stopped and stood still for a moment with his eyes closed.

"I sense the one you call Kal has begun the passive defenses."

"Yes, just as you came in, I got a flash that I had a visitor."

"Impressive. I have detected nothing until now. That will tie in nicely with my system. However, I believe there is a weakness if something arrives by air. I will have a flock of crows patrol to observe by day. I suggest you talk to Kal about having night coverage, probably by owls."

"Good idea, and I'll talk to him about the owls." I called out for Henry and Simon to come over, since they knew more than me about any other blind spots.

Simon and Henry jogged over, but when Henry got ten steps away, he stopped and stared at Odin, who reciprocated the stare. They both became still. Simon picked up on the atmosphere and I noticed the almost imperceptible change in his stance as he loosened his muscles to ready for battle. I wasn't sure what was going on, but it just got tense and dangerous.

"Henry and Simon, this is our guest, Odin, who is going to help us with Farm defenses." I slightly emphasized "guest" in that sentence. Henry picked that up and immediately relaxed, and Simon did a second later.

"Odin," Henry said, as he gave a slight nod.

"Wol," Odin replied. I thought that was going to require an explanation later.

Simon and Odin also traded nods of acknowledgement.

"I would like us to take a quick walk around the perimeter, as we need to discuss what we can do to improve the security and readiness of our people," I said.

Everyone agreed and off we went. After a half hour, we were back at the buildings. Odin had said little, but I could tell he was highly alert and could sense Kal's "sensors". We went into the less-destroyed barn and opened up beer, cider, and mead. Odin then explained what he wanted to do for us.

"Once an alarm passes through Kal's passive network, the einherjar, soldiers that have fallen in battle and residing in Valhalla, will issue from different sites along the periphery of the property. Since they are already dead, and have been training daily for hundreds or thousands of years, they will be hard to kill. Since they were all originally soldiers, they know what to do, and do it with extreme prejudice."

"That sounds like a great plan," Simon said. "But if we have a sizable battle, how will the einherjar know us from the attackers?" Simon asked.

"Excellent question. They will instinctively know the difference. However, they are so fierce, mistakes could happen. Since the battle-killed all come to Valhalla, they may not be as judicious in separating out the mortals from enemies. No harm, no foul, once they join battle. I will furnish you with runic medallions that I suggest your people, as well as any guests, wear and not remove. That will protect you from all einherjar, as they cannot attack anyone wearing the runes."

"What about the cost?" I asked.

"That will be determined at a later date, but it won't be anything that you cannot afford. Each time the einherjar are called into battle on your behalf, you will owe me a favor. I can't tell what it might be, as that time has not come to pass. But it will be something easily within you purview."

"How many will arrive?" Henry asked.

"A minimum of twenty-four. They fight in groups of four, so there will be six kill teams, even if there is only one trespasser. If more come for the attack, multiples of twenty-four of my soldiers will arrive every few seconds."

"That sounds impressive," Simon said.

"The plan is to swarm any intruders before they can cause harm. The Kal network will allow my men to issue from portals nearest the point of incursion. I believe the terms are 'interactive' and 'real-time' in your vernacular."

Henry and Simon had a brief side conversation about practice training.

"Can we schedule the einherjar to stage attacks against us so we can practice our defenses and train our people?" Simon asked.

Odin considered, then responded, "Yes, that will be acceptable. The soldiers will consider it light duty, but will give them a chance to learn about your people and the grounds. Some will be happy to be back on earth, just as a diversion. But your people must wear the medallions at all times."

"That seems like a great idea, and a small price to pay for making us better," I said.

Shortly afterward, Odin left. We met and decided to begin the einherjar program the following week. It would be an exciting few days or weeks, we thought. We didn't consider how it would feel to "die" every day, however. But our people improved immensely after just two weeks of constant assaults.

We had our usual fire that evening. I steered Henry away from the others for a few minutes. "OK, Henry, today was a little weird. Seemed like you already knew Odin, and he seemed to know you, at least under a different name. Pretty unusual for a regular guy from Oklahoma. Care to elaborate?"

"We once had a dustup out on the Bering Plains. He was chasing something toward us I didn't want around. We agreed to disagree about that plan, but we then worked it out by agreeing to kill that third party. Since then, we normally keep to our respective continents."

"That is... interesting? Possibly disturbing? But anyway, I don't think there is any place called the Bering Plains."

"Not anymore. The closest thing to it now is the Bering Strait."

"Damn Henry, that just opens up all kinds of questions."

"Yeah, but we can go over all that once you get back from Europe."

"I'm not going to Europe, at least not soon."

"Yeah, you are. We will talk then."

"A year ago, I was the oldest and most interesting person I knew. Now I'm surrounded by people, all of whom are older and more interesting than me."

"Yeah, well, hate to bust that bubble again, but you finally got something right."

"Ass."

www.ingramcontent.com/pod-product-compliance
Lightning Source LLC
Chambersburg PA
CBHW051131190726
48290CB00006B/1790